THE WORLDS OF H. BEAM PIPER

FOUR-DAY PLANET . . . where the killing heat of a thousand-hour "day" drives men underground, and the glorious hundred-hour sunset is followed by a thousand-hour night so cold that only an Extreme Environment Suit can preserve the life of anyone caught outside.

and

LONE STAR PLANET . . . a planet-full of Texans—they firmly believe they live on the biggest, strongest, best planet in the galaxy. They herd cattle the size of boxcars for a living, and they defy the Solar League to prove that New Texas has even the slightest need of the "protection" that a bunch of diplomatic sissies can offer.

BRAVE NEW WORLDS FROM THE CREATOR OF "LITTLE FUZZY"

—TOGETHER IN ONE VOLUME—

Four-Day Planet
Lone Star Planet

ACE SCIENCE FICTION BOOKS
NEW YORK

FOUR-DAY PLANET
and
LONE STAR PLANET

An Ace Science Fiction Book

PRINTING HISTORY
First Ace edition / April 1979
Second Ace printing / September 1984

Cover art by Michael Whelan

ISBN: 0-441-24892-6

Ace Science Fiction Books are published by The Berkley Publishing Group,
200 Madison Avenue, New York, New York 10016.
PRINTED IN THE UNITED STATES OF AMERICA

DEDICATION

**For Betty and Vall, with
loving remembrance**

Four-Day Planet

CONTENTS

1

THE SHIP FROM TERRA

I WENT THROUGH the gateway, towing my equipment in a contragravity hamper over my head. As usual, I was wondering what it would take, short of a revolution, to get the city of Port Sandor as clean and tidy and well lighted as the spaceport area. I knew Dad's editorials and my sarcastic news stories wouldn't do it. We'd been trying long enough.

The two girls in bikinis in front of me pushed on, still gabbling about the fight one of them had had with her boy friend, and I closed up behind the half dozen monster-hunters in long trousers, ankle boots and short boat-jackets, with big knives on their belts. They must have all been from the same crew, because they weren't arguing about whose ship was fastest, had the toughest skipper, and made the most money. They were talking about the price of tallow-wax, and they seemed to have picked up a rumor that it was going to be cut another ten centisols a pound. I eavesdropped shamelessly, but it was the same rumor I'd picked up, myself, a little earlier.

"Hi, Walt," somebody behind me called out. "Looking for some news that's fit to print?"

I turned my head. It was a man of about thirty-five with curly brown hair and a wide grin. Adolf Lautier, the entertainment promoter. He and Dad each owned a share in the Port Sandor telecast station, and split their time between his music and drama-films and Dad's newscasts.

"All the news is fit to print, and if it's news the Times prints it," I told him. "Think you're going to get some good thrillers this time?"

He shrugged. I'd just asked that to make conversation; he never had any way of knowing what sort of films would come in. The ones the Peenemünde was bringing should be fairly new, because she was outbound from Terra. He'd go over what was aboard, and trade one for one for the old films he'd shown already.

"They tell me there's a real Old-Terran-style Western been showing on Völund that ought to be coming our way this time," he said. "It was filmed in South America, with real horses."

That would go over big here. Almost everybody thought horses were as extinct as dinosaurs. I've seen so-called Westerns with the cowboys riding Freyan oukry. I mentioned that, and then added:

"They'll think the old cattle towns like Dodge and Abilene were awful sissy places, though."

"I suppose they were, compared to Port Sandor," Lautier said. "Are you going aboard to interview the distinguished visitor?"

"Which one?" I asked. "Glenn Murell or Leo Belsher?"

Lautier called Leo Belsher something you won't find in the dictionary but which nobody needs to look up. The hunters, ahead of us, heard him and laughed. They couldn't possibly have agreed more. He was going to continue with the fascinating subject of Mr. Leo Belsher's ancestry and personal characteristics, and then bit it off short. I followed his eyes, and saw old Professor Hartzenbosch, the principal of the school, approaching.

"Ah, here you are, Mr. Lautier," he greeted. "I trust that I did not keep you waiting." Then he saw me. "Why, it's Walter Boyd. How is your father, Walter?"

I assured him as to Dad's health and inquired about his own, and then asked him how things were going at school. As well as could be expected, he told me, and I gathered that he kept his point of expectation safely low. Then he wanted to know if I were going aboard to interview Mr. Murell.

"Really, Walter, it is a wonderful thing that a famous author like Mr. Murell should come here to write a book about our planet," he told me, very seriously, and added, as an afterthought: "Have you any idea where he intends staying while he is among us?"

"Why, yes," I admitted. "After the *Peenmünde* radioed us their passenger list, Dad talked to him by screen, and invited him to stay with us. Mr. Murell accepted, at least until he can find quarters of his own."

There are a lot of good poker players in Port Sandor, but Professor Jan Hartzenbosch is not one of them. The look of disappointment would have been comical if it hadn't been so utterly pathetic. He'd been hoping to lasso Murell himself.

"I wonder if Mr. Murell could spare time to

come to the school and speak to the students," he said, after a moment.

"I'm sure he could. I'll mention it to him, Professor," I promised.

Professor Hartzenbosch bridled at that. The great author ought to be coming to his school out of respect for him, not because a seventeen-year-old cub reporter sent him. But then, Professor Hartzenbosch always took the attitude that he was conferring a favor on the *Times* when he had anything he wanted publicity on.

The elevator door opened, and Lautier and the professor joined in the push to get into it. I hung back, deciding to wait for the next one so that I could get in first and get back to the rear, where my hamper wouldn't be in people's way. After a while, it came back empty and I got on, and when the crowd pushed off on the top level, I put my hamper back on contragravity and towed it out into the outdoor air, which by this time had gotten almost as cool as a bake-oven.

I looked up at the sky, where everybody else was looking. The Peenemünde wasn't visible; it was still a few thousand miles off-planet. Big ragged clouds were still blowing in from the west, very high, and the sunset was even brighter and redder than when I had seen it last, ten hours before. It was now about 1630.

Now, before anybody starts asking just who's crazy, let me point out that this is not on Terra, nor on Baldur nor Thor nor Odin nor Freya, nor any other rational planet. This is Fenris, and on Fenris the sunsets, like many other things, are somewhat peculiar.

Fenris is the second planet of a G4 star, six

hundred and fifty light-years to the Galactic southwest of the Sol System. Everything else equal, it should have been pretty much Terra type; closer to a cooler primary and getting about the same amount of radiation. At least, that's what the book says. I was born on Fenris, and have never been off it in the seventeen years since.

Everything else, however, is not equal. The Fenris year is a trifle shorter than the Terran year we use for Atomic Era dating, eight thousand and a few odd Galactic Standard hours. In that time, Fenris makes almost exactly four axial rotations. This means that on one side the sun is continuously in the sky for a thousand hours, pouring down unceasing heat, while the other side is in shadow. You sleep eight hours, and when you get up and go outside—in an insulated vehicle, or an extreme-environment suit—you find that the shadows have moved only an inch or so, and it's that much hotter. Finally, the sun crawls down to the horizon and hangs there for a few days— periods of twenty-four G.S. hours—and then slides slowly out of sight. Then, for about a hundred hours, there is a beautiful unfading sunset, and it's really pleasant outdoors. Then it gets darker and colder until, just before sunrise, it gets almost cold enough to freeze CO_2. Then the sun comes up, and we begin all over again.

You are picking up the impression, I trust, that as planets go, Fenris is nobody's bargain. It isn't a real hell-planet, and spacemen haven't made a swear word out of its name, as they have with the name of fluorine-atmosphere Nifflheim, but even the Reverend Hiram Zilker, the Orthodox-Monophysite preacher, admits that it's one of

those planets the Creator must have gotten a trifle
absent-minded with.

The chartered company that colonized it, back
at the end of the Fourth Century A.E., went bankrupt in ten years, and it wouldn't have taken that
long if communication between Terra and Fenris
hadn't been a matter of six months each way.
When the smash finally came, two hundred and
fifty thousand colonists were left stranded. They
lost everything they'd put into the company,
which, for most of them, was all they had. Not
a few lost their lives before the Federation
Space Navy could get ships here to evacuate
them.

But about a thousand, who were too poor to
make a fresh start elsewhere and too tough for
Fenris to kill, refused evacuation, took over all the
equipment and installations the Fenris Company
had abandoned, and tried to make a living out of
the planet. At least, they stayed alive. There are
now twenty-odd thousand of us, and while we are
still very poor, we are very tough, and we brag
about it.

There were about two thousand people—ten
per cent of the planetary population—on the wide
concrete promenade around the spaceport landing pit. I came out among them and set down the
hamper with my telecast cameras and recorders,
wishing, as usual, that I could find some ten- or
twelve-year-old kid weak-minded enough to
want to be a reporter when he grew up, so that I
could have an apprentice to help me with my
junk.

As the star—and only—reporter of the great-
est—and only—paper on the planet, I was al-

ways on hand when either of the two ships on the Terra-Odin milk run, the *Peenemünde* and the *Cape Canaveral*, landed. Of course, we always talk to them by screen as soon as they come out of hyperspace and into radio range, and get the passenger list, and a speed-recording of any news they are carrying, from the latest native uprising on Thor to the latest political scandal on Venus. Sometime the natives of Thor won't be fighting anybody at all, or the Federation Member Republic of Venus will have some nonscandalous politics, and either will be the man-bites-dog story to end man-bites-dog stories. All the news is at least six months old, some more than a year. A spaceship can log a light-year in sixty-odd hours, but radio waves still crawl along at the same old 186,000 mps.

I still have to meet the ships. There's always something that has to be picked up personally, usually an interview with some VIP traveling through. This time, though, the big story coming in on the *Peenemünde* was a local item. Paradox? Dad says there is no such thing. He says a paradox is either a verbal contradiction, and you get rid of it by restating it correctly, or it's a structural contradiction, and you just call it an impossibility and let it go at that. In this case, what was coming in was a real live author, who was going to write a travel book about Fenris, the planet with the four-day year. Glenn Murell, which sounded suspiciously like a nom de plume, and nobody here had ever heard of him.

That was odd, too. One thing we can really be proud of here, besides the toughness of our citizens, is our public library. When people have to

stay underground most of the time to avoid being
fried and/or frozen to death, they have a lot of time
to kill, and reading is one of the cheaper and more
harmless and profitable ways of doing it. And
travel books are a special favorite here. I suppose
because everybody is hoping to read about a
worse place than Fenris. I had checked on Glenn
Murell at the library. None of the librarians had
ever heard of him, and there wasn't a single mention of him in any of the big catalogues of publications.

The first and obvious conclusion would be that
Mr. Glenn Murell was some swindler posing as an
author. The only objection to that was that I
couldn't quite see why any swindler would come
to Fenris, or what he'd expect to swindle the Fen-
risians out of. Of course, he could be on the lam
from somewhere, but in that case why bother with
all the cover story? Some of our better-known
citizens came here dodging warrants on other
planets.

I was still wondering about Murell when somebody behind me greeted me, and I turned around.
It was Tom Kivelson.

Tom and I are buddies, when he's in port. He's
just a shade older than I am; he was eighteen
around noon, and my eighteenth birthday won't
come till midnight, Fenris Standard Sundial
Time. His father is Joe Kivelson, the skipper of the
Javelin; Tom is sort of junior engineer, second
gunner, and about third harpooner. We went to
school together, which is to say a couple of years
at Professor Hartzenbosch's, learning to read and
write and put figures together. That is all the
schooling anybody on Fenris gets, although Joe

Kivelson sent Tom's older sister, Linda, to school on Terra. Anybody who stays here has to dig out education for himself. Tom and I were still digging for ours.

Each of us envied the other, when we weren't thinking seriously about it. I imagined that sea-monster hunting was wonderfully thrilling and romantic, and Tom had the idea that being a newsman was real hot stuff. When we actually stopped to think about it, though, we realized that neither of us would trade jobs and take anything at all for boot. Tom couldn't string three sentences—no, one sentence—together to save his life, and I'm just a town boy who likes to live in something that isn't pitching end-for-end every minute.

Tom is about three inches taller than I am, and about thirty pounds heavier. Like all monster-hunters, he's trying to grow a beard, though at present it's just a blond chin-fuzz. I was surprised to see him dressed as I was, in shorts and sandals and a white shirt and a light jacket. Ordinarily, even in town, he wears boat-clothes. I looked around behind him, and saw the brass tip of a scabbard under the jacket. Any time a hunter-ship man doesn't have his knife on, he isn't wearing anything else. I wondered about his being in port now. I knew Joe Kivelson wouldn't bring his ship in just to meet the Peenemünde, with only a couple of hundred hours' hunting left till the storms and the cold.

"I thought you were down in the South Ocean," I said.

"There's going to be a special meeting of the Co-op," he said. "We only heard about it last evening," by which he meant after 1800 of the previous Galactic Standard day. He named another hunter-ship captain who had called the *Javelin* by screen. "We screened everybody else we could."

That was the way they ran things in the Hunters' Co-operative. Steve Ravick would wait till everybody had their ships down on the coast of Hermann Reuch's Land, and then he would call a meeting and pack it with his stooges and hooligans, and get anything he wanted voted through. I had always wondered how long the real hunters were going to stand for that. They'd been standing for it ever since I could remember anything outside my own playpen, which, of course, hadn't been too long.

I was about to say something to that effect, and then somebody yelled, "There she is!" I took a quick look at the radar bowls to see which way they were pointed and followed them up to the sky, and caught a tiny twinkle through a cloud rift. After a moment's mental arithmetic to figure how high she'd have to be to catch the sunlight, I relaxed. Even with the telephoto, I'd only get a picture the size of a pinhead, so I fixed the position in my mind and then looked around at the crowd.

Among them were two men, both well dressed. One was tall and slender, with small hands and feet; the other was short and stout, with a scrubby gray-brown mustache. The slender one had a bulge under his left arm, and the short-and-stout job bulged over the right hip. The former was Steve Ravick, the boss of the Hunters' Co-operative, and his companion was the Honorable

Morton Hallstock, mayor of Port Sandor and consequently the planetary government of Fenris.

They had held their respective positions for as long as I could remember anything at all. I could never remember an election in Port Sandor, or an election of officers in the Co-op. Ravick had a bunch of goons and triggermen—I could see a couple of them loitering in the background—who kept down opposition for him. So did Hallstock, only his wore badges and called themselves police.

Once in a while, Dad would write a blistering editorial about one or the other or both of them. Whenever he did, I would put my gun on, and so would Julio Kubanoff, the one-legged compositor who is the third member of the Times staff, and we would take turns making sure nobody got behind Dad's back. Nothing ever happened, though, and that always rather hurt me. Those two racketeers were in so tight they didn't need to care what the Times printed or 'cast about them.

Hallstock glanced over in my direction and said something to Ravick. Ravick gave a sneering laugh, and then he crushed out the cigarette he was smoking on the palm of his left hand. That was a regular trick of his. Showing how tough he was. Dad says that when you see somebody showing off, ask yourself whether he's trying to impress other people, or himself. I wondered which was the case with Steve Ravick.

Then I looked up again. The Peenemünde was coming down as fast as she could without overheating from atmosphere friction. She was almost buckshot size to the naked eye, and a couple of tugs were getting ready to go up and meet her. I got the telephoto camera out of the hamper, checked it, and aimed it. It has a shoulder stock and handgrips and a trigger like a submachine gun. I caught the ship in the finder and squeezed the trigger for a couple of seconds. It would be about five minutes till the tugs got to her and anything else happened, so I put down the camera and looked around.

Coming through the crowd, walking as though the concrete under him was pitching and rolling like a ship's deck on contragravity in a storm, was Bish Ware. He caught sight of us, waved, overbalanced himself and recovered, and then changed course to starboard and bore down on us. He was carrying about his usual cargo, and as usual the manifest would read, *Baldur honey-rum, from Harry Wong's bar.*

Bish wasn't his real name. Neither, I suspected, was Ware. When he'd first landed on Fenris, some five years ago, somebody had nicknamed him the Bishop, and before long that had gotten cut to one syllable. He looked like a bishop, or at least like what anybody who's never seen a bishop outside a screen-play would think a bishop looked like. He was a big man, not fat, but tall and portly; he had a ruddy face that always wore an expression of benevolent wisdom, and the more cargo he took on the wiser and more benevolent he looked.

He had iron-gray hair, but he wasn't old. You could tell that by the backs of his hands; they weren't wrinkled or crepy and the veins didn't protrude. And drunk or sober—though I never remembered seeing him in the latter condition—he had the fastest reflexes of anybody I knew. I saw him, once, standing at the bar in Harry

Wong's, knock over an open bottle with his left elbow. He spun half around, grabbed it by the neck and set it up, all in one motion, without spilling a drop, and he went on talking as though nothing had happened. He was quoting Homer, I remembered, and you could tell that he was thinking in the original ancient Greek and translating to Lingua Terra as he went.

He was always dressed as he was now, in a conservative black suit, the jacket a trifle longer than usual, and a black neckcloth with an Uller organic-opal pin. He didn't work at anything, but quarterly—once every planetary day—a draft on the Banking Cartel would come in for him, and he'd deposit it with the Port Sandor Fidelity & Trust. If anybody was unmannerly enough to ask him about it, he always said he had a rich uncle on Terra.

When I was a kid—well, more of a kid than I am now—I used to believe he really was a bishop—unfrocked, of course, or ungaitered, or whatever they call it when they give a bishop the heave-ho. A lot of people who weren't kids still believed that, and they blamed him on every denomination from Anglicans to Zen Buddhists, not even missing the Satanists, and there were all sorts of theories about what he'd done to get excommunicated, the mildest of which was that somewhere there was a cathedral standing unfinished because he'd hypered out with the building fund. It was generally agreed that his ecclesiastical organization was paying him to stay out there in the boondocks where he wouldn't cause them further embarrassment.

I was pretty sure, myself, that he was being paid

by somebody, probably his family, to stay out of sight. The colonial planets are full of that sort of remittance men.

Bish and I were pretty good friends. There were certain old ladies, of both sexes and all ages, of whom Professor Hartzenbosch was an example, who took Dad to task occasionally for letting me associate with him. Dad simply ignored them. As long as I was going to be a reporter, I'd have to have news sources, and Bish was a dandy. He knew all the disreputable characters in town, which saved me having to associate with all of them, and it is sad but true that you get very few news stories in Sunday school. Far from fearing that Bish would be a bad influence on me, he rather hoped I'd be a good one on Bish.

I had that in mind, too, if I could think of any way of managing it. Bish had been a good man, once. He still was, except for one thing. You could tell that before he'd started drinking, he'd really been somebody, somewhere. Then something pretty bad must have happened to him, and now he was here on Fenris, trying to hide from it behind a bottle. Something ought to be done to give him a shove up on his feet again. I hate waste, and a man of the sort he must have been turning himself into the rumpot he was now was waste of the worst kind.

It would take a lot of doing, though, and careful tactical planning. Preaching at him would be worse than useless, and so would simply trying to get him to stop drinking. That would be what Doc Rojansky, at the hospital, would call treating the symptoms. The thing to do was make him *want* to stop drinking, and I didn't know how I was going to manage that. I'd thought, a couple of times, of getting him to work on the *Times*, but we barely made enough money out of it for ourselves, and with his remittance he didn't need to work. I had a lot of other ideas, now and then, but every time I took a second look at one, it got sick and died.

2

REPORTER WORKING

BISH CAME OVER and greeted us solemnly.

"Good afternoon, gentlemen. Captain Ahab, I believe," he said, bowing to Tom, who seemed slightly puzzled; the education Tom had been digging out for himself was technical rather than literary. "And Mr. Pulitzer. Or is it Horace Greeley?"

"Lord Beaverbrook, your Grace," I replied. "Have you any little news items for us from your diocese?"

Bish teetered slightly, getting out a cigar and inspecting it carefully before lighting it.

"We-el," he said carefully, "my diocese is full to the hatch covers with sinners, but that's scarcely news." He turned to Tom. "One of your hands on the *Javelin* got into a fight in Martian Joe's, a while ago. Lumped the other man up pretty badly." He named the *Javelin* crewman, and the man who had been pounded. The latter was one of Steve Ravick's goons. "But not fatally, I regret to say," Bish added. "The local Gestapo are looking for your man, but he made it aboard Nip

16

Spazoni's *Bulldog*, and by this time he's halfway to Hermann Reuch's Land."

"Isn't Nip going to the meeting, tonight?" Tom asked.

Bish shook his head. "Nip is a peace-loving man. He has a well-founded suspicion that peace is going to be in short supply around Hunters' Hall this evening. You know, of course, that Leo Belsher's coming in on the *Pennemünde* and will be there to announce another price cut. The new price, I understand, will be thirty-five centisols a pound."

Seven hundred sols a ton, I thought; why, that would barely pay ship expenses.

"Where did you get that?" Tom asked, a trifle sharply.

"Oh, I have my spies and informers," Bish said. "And even if I hadn't, it would figure. The only reason Leo Belsher ever comes to this Eden among planets is to negotiate a new contract, and who ever heard of a new contract at a higher price?"

That had all happened before, a number of times. When Steve Ravick had gotten control of the Hunters' Co-operative, the price of tallow-wax, on the loading floor at Port Sandor spaceport, had been fifteen hundred sols a ton. As far as Dad and I could find out, it was still bringing the same price on Terra as it always had. It looked to us as if Ravick and Leo Belsher, who was the Co-op representative on Terra, and Mort Hallstock were simply pocketing the difference. I was just as sore about what was happening as anybody who went out in the hunter-ships. Tallow-wax is our only export. All our imports are paid for with credit from the sale of wax.

It isn't really wax, and it isn't tallow. It's a growth on the Jarvis's sea-monster; there's a layer of it under the skin, and around organs that need padding. An average-sized monster, say a hundred and fifty feet long, will yield twelve to fifteen tons of it, and a good hunter kills about ten monsters a year. Well, at the price Belsher and Ravick were going to cut from, that would run a little short of a hundred and fifty thousand sols for a year. If you say it quick enough and don't think, that sounds like big money, but the upkeep and supplies for a hunter-ship are big money, too, and what's left after that's paid off is divided, on a graduated scale, among ten to fifteen men, from the captain down. A hunter-boat captain even a good one like Joe Kivelson, won't make much more in a year than Dad and I make out of the Times.

Chemically, tallow-wax isn't like anything else in the known Galaxy. The molecules are huge; they can be seen with an ordinary optical microscope, and a microscopically visible molecule is a curious-looking object, to say the least. They use the stuff to treat fabric for protective garments. It isn't anything like collapsium, of course, but a suit of waxed coveralls weighing only a couple of pounds will stop as much radiation as half an inch of lead.

Back when they were getting fifteen hundred a ton, the hunters had been making good money, but that was before Steve Ravick's time.

It was slightly before mine, too. Steve Ravick had showed up on Fenris about twelve years ago. He'd had some money, and he'd bought shares in a couple of hunter-ships and staked a few captains who'd had bad luck and got them in debt to him. He also got in with Morton Hallstock, who controlled what some people were credulous enough to take for a government here. Before long, he was secretary of the Hunters' Co-operative. Old Simon MacGregor, who had been president then, was a good hunter, but he was no businessman. He came to depend very heavily on Ravick, up till his ship, the *Claymore*, was lost with all hands down in Fitzwilliam Straits. I think that was a time bomb in the magazine, but I have a low and suspicious mind. Professor Hartzenbosch has told me so repeatedly. After that, Steve Ravick was president of the Co-op. He immediately began a drive to increase the membership. Most of the new members had never been out in a hunter-ship in their lives, but they could all be depended on to vote the way he wanted them to.

First, he jacked the price of wax up, which made everybody but the wax buyers happy. Everybody who wasn't already in the Co-op hurried up and joined. Then he negotiated an exclusive contract with Kapstaad Chemical Products, Ltd., in South Africa, by which they agreed to take the entire output for the Co-op. That ended competitive wax buying, and when there was nobody to buy the wax but Kapstaad, you had to sell it through the Co-operative or you didn't sell it at all. After that, the price started going down. The Co-operative, for which read Steve Ravick, had a sales representative on Terra, Leo Belsher. He wrote all the contracts, collected all the money, and split with Ravick. What was going on was pretty generally understood, even if it couldn't be proven, but what could anybody do about it?

Maybe somebody would try to do something about it at the meeting this evening. I would be there to cover it. I was beginning to wish I owned a bullet-proof vest.

Bish and Tom were exchanging views on the subject, some of them almost printable. I had my eyes to my binoculars, watching the tugs go up to meet the Peenemünde.

"What we need for Ravick, Hallstock and Belsher," Tom was saying, "is about four fathoms of harpoon line apiece, and something to haul up to."

That kind of talk would have shocked Dad. He is very strong for law and order, even when there is no order and the law itself is illegal. I'd always thought there was a lot of merit in what Tom was suggesting. Bish Ware seemed to have his doubts, though.

"Mmm, no; there ought to be some better way of doing it than that."

"Can you think of one?" Tom challenged.

I didn't hear Bish's reply. By that time, the tugs were almost to the ship. I grabbed up the tele-photo camera and aimed it. It has its own power unit, and transmits directly. In theory, I could tune it to the telecast station and put what I was getting right on the air, and what I was doing was transmitting to the Times, to be recorded and 'cast later. Because it's not a hundred per cent reliable, though, it makes its own audiovisual record, so if any of what I was sending didn't get through, it could be spliced in after I got back.

I got some footage of the tugs grappling the ship, which was now completely weightless, and pulling her down. Through the finder, I could see that she had her landing legs extended; she looked like a big overfed spider being hauled in by a couple of gnats. I kept the butt of the camera to my shoulder, and whenever anything interesting happened, I'd squeeze the trigger. The first time I ever used a real submachine gun had been to kill a blue slasher that had gotten into one of the ship pools at the waterfront. I used three one-second bursts, and threw bits of slasher all over the place, and everybody wondered how I'd gotten the practice.

A couple more boats, pushers, went up to help hold the ship against the wind, and by that time she was down to a thousand feet, which was half her diameter. I switched from the shoulder-stock telephoto to the big tripod job, because this was the best part of it. The ship was weightless, of course, but she had mass and an awful lot of it. If anybody goofed getting her down, she'd take the side of the landing pit out, and about ten per cent of the population of Fenris, including the ace reporter for the *Times*, along with it.

At the same time, some workmen and a couple of spaceport cops had appeared, taken out a section of railing and put in a gate. The *Peenemünde* settled down, turned slowly to get her port in line with the gate, and lurched off contragravity and began running out a bridge to the promenade. I got some shots of that, and then began packing my stuff back in the hamper.

"You going aboard?" Tom asked. "Can I come along? I can carry some of your stuff and let on I'm your helper."

Glory be, I thought; I finally got that apprentice.

"Why, sure," I said. "You tow the hamper; I'll

carry this." I got out what looked like a big camera case and slung it over my shoulder. "But you'll have to take me out on the *Javelin*, sometime, and let me shoot a monster."

He said it was a deal, and we shook on it. Then I had another idea.

"Bish, suppose you come with us, too," I said. "After all, Tom and I are just a couple of kids. If you're with us, it'll look a lot more big-paperish."

That didn't seem to please Tom too much. Bish shook his head, though, and Tom brightened.

"I'm dreadfully sorry, Walt," Bish said. "But I'm going aboard, myself, to see a friend who is en route through to Odin. A Dr. Watson; I have not seen him for years."

I'd caught that name, too, when we'd gotten the passenger list. Dr. John Watson. Now, I know that all sorts of people call themselves Doctor, and Watson and John aren't too improbable a combination, but I'd read *Sherlock Holmes* long ago, and the name had caught my attention. And this was the first, to my knowledge, that Bish Ware had ever admitted to any off-planet connections.

We started over to the gate. Hallstock and Ravick were ahead of us. So was Sigurd Ngozori, the president of the Fidelity & Trust, carrying a heavy briefcase and accompanied by a character with a submachine gun, and Adolf Lautier and Professor Hartzenbosch. There were a couple of spaceport cops at the gate, in olive-green uniforms that looked as though they had been sprayed on, and steel helmets. I wished we had a city police force like that. They were Odin Dock & Shipyard Company men, all former Federation Regular Army or Colonial Constabulary. The spaceport wasn't part of Port Sandor, or even Fenris; the Odin Dock & Shipyard Company was the government there, and it was run honestly and efficiently.

They knew me, and when they saw Tom towing my hamper they cracked a few jokes about the new *Times* cub reporter and waved us through. I thought they might give Bish an argument, but they just nodded and let him pass, too. We all went out onto the bridge, and across the pit to the equator of the two-thousand-foot globular ship.

We went into the main lounge, and the captain introduced us to Mr. Glenn Murell. He was fairly tall, with light gray hair, prematurely so, I thought, and a pleasant, noncommittal face. I'd have pegged him for a businessman. Well, I suppose authoring is a business, if that *was* his business. He shook hands with us, and said:

"Aren't you rather young to be a newsman?"

I started to burn on that. I get it all the time, and it burns me all the time, but worst of all on the job. Maybe I am only going-on-eighteen, but I'm doing a man's work, and I'm doing it competently.

"Well, they grow up young on Fenris, Mr. Murell," Captain Marshak earned my gratitude by putting in. "Either that or they don't live to grow up."

Murell unhooked his memophone and repeated the captain's remark into it. Opening line for one of his chapters. Then he wanted to know if I'd been born on Fenris. I saw I was going to have to get firm with Mr. Murell, right away. The time to stop that sort of thing is as soon as it starts.

"Who," I wanted to know, "is interviewing whom? You'll have at least five hundred hours till

the next possible ship out of here; I only have two
and a half to my next deadline. You want cover-
age, don't you? The more publicity you get, the
easier your own job's going to be."

Then I introduced Tom, carefully giving the
impression that while I handled all ordinary as-
signments, I needed help to give him the full VIP
treatment. We went over to a quiet corner and sat
down, and the interview started.

The camera case I was carrying was a snare and
a deceit. Everybody knows that reporters use recorders in interviews, but it never pays to be too
obtrusive about them, or the subject gets re-
corder-conscious and stiffens up. What I had
was better than a recorder; it was a recording
radio. Like the audiovisuals, it not only transmitted in to the *Times*, but made a recording as insur-
ance against transmission failure. I reached into a
slit on the side and snapped on the switch while I
was fumbling with a pencil and notebook with the
other hand, and started by asking him what had
decided him to do a book about Fenris.

After that, I fed a question every now and then
to keep him running, and only listened to every
third word. The radio was doing a better job than I
possibly could have. At the same time, I was
watching Steve Ravick, Morton Hallstock and Leo
Belsher at one side of the room, and Bish Ware at
the other. Bish was within ear-straining range.
Out of the corner of my eye, I saw another man,
younger in appearance and looking like an Army
officer in civvies, approach him.

"My dear Bishop!" this man said in greeting.

As far as I knew, that nickname had originated
on Fenris. I made a mental note of that.

"How are you?" Bish replied, grasping the other's hand. "You have been in Afghanistan, I perceive."

That did it. I told you I was an old 'Sherlock Holmes' reader; I recognized that line. This meeting was prearranged, neither of them had ever met before, and they needed a recognition code. Then I returned to Murell, and decided to wonder about Bish Ware and "Dr. Watson" later.

It wasn't long before I was noticing a few odd things about Murell, too, which confirmed my original suspicions of him. He didn't have the firm name of his alleged publishers right, he didn't know what a literary agent was and, after claiming to have been a newsman, he consistently used the expression "news service." I know, everybody says that—everybody but newsmen. They always call a news service a "paper," especially when talking to other newsmen.

Of course, there isn't any paper connected with it, except the pad the editor doodles on. What gets to the public is photoprint, out of a teleprinter. As small as our circulation is, we have four or five hundred of them in Port Sandor and around among the small settlements in the archipelago, and even on the mainland. Most of them are in bars and cafés and cigar stores and places like that, operated by a coin in a slot and leased by the proprietor, and some of the big hunter-ships like Joe Kivelson's *Javelin* and Nip Spazoni's *Bulldog* have them.

But long ago, back in the First Centuries, Pre-Atomic and Atomic Era, they were actually printed on paper, and the copies distributed and sold. They used printing presses as heavy as a

spaceship's engines. That's why we still call ourselves the Press. Some of the old papers on Terra,
like *La Prensa* in Buenos Aires, and the Mel-
bourne *Times*, which used to be the London
Times when there was still a London, were
printed that way originally.

Finally I got through with my interview, and
then shot about fifteen minutes of audiovisual,
which would be cut to five for the 'cast. By this
time Bish and "Dr. Watson" had disappeared, I
supposed to the ship's bar, and Ravick and his
accomplices had gotten through with their conspiracy to defraud the hunters. I turned Murell
over to Tom, and went over to where they were
standing together. I'd put away my pencil and pad
long ago with Murell; now I got them out ostentatiously as I approached.

"Good day, gentlemen," I greeted them. "I'm
representing the Port Sandor *Times*."

"Oh, run along, sonny; we haven't time to
bother with you," Hallstock said.

"But I want to get a story from Mr. Belsher," I
began.

"Well, come back in five or six years, when
you're dry behind the ears, and you can get it,"
Ravick told me.

"Our readers aren't interested in the condition
of my ears," I said sweetly. "They want to read
about the price of tallow-wax. What's this about
another price cut? To thirty-five centisols a
pound, I understand."

"Oh, Steve, the young man's from the news
service, and his father will publish whatever he
brings home," Belsher argued. "We'd better give
him something." He turned to me. "I don't know

how this got out, but it's quite true," he said. He had a long face, like a horse's. At least, he looked like pictures of horses I'd seen. As he spoke, he pulled it even longer and became as doleful as an undertaker at a ten-thousand-sol funeral.

"The price has gone down, again. Somebody has developed a synthetic substitute. Of course, it isn't anywhere near as good as real Fenris tallow-wax, but try and tell the public that. So Kapstaad Chemical is being undersold, and the only way they can stay in business is cut the price they have to pay for wax . . ."

It went on like that, and this time I had real trouble keeping my anger down. In the first place, I was pretty sure there was no substitute for Fenris tallow-wax, good, bad or indifferent. In the second place, it isn't sold to the gullible public, it's sold to equipment manufacturers who have their own test engineers and who have to keep their products up to legal safety standards. He didn't know this balderdash of his was going straight to the *Times* as fast as he spouted it; he thought I was taking it down in shorthand. I knew exactly what Dad would do with it. He'd put it on telecast in Belsher's own voice.

Maybe the monster-hunters *would* start looking around for a rope, then.

When I got through listening to him, I went over and got a short audiovisual of Captain Marshak of the *Peenemünde* for the 'cast, and then I rejoined Tom and Murell.

"Mr. Murell says he's staying with you at the *Times*," Tom said. He seemed almost as disappointed as Professor Hartzenbosch. I wondered, for an incredulous moment, if Tom had been trying to kidnap Murell away from me. "He wants to go out on the *Javelin* with us for a monster-hunt."

"Well, that's swell!" I said. "You can pay off on that promise to take me monster-hunting, too. Right now, Mr. Murell is my big story." I reached into the front pocket of my "camera" case for the handphone, to shift to two-way. "I'll call the *Times* and have somebody come up with a car to get us and Mr. Murell's luggage."

"Oh, I have a car. Jeep, that is," Tom said. "It's down on the Bottom Level. We can use that."

Funny place to leave a car. And I was sure that he and Murell had come to some kind of an understanding, while I was being lied to by Belsher. I didn't get it. There was just too much going on around me that I didn't get, and me, I'm supposed to be the razor-sharp newshawk who gets everything.

3

BOTTOM LEVEL

IT DIDN'T TAKE long to get Murell's luggage assembled. There was surprisingly little of it, and nothing that looked like photographic or recording equipment. When he returned from a final gathering-up in his stateroom, I noticed that he was bulging under his jacket, too, on the left side at the waist. About enough for an 8.5-mm pocket automatic. Evidently he had been briefed on the law-and-order situation in Port Sandor.

Normally, we'd have gone off onto the Main City Level, but Tom's jeep was down on the Bottom Level, and he made no suggestion that we go off and wait for him to bring it up. I didn't suggest it, either. After all, it was his jeep, and he wasn't our hired pilot. Besides, I was beginning to get curious. An abnormally large bump of curiosity is part of every newsman's basic equipment.

We borrowed a small handling-lifter and one of the spaceport roustabouts to tow it for us, loaded Murell's luggage and my things onto it, and started down to the bottomside cargo hatches, from which the ship was discharging. There was no cargo at all to go aboard, except mail and

29

things like Adolf Lautier's old film and music tapes. Our only export is tallow-wax, and it all goes to Terra. It would be picked up by the *Cape Canaveral* when she got in from Odin five hundred hours from now. But except for a few luxury items from Odin, everything we import comes from Terra, and the *Peenemünde* had started discharging that already. We rode down on a contragravity skid loaded with ammunition. I saw Murell looking curiously at the square cases, marked TERRAN FEDERATION ARMED FORCES, and 50-MM, MK. 608, ANTIVEHICLE AND ANTIPERSONNEL, 25 ROUNDS, and OVERAGE. PRACTICE ONLY. NOT TO BE ISSUED FOR SERVICE, and INSPECTED AND CONDEMNED. The hunters bought that stuff through the Co-op. It cost half as much as new ammo, but that didn't help them any. The difference stopped with Steve Ravick. Murrell didn't comment, and neither did Tom or I.

We got off at the bottom of the pit, a thousand feet below the promenade from which I had come aboard, and stopped for a moment. Murell was looking about the great amphitheater in amazement.

"I knew this spaceport would be big when I found out that the ship landed directly on the planet," he said, "but I never expected anything like this. And this serves a population of twenty thousand?"

"Twenty-four thousand, seven hundred and eight, if the man who got pounded in a barroom fight around 1330 hasn't died yet," I said. "But you have to remember that this place was built close to a hundred years ago, when the population was ten times that much." I'd gotten my story from him; now it was his turn to interview me. "You know something about the history of Fenris, I suppose?"

"Yes. There are ample sources for it on Terra, up to the collapse of the Fenris Company," he said. "Too much isn't known about what's been happening here since, which is why I decided to do this book."

"Well, there were several cities built, over on the mainland," I told him. "They're all abandoned now. The first one was a conventional city, the buildings all on the surface. After one day-and-night cycle, they found that it was uninhabitable. It was left unfinished. Then they started digging in. The Chartered Fenris Company shipped in huge quantities of mining and earth-moving equipment—that put the company in the red more than anything else—and they began making burrow-cities, like the ones built in the Northern Hemisphere of Terra during the Third and Fourth World Wars, or like the cities on Luna and Mercury Twilight Zone and Titan. There are a lot of valuable mineral deposits over on the mainland; maybe in another century our grandchildren will start working them again.

"But about six years before the Fenris Company went to pieces, they decided to concentrate in one city, here in the archipelago. The sea water stays cooler in the daytime and doesn't lose heat so rapidly in the nighttime. So they built Port Sandor, here on Oakleaf Island."

"And for convenience in monster-hunting?"

I shook my head. "No. The Jarvis's sea-monster wasn't discovered until after the city was built, and it was years after the company had gone bankrupt before anybody found out about what tallow-wax was good for."

I started telling him about the native life-forms of Fenris. Because of the surface temperature extremes, the marine life is the most highly developed. The land animals are active during the periods after sunset and after sunrise; when it begins getting colder or hotter, they burrow, or crawl into caves and crevices among the rocks, and go into suspended animation. I found that he'd read up on that, and not too much of his information was incorrect.

He seemed to think, though, that Port Sandor had also been mined out below the surface. I set him right on that.

"You saw what it looked like when you were coming down," I said. "Just a flat plateau, with a few shaft-head domes here and there, and the landing pit of the spaceport. Well, originally it was a valley, between two low hills. The city was built in the valley, level by level, and then the tops of the hills were dug off and bulldozed down on top of it. We have a lot of film at the public library of the construction of the city, step by step. As far as I know, there are no copies anywhere off-planet."

He should have gotten excited about that, and wanted to see them. Instead, he was watching the cargo come off—food-stuffs, now—and wanted to know if we had to import everything we needed.

"Oh, no. We're going in on the Bottom Level, which is mainly storage, but we have hydroponic farms for our vegetables and carniculture plants for meat on the Second and Third Levels. That's counting down from the Main City Level. We make our own lumber, out of reeds harvested in the swamps after sunrise and converted to pulpwood, and we get some good hardwood from the native trees which only grow in four periods of two hundred hours a year. We only use that for furniture, gunstocks, that sort of thing. And there are a couple of mining camps and smelters on the mainland; they employ about a thousand of our people. But every millisol that's spent on this planet is gotten from the sale of tallow-wax, at second or third hand if not directly."

That seemed to interest him more. Maybe his book, if he was really writing one, was going to be an economic study of Fenris. Or maybe his racket, whatever it was, would be based on something connected with our local production. I went on telling him about our hydroponic farms, and the carniculture plant where any kind of animal tissue we wanted was grown—Terran pork and beef and poultry, Freyan *zhoumy* meat, Zarathustran veldbeest. . . . He knew, already, that none of the native life-forms, animal or vegetable, were edible by Terrans.

"You can get all the *paté de foie gras* you want here," I said. "We have a chunk of goose liver about fifty feet in diameter growing in one of our vats."

By this time, we'd gotten across the bottom of the pit, Murell's luggage and my equipment being towed after us, and had entered the Bottom Level. It was cool and pleasant here, lighted from the ceiling fifty feet overhead, among the great column bases, two hundred feet square and two hundred yards apart, that supported the upper city and the thick roof of rock and earth that insu-

lated it. The area we were entering was stacked
with tallow-wax waiting to be loaded onto the
Cape Canaveral when she came in; it was
vacuum-packed in plastic skins, like big half-ton
Bologna sausages, each one painted with the blue
and white emblem of the Hunters' Co-operative.
He was quite interested in that, and was figuring,
mentally, how much wax there was here and how
much it was worth.

"Who does this belong to?" he wanted to know.
"The Hunters' Co-operative?"

Tom had been letting me do the talking up to
now, but he answered that question, very emphatically.

"No, it doesn't. It belongs to the hunters," he
said. "Each ship crew owns the wax they bring in
in common, and it's sold for them by the Co-op.
When the captain gets paid for the wax he's
turned over to the Co-op, he divides the money
among the crew. But every scrap of this belongs to
the ships that took it, up till it's bought and paid
for by Kapstaad Chemical."

"Well, if a captain wants his wax back, after it's
been turned over for sale to the Co-op, can he get
it?" Murell asked.

"Absolutely!"

Murell nodded, and we went on. The roustabout who had been following us with the lifter
had stopped to chat with a couple of his fellows.
We went on slowly, and now and then a vehicle,
usually a lorry, would pass above us. Then I saw
Bish Ware, ahead, sitting on a sausage of wax,
talking to one of the Spaceport Police. They were
both smoking, but that was all right. Tallow-wax
will burn, and a wax fire is something to get really

excited about, but the ignition point is 750° C., and that's a lot hotter than the end of anybody's cigar. He must have come out the same way we did, and I added that to the "wonder-why" file. Pretty soon, I'd have so many questions to wonder about that they'd start answering each other. He saw us and waved to us, and then suddenly the spaceport cop's face got as white as my shirt and he grabbed Bish by the arm. Bish didn't change color; he just shook off the cop's hand, got to his feet, dropped his cigar, and took a side skip out into the aisle.

"Murell!" he yelled. "Freeze! On your life; don't move a muscle!"

Then there was a gun going off in his hand. I didn't see him reach for it, or where he drew it from. It was just in his hand, firing, and the empty brass flew up and came down on the concrete with a jingle on the heels of the report. We had all stopped short, and the roustabout who was towing the lifter came hurrying up. Murell simply stood gaping at Bish.

"All right," Bish said, slipping his gun back into a shoulder holster under his coat. "Step carefully to your left. Don't move right at all."

Murell, still in a sort of trance, obeyed. As he did I looked past his right shin and saw what Bish had been shooting at. It was an irregular gray oval, about sixteen inches by four at its widest and tapering up in front to a cone about six inches high, into which a rodlike member, darker gray, was slowly collapsing and dribbling oily yellow stuff. The bullet had gone clear through and made a mess of dirty gray and black and green body fluids on the concrete.

It was what we call a tread-snail, because it moves on a double row of pads like stumpy feet and leaves a trail like a tractor. The fishpole-aerial thing it had erected out of its head was its stinger, and the yellow stuff was venom. A tenth of a milligram of it in your blood and it's "Get the Gate open, St. Peter; here I come."

Tom saw it as soon as I did. His face got the same color as the cop's. I don't suppose mine looked any better. When Murell saw what had been buddying up to him, I will swear, on a warehouse full of Bibles, Korans, Torah scrolls, Satanist grimoires, Buddhist prayer wheels and Thoran Grandfather-God images, that his hair literally stood on end. I've heard that expression all my life; well, this time I really saw it happen. I mentioned that he seemed to have been reading up on the local fauna.

I looked down at his right leg. He hadn't been stung—if he had, he wouldn't be breathing now—but he had been squirted, and there were a couple of yellow stains on the cloth of his trouser leg. I told him to hold still, used my left hand to pull the cloth away from his leg, and got out my knife and flipped it open with the other hand, cutting away the poisoned cloth and dropping it on the dead snail.

Murell started making an outcry about cutting up his trousers, and said he could have had them cleaned. Bish Ware, coming up, told him to stop talking like an imbecile.

"No cleaner would touch them, and even if they were cleaned, some of the poison would remain in the fabric. Then, the next time you were caught in the rain with a scratch on your leg, Walt, here, would write you one of his very nicest obituaries."

Then he turned to the cop, who was gabbling into his belt radio, and said: "Get an ambulance, quick. Possible case of tread-snail skin poisoning." A moment later, looking at Murell's leg, he added, "Omit 'possible.'"

There were a couple of little spots on Murell's skin that were beginning to turn raw-liver color. The raw poison hadn't gotten into his blood, but some of it, with impurities, had filtered through the cloth, and he'd absorbed enough of it through his skin to make him seriously ill. The cop jabbered some more into the radio, and the laborer with the lifter brought it and let it down, and Murell sat down on his luggage. Tom lit a cigarette and gave it to him, and told him to remain perfectly still. In a couple of minutes, an ambulance was coming, its siren howling.

The pilot and his helper were both jackleg medics, at least as far as first aid. They gave him a drink out of a flask, smeared a lot of gunk on the spots and slapped plasters over them, and helped him into the ambulance, after I told him we'd take his things to the Times building.

By this time, between the shot and the siren, quite a crowd had gathered, and everybody was having a nice little recrimination party. The labor foreman was chewing the cop out. The warehouse superintendent was chewing him out. And somebody from the general superintendent's office was chewing out everybody indiscriminately, and at the same time mentioning to me that Mr. Fieschi, the superintendent, would be very much pleased if the Times didn't mention the incident at all. I

told him that was editorial policy, and to talk to
Dad about it. Nobody had any idea how the thing
had gotten in, but that wasn't much of a mystery.
The Bottom Level is full of things like that; they
can stay active all the time because the temperature is constant. I supposed that eventually they'd
pick the dumbest day laborer in the place and
make him the patsy.

Tom stood watching the ambulance whisk
Murell off, dithering in indecision. The poisoning
of Murell seemed like an unexpected blow to
him. That fitted what I'd begun to think. Finally,
he motioned the laborer to pick up the lifter, and
we started off toward where he had parked his
jeep, outside the spaceport area.

Bish walked along with us, drawing his pistol
and replacing the fired round in the magazine. I
noticed that it was a 10-mm Colt-Argentine Federation Service, commercial type. There aren't
many of those on Fenris. A lot of 10-mm's, but
mostly South African Sterbergs or Vickers-
Bothas, or Mars-Consolidated Police Specials.
Mine, which I wasn't carrying at the moment, was
a Sterberg 7.7-mm Olympic Match.

"You know," he said, sliding the gun back
under his coat, "I would be just as well pleased as
Mr. Fieschi if this didn't get any publicity. If you
do publish anything about it, I wish you'd
minimize my own part in it. As you have noticed,
I have some slight proficiency with lethal
hardware. This I would prefer not to advertise. I
can usually avoid trouble, but when I can't, I
would like to retain the advantage of surprise."

We all got into the jeep. Tom, not too gracious-
ly, offered to drop Bish wherever he was going.

Bish said he was going to the *Times,* so Tom lifted the jeep and cut in the horizontal drive. We got into a busy one-way aisle, crowded with lorries hauling foodstuffs to the refrigeration area. He followed that for a short distance, and then turned off into a dimly lighted, disused area.

Before long, I began noticing stacks of tallow-wax, put up in the regular outside sausage skins but without the Co-op markings. They just had the names of hunter-ships—*Javelin, Bulldog, Helldiver, Slasher,* and so on.

"What's that stuff doing in here?" I asked. "It's a long way from the docks, and a long way from the spaceport."

"Oh, just temporary storage," Tom said. "It hasn't been checked in with the Co-op yet."

That wasn't any answer—or maybe it was. I let it go at that. Then we came to an open space about fifty feet square. There was a jeep, with a 7-mm machine gun mounted on it, and half a dozen men in boat-clothes were playing cards at a table made out of empty ammunition boxes. I noticed they were all wearing pistols, and when a couple of them saw us, they got up and grabbed rifles. Tom let down and got out of the jeep, going over and talking with them for a few minutes. What he had to tell them didn't seem to bring any noticeable amount of sunlight into their lives. After a while he came back, climbed in at the controls, and lifted the jeep again.

4

MAIN CITY LEVEL

THE CEILING on Main City Level is two hundred feet high; in order to permit free circulation of air and avoid traffic jams, nothing is built higher than a hundred and fifty feet except the square buildings, two hundred yards apart, which rest on foundations on the Bottom Level and extend up to support the roof. The *Times* has one of these pillar-buildings, and we have the whole thing to ourselves. In a city built for a quarter of a million, twenty thousand people don't have to crowd very closely on one another. Naturally, we don't have a top landing stage, but except for the buttresses at the corners and solid central column, the whole street floor is open.

Tom hadn't said anything after we left the stacks of wax and the men guarding them. We came up a vehicle shaft a few blocks up Broadway, and he brought the jeep down and floated it in through one of the archways. As usual, the place was cluttered with equipment we hadn't gotten around to repairing or installing, merchandise we'd taken in exchange for advertising, and vehicles, our own and everybody else's. A

couple of mechanics were tinkering on one of
them. I decided, for the oomptieth time, to do
something about cleaning it up. Say in another
two or three hundred hours, when the ships
would all be in port and work would be slack, and
I could hire a couple of good men to help.

We got Murell's stuff off the jeep, and I hunted
around till I found a hand-lifter.

"Want to stay and have dinner with us, Tom?" I
asked.

"Uh?" It took him a second or so to realize what
I'd said. "Why, no, thanks, Walt. I have to get back
to the ship. Father wants to see me before the
meeting."

"How about you, Bish? Want to take potluck
with us?"

"I shall be delighted," he assured me.

Tom told us good-by absent-mindedly, lifted
the jeep, and floated it out into the street. Bish and
I watched him go; Bish looked as though he had
wanted to say something and then thought better
of it. We floated Murell's stuff and mine over to
the elevator beside the central column, and I ran it
up to the editorial offices on the top floor.

We came out in a big room, half the area of the
floor, full of worktables and radios and screens
and photoprinting machines. Dad, as usual, was
in a gray knee-length smock, with a pipe jutting
out under his ragged mustache, and, as usual, he
was stopping every minute or so to relight it. He
was putting together the stuff I'd transmitted in
for the audio-visual newscast. Over across the
room, the rest of the Times staff, Julio Kubanoff,
was sitting at the composing machine, his peg leg
propped up and an earphone on, his fingers

punching rapidly at the keyboard as he burned letters onto the white plastic sheet with ultraviolet rays for photographing. Julio was an old hunter-ship man who had lost a leg in an accident and taught himself his new trade. He still wore the beard, now white, that was practically the monster-hunters' uniform.

"The stuff come in all right?" I asked Dad, letting down the lifter.

"Yes. What do you think of that fellow Belsher?" he asked. "Did you ever hear such an impudent string of lies in your life?" Then, out of the corner of his eye, he saw the lifter full of luggage, and saw somebody with me. "Mr. Murell? Please excuse me for a moment, till I get this blasted thing together straight." Then he got the film spliced and the sound record matched, and looked up. "Why, Bish? Where's Mr. Murell, Walt?"

"Mr. Murell has had his initiation to Fenris," I said. "He got squirted by a tread-snail almost as soon as he got off the ship. They have him at the spaceport hospital; it'll be 2400 before they get all the poison sweated out of him."

I went on to tell him what had happened. Dad's eyes widened slightly, and he took the pipe out of his mouth and looked at Bish with something very reasonably like respect.

"That was mighty sharp work," he said. "If you'd been a second slower, we'd be all out of visiting authors. That would have been a nice business; story would have gotten back to Terra, and been most unfortunate publicity for Fenris. And, of course," he afterthoughted, "most unfortunate for Mr. Murell, too."

"Well, if you give this any publicity, I would rather you passed my own trifling exploit over in silence," Bish said. "I gather the spaceport people wouldn't be too happy about giving the public the impression that their area is teeming with tread-snails, either. They have enough trouble hiring shipping-floor help as it is."

"But don't you want people to know what you did?" Dad demanded, incredulously. Everybody wanted their names in print or on 'cast; that was one of his basic articles of faith. "If the public learned about this—" he went on, and then saw where he was heading and pulled up short. It wouldn't be tactful to say something like, "Maybe they wouldn't think you were just a worthless old soak."

Bish saw where Dad was heading, too, but he just smiled, as though he were about to confer his episcopal blessing.

"Ah, but that would be a step out of character for me," he said. "I must not confuse my public. Just as a favor to me, Ralph, say nothing about it."

"Well, if you'd rather I didn't . . . Are you going to cover this meeting at Hunters' Hall, to-night, Walt?" he asked me.

"Would I miss it?"

He frowned. "I could handle that myself," he said. "I'm afraid this meeting's going to get a little rough."

I shook my head. "Let's face it, Dad," I said. "I'm a little short of eighteen, but you're sixty. I can see things coming better than you can, and dodge them quicker."

Dad gave a rueful little laugh and looked at Bish.

"See how it goes?" he asked. "We spend our lives shielding our young and then, all of a sudden, we find they're shielding us." His pipe had gone out again and he relit it. "Too bad you didn't get an audiovisual of Belsher making that idiotic statement."

"He didn't even know I was getting a voice-only. All the time he was talking, I was doodling in a pad with a pencil."

"Synthetic substitutes!" Dad snorted. "Putting a synthetic tallow-wax molecule together would be like trying to build a spaceship with a jackknife and a tack hammer." He puffed hard on his pipe, and then excused himself and went back to his work.

Editing an audiovisual telecast is pretty much a one-man job. Bish wanted to know if he could be of assistance, but there was nothing either of us could do, except sit by and watch and listen. Dad handled the Belsher thing by making a film of himself playing off the recording, and interjecting sarcastic comments from time to time. When it went on the air, I thought, Ravick wasn't going to like it. I would have to start wearing my pistol again. Then he made a tape on the landing of the Peenemünde and the arrival of Murell, who he said had met with a slight accident after leaving the ship. I took that over to Julio when Dad was finished, along with a tape on the announced tallow-wax price cut. Julio only grunted and pushed them aside. He was setting up the story of the fight in Martian Joe's—a "local bar," of course; nobody ever gets shot or stabbed or slashed or slugged in anything else. All the news *is* fit to print, sure, but you can't give your advertisers and teleprinter customers any worse name than they have already. A paper has to use some judgment.

Then Dad and Bish and I went down to dinner. Julio would have his a little later, not because we're too good to eat with the help but because, around 1830, the help is too busy setting up the next paper to eat with us. The dining room, which is also the library, living room, and general congregating and loafing place, is as big as the editorial room above. Originally, it was an office, at a time when a lot of Fenris Company office work was being done here. Some of the furniture is original, and some was made for us by local cabinetmakers out of native hardwood. The dining table, big enough for two ships' crews to eat at, is an example of the latter. Then, of course, there are screens and microbook cabinets and things like that, and a refrigerator to save going a couple of hundred feet to the pantry in case anybody wants a snack.

I went to that and opened it, and got out a bulb of concentrated fruit juice and a bottle of carbonated water. Dad, who seldom drinks, keeps a few bottles around for guests. Seems most of our "guests" part with information easier if they have something like the locally made hydroponic potato schnapps inside them for courage.

"You drink Baldur honey-rum, don't you, Bish?" he said, pawing among the bottles in the liquor cabinet next to the refrigerator. "I'm sure I have a bottle of it. Now wait a minute; it's here somewhere."

When Dad passes on and some medium claims to have produced a spirit communication from him, I will not accept it as genuine without the

expression: "Now wait a minute; it's here somewhere."

Bish wanted to know what I was fixing for myself, and I told him.

"Never mind the rum, Ralph. I believe," he
said, "that I shall join Walt in a fruit fizz."

Well, whattaya know! Maybe my stealthy tem-
perance campaign was having results. Dad looked
positively startled, and then replaced the bottle he
was holding.

"I believe I'll make it unanimous," he said. "Fix
me up a fruit fizz, too, Walt."

I mixed two more fruit fizzes, and we carried
them over to the table. Bish sipped at his critical-
ly.

"Palatable," he pronounced it. "Just a trifle on
the mild side, but definitely palatable."

Dad looked at him as though he still couldn't
believe the whole thing. Dinner was slow coming.
We finished our fizzes, and Bish and I both
wanted repeats, and Dad felt that he had to go
along. So I made three more. We were finishing
them when Mrs. Laden started bringing in the
dinner. Mrs. Laden is a widow; she has been
with us since my mother died, the year after I was
born. She is violently anti-liquor. Reluctantly, she
condones Dad taking a snort now and then, but as
soon as she saw Bish Ware, her face started to
stiffen.

She put the soup on the table and took off for the
kitchen. She always has her own dinner with
Julio. That way, while they're eating he can tell
her all the news that's fit to print, and all the
gossip that isn't.

For the moment, the odd things I'd been noticing about our distinguished and temporarily in-

capacitated visitor came under the latter head. I told Dad and Bish about my observations, beginning with the deafening silence about Glenn Murell at the library. Dad began popping immediately.

"Why, he must be an impostor!" he exlaimed. "What kind of a racket do you think he's up to?"

"Mmm-mm; I wouldn't say that, not right away," Bish said. "In the first place, Murell may be his true name and he may publish under a nom de plume. I admit, some of the other items are a little suspicious, but even if he isn't an author, he may have some legitimate business here and, having heard a few stories about this planetary Elysium, he may be exercising a little caution. Walt, tell your father about that tallow-wax we saw, down in Bottom Level Fourth Ward."

I did, and while I was talking Dad sat with his soup spoon poised halfway to his mouth for at least a minute before he remembered he was holding it.

"Now, that is funny," he said when I was through. "Why do you suppose . . .?"

"Somebody," Bish said, "some group of ship captains, is holding wax out from the Co-operative. There's no other outlet for it, so my guess is that they're holding it for a rise in price. There's only one way that could happen, and that, literally, would be over Steve Ravick's dead body. It could be that they expect Steve's dead body to be around for a price rise to come in over."

I was expecting Dad to begin spouting law-and-order. Instead, he hit the table with his fist; not, fortunately, the one that was holding the soup spoon.

"Well, I hope so! And if they do it before the

Cape Canaveral gets in, they may fix Leo Belsher, too, and then, in the general excitement, somebody might clobber Mort Hallstock, and that'd be grand slam. After the triple funeral, we could go to work on setting up an honest co-operative and an honest government."

"Well, I never expected to hear you advocating lynch law, Dad," I said.

He looked at me for a few seconds.

"Tell the truth, Walt, neither did I," he admitted. "Lynch law is a horrible thing; don't make any mistake about that. But there's one thing more horrible, and that's no law at all. And that is the present situation in Port Sandor.

"You know what the trouble is, here? We have no government. No legal government, anyhow; no government under Federation law. We don't even have a Federation Resident-Agent. Before the Fenris Company went broke, it was the government here; when the Space Navy evacuated the colonists, they evacuated the government along with them. The thousand who remained were all too busy keeping alive to worry about that. They didn't even care when Fenris was reclassified from Class III, uninhabited but inhabitable, to Class II, inhabitable only in artificial environment, like Mercury or Titan. And when Mort Hallstock got hold of the town-meeting pseudo government they put together fifty years ago and turned it into a dictatorship, nobody realized what had happened till it was too late. Lynch law's the only recourse we have."

"Ralph," Bish told him, "if anything like that starts, Belsher and Hallstock and Ravick won't be the only casualties. Between Ravick's goons and

Hallstock's police, they have close to a hundred men. I won't deny that they could be cleaned out, but it wouldn't be a lynching. It would be a civil war."

"Well, that's swell!" Dad said. "The Federation Government has never paid us any attention; the Federation planets are scattered over too many million cubic light-years of space for the Government to run around to all of them wiping everybody's noses. As long as things are quiet here, they'll continue to do nothing for us. But let a story hit the big papers on Terra, *Revolution Breaks Out on Fenris*—and that'll be the story I'll send to Interworld News—and watch what happens."

"I will tell you what will happen," Bish Ware said. "A lot of people will get killed. That isn't important, in itself. People are getting killed all the time, in a lot worse causes. But these people will all have friends and relatives who will take it up for them. Start killing people here in a faction fight, and somebody will be shooting somebody in the back out of a dark passage a hundred years from now over it. You want this planet poisoned with blood feuds for the next century?"

Dad and I looked at one another. That was something that hadn't occurred to either of us, and it should have. There were feuds, even now. Half the little settlements on the other islands and on the mainland had started when some group or family moved out of Port Sandor because of the enmity of some larger and more powerful group or family, and half our shootings and knife fights grew out of old grudges between families or hunting crews.

"We don't want it poisoned for the next century with the sort of thing Mort Hallstock and Steve Ravick started here, either," Dad said.

"Granted." Bish nodded. "If a civil war's the only possible way to get rid of them, that's what you'll have to have, I suppose. Only make sure you don't leave a single one of them alive when it's over. But if you can get the Federation Government in here to clean the mess up, that would be better. Nobody starts a vendetta with the Terran Federation."

"But how?" Dad asked. "I've sent story after story off about crime and corruption on Fenris. They all get the file-and-forget treatment."

Mrs. Laden had taken away the soup plates and brought us our main course. Bish sat toying with his fork for a moment.

"I don't know what you can do," he said slowly. "If you can stall off the blowup till the *Cape Canaveral* gets in, and you can send somebody to Terra . . ."

All of a sudden, it hit me. Here was something that would give Bish a purpose; something to make him want to stay sober.

"Well, don't say, 'If *you* can,' " I said. "Say, 'If *we* can.' You live on Fenris, too, don't you?"

5

MEETING OUT OF ORDER

DAD CALLED THE spaceport hospital, after dinner, and talked to Doc Rojansky. Murell was asleep, and in no danger whatever. They'd given him a couple of injections and a sedative, and his system was throwing off the poison satisfactorily. He'd be all right, but they thought he ought to be allowed to rest at the hospital for a while.

By then, it was time for me to leave for Hunters' Hall. Julio and Mrs. Laden were having their dinner, and Dad and Bish went up to the editorial office. I didn't take a car. Hunters' Hall was only a half dozen blocks south of the *Times*, toward the waterfront. I carried my radio-under-false-pretense slung from my shoulder, and started downtown on foot.

The business district was pretty well lighted, both from the ceiling and by the stores and restaurants. Most of the latter were in the open, with small kitchen and storage buildings. At a table at one of them I saw two petty officers from the *Pennemünde* with a couple of girls, so I knew the ship wasn't leaving immediately. Going past the

Municipal Building, I saw some activity, and an unusually large number of police gathered around the vehicle port. Ravick must have his doubts about how the price cut was going to be received, and Mort Hallstock was mobilizing his storm troopers to give him support in case he needed it. I called in about that, and Dad told me fretfully to be sure to stay out of trouble.

Hunters' Hall was a four-story building, fairly substantial as buildings that don't have to support the roof go, with a landing stage on top and a vehicle park underneath. As I came up, I saw a lot of cars and jeeps and ships' boats grounded in and around it, and a crowd of men, almost all of them in boat-clothes and wearing whiskers, including quite a few characters who had never been out in a hunter-ship in their lives but were members in the best of good standing of the Co-operative. I also saw a few of Hallstock's uniformed thugs standing around with their thumbs in their gun belts or twirling their truncheons.

I took an escalator up to the second floor, which was one big room, with the escalators and elevators in the rear. It was the social room, decorated with photos and models and solidigraphs of hunter-ships, photos of record-sized monsters lashed alongside ships before cutting-up, group pictures of ships's crews, monster tusks, dried slashers and halberd fish, and a whole monster head, its tusked mouth open. There was a big crowd there, too, at the bar, at the game machines, or just standing around in groups talking.

I saw Tom Kivelson and his father and Oscar Fujisawa, and went over to join them. Joe Kivelson is just an outsize edition of his son, with a blond beard that's had thirty-five years' more growth. Oscar is skipper of the Pequod—he wouldn't have looked baffled if Bish Ware called him Captain Ahab—and while his family name is Old Terran Japanese, he had blue eyes and red hair and beard. He was almost as big as Joe Kivelson.

"Hello, Walt," Joe greeted me. "What's this Tom's been telling me about Bish Ware shooting a tread-snail that was going to sting Mr. Murell?"

"Just about that," I said. "That snail must have crawled out from between two stacks of wax as we came up. We never saw it till it was all over. It was right beside Murell and had its stinger up when Bish shot it."

"He took an awful chance," Kivelson said. "He might of shot Mr. Murell."

I suppose it would look that way to Joe. He is the planet's worst pistol shot, so according to him nobody can hit anything with a pistol.

"He wouldn't have taken any chance not shooting," I said. "If he hadn't, we'd have been running the Murell story with black borders."

Another man came up, skinny, red hair, sharp-pointed nose. His name was Al Devis, and he was Joe Kivelson's engineer's helper. He wanted to know about the tread-snail shooting, so I had to go over it again. I hadn't anything to add to what Tom had told them already, but I was the Times, and if the Times says so it's true.

"Well, I wouldn't want any drunk like Bish Ware shooting around me with a pistol," Joe Kivelson said.

That's relative, too. Joe doesn't drink.

"Don't kid yourself, Joe," Oscar told him. "I saw

Bish shoot a knife out of a man's hand, one time, in One Eye Swanson's. Didn't scratch the guy; hit the blade. One Eye has the knife, with the bullet mark on it, over his back bar, now."

"Well, was he drunk then?" Joe asked.

"Well, he had to hang onto the bar with one hand while he fired with the other." Then he turned to me. "How is Murell, now?" he asked.

I told him what the hospital had given us. Everybody seemed much relieved. I wouldn't have thought that a celebrated author of whom nobody had ever heard before would be the center of so much interest in monster-hunting circles. I kept looking at my watch while we were talking. After a while, the *Times* newscast came on the big screen across the room, and everybody moved over toward it.

They watched the *Peenemünde* being towed down and berthed, and the audiovisual interview with Murell. Then Dad came on the screen with a record player in front of them, and gave them a play-off of my interview with Leo Belsher.

Ordinary bad language I do not mind. I'm afraid I use a little myself, while struggling with some of the worn-out equipment we have at the paper. But when Belsher began explaining about how the price of wax had to be cut again, to thirty-five centisols a pound, the language those hunters used positively smelled. I noticed, though, that a lot of the crowd weren't saying anything at all. They would be Ravick's boys, and they would have orders not to start anything before the meeting.

"Wonder if he's going to try to give us that stuff about substitutes?" Oscar said.

"Well, what are you going to do?" I asked.

"I'll tell you what we're not going to do," Joe Kivelson said. "We're not going to take his price cut. If he won't pay our price, he can use his [deleted by censor] substitutes."

"You can't sell wax anywhere else, can you?"

"Is that so, we can't?" Joe started.

Before he could say anything else, Oscar was interrupting:

"We can eat for a while, even if we don't sell wax. Sigurd Ngozori'll carry us for a while and make loans on wax. But if the wax stops coming in, Kapstaad Chemical's going to start wondering why . . ."

By this time, other *Javelin* men came drifting over—Ramón Llewellyn, the mate, and Abdullah Monnahan, the engineer, and Abe Clifford, the navigator, and some others. I talked with some of them, and then drifted off in the direction of the bar, where I found another hunter captain, Mohandas Gandhi Feinberg, whom everybody simply called the Mahatma. He didn't resemble his namesake. He had a curly black beard with a twisted black cigar sticking out of it, and nobody, after one look at him, would have mistaken him for any apostle of nonviolence.

He had a proposition he was enlisting support for. He wanted balloting at meetings to be limited to captains of active hunter-ships, the captains to vote according to expressed wishes of a majority of their crews. It was a good scheme, though it would have sounded better if the man who was advocating it hadn't been a captain himself. At least, it would have disenfranchised all Ravick's permanently unemployed "unemployed hunters." The only trouble was, there was no conceivable way of getting it passed. It was too much like trying to curtail the powers of Parliament by act of Parliament.

The gang from the street level started coming up, and scattered in twos and threes around the hall, ready for trouble. I'd put on my radio when I'd joined the Kivelsons and Oscar, and I kept it on, circulating around and letting it listen to the conversations. The Ravick people were either saying nothing or arguing that Belsher was doing the best he could, and if Kapstaad wouldn't pay more than thirty-five centisols, it wasn't his fault. Finally, the call bell for the meeting began clanging, and the crowd began sliding over toward the elevators and escalators.

The meeting room was on the floor above, at the front of the building, beyond a narrow hall and a door at which a couple of Ravick henchmen wearing guns and sergeant-at-arms brassards were making everybody check their knives and pistols. They passed me by without getting my arsenal, which consisted of a sleep-gas projector camouflaged as a jumbo-sized lighter and twenty sols in two rolls of forty quarter sols each. One of these inside a fist can make a big difference.

Ravick and Belsher and the secretary of the Co-op, who was a little scrawny henpecked-husband type who never had an opinion of his own in his life, were all sitting back of a big desk on a dais in front. After as many of the crowd who could had found seats and the rest, including the Press, were standing in the rear, Ravick pounded with the chunk of monster tusk he used for a gavel and called the meeting to order.

"There's a bunch of old business," he said, "but I'm going to rule that aside for the moment. We have with us this evening our representative on Terra, Mr. Leo Belsher, whom I wish to present. Mr. Belsher."

Belsher got up. Ravick started clapping his hands to indicate that applause was in order. A few of his zombies clapped their hands; everybody else was quiet. Belsher held up a hand.

"Please don't applaud," he begged. "What I have to tell you isn't anything to applaud about."

"You're tootin' well right it isn't!" somebody directly in front of me said, very distinctly.

"I'm very sorry to have to bring this news to you, but the fact is that Kapstaad Chemical Products, Ltd., is no longer able to pay forty-five centisols a pound. This price is being scaled down to thirty-five centisols. I want you to understand that Kapstaad Chemical wants to give you every cent they can, but business conditions no longer permit them to pay the old price. Thirty-five is the absolute maximum they can pay and still meet competition—"

"Aaah, knock it off, Belsher!" somebody shouted. "We heard all that rot on the screen."

"How about our contract?" somebody else asked. "We do have a contract with Kapstaad, don't we?"

"Well, the contract will have to be re-negotiated. They'll pay thirty-five centisols or they'll pay nothing."

"They can try getting along without wax. Or try buying it somewhere else!"

"Yes; those wonderful synthetic substitutes!"

"Mr. Chairman," Oscar Fujisawa called out. "I

move that this organization reject the price of thirty-five centisols a pound for tallow-wax, as offered by, or through, Leo Belsher at this meeting."

Ravick began clamoring that Oscar was out of order, that Leo Belsher had the floor.

"I second Captain Fujisawa's motion," Mohandas Feinberg said.

"And Leo Belsher doesn't have the floor; he's not a member of the Co-operative," Tom Kivelson declared. "He's our hired employee, and as soon as this present motion is dealt with, I intend moving that we fire him and hire somebody else."

"I move to amend Captain Fujisawa's motion," Joe Kivelson said. "I move that the motion, as amended, read, '—and stipulate a price of seventy-five centisols a pound.'"

"You're crazy!" Belsher almost screamed.

Seventy-five was the old price, from which he and Ravick had been reducing until they'd gotten down to forty-five.

Just at that moment, my radio began making a small fuss. I unhooked the handphone and brought it to my face.

"Yeah?"

It was Bish Ware's voice: "Walt, get hold of the Kivelsons and get them out of Hunters' Hall as fast as you can," he said. "I just got a tip from one of my . . . my parishioners. Ravick's going to stage a riot to give Hallstock's cops an excuse to raid the meeting. They want the Kivelsons."

"Roger." I hung up, and as I did I could hear Joe Kivelson shouting:

"You think we don't get any news on this planet? Tallow-wax has been selling for the same price on Terra that it did eight years ago, when you two crooks started cutting the price. Why, the very ship Belsher came here on brought the quotations on the commodity market—"

I edged through the crowd till I was beside Oscar Fujisawa. I decided the truth would need a little editing; I didn't want to use Bish Ware as my source.

"Oscar, Dad just called me," I told him. "A tip came in to the *Times* that Ravick's boys are going to fake a riot and Hallstock's cops are going to raid the meeting. They want Joe and Tom. You know what they'll do if they get hold of them."

"Shot while resisting arrest. You sure this is a good tip, though?"

Across the room, somebody jumped to his feet, kicking over a chair.

"That's a double two-em-dashed lie, you etaoin shrdlu so-and-so!" somebody yelled.

"Who are you calling a so-and-so, you thus-and-so-ing such-and-such?" somebody else yelled back, and a couple more chairs got smashed and a swirl of fighting started.

"Yes, it is," Oscar decided. "Let's go."

We started plowing through the crowd toward where the Kivelsons and a couple more of the *Javelin* crew were clumped. I got one of the rolls of quarter sols into my right fist and let Oscar go ahead. He has more mass than I have.

It was a good thing I did, because before we had gone ten feet, some character got between us, dragged a two-foot length of inch-and-a-half high-pressure hose out of his pant leg, and started to swing at the back of Oscar's head. I promptly clipped him behind the ear with a fist full of money, and down he went. Oscar, who must have eyes in the back of his head, turned and grabbed the hose out of his hand before he dropped it, using it to clout somebody in front of him. Somebody else came pushing toward us, and I was about to clip him, too, when he yelled, "Watch it, Walt; I'm with it!" It was Cesário Vieira, another *Javelin* man; he's engaged to Linda Kivelson, Joe's daughter and Tom's sister, the one going to school on Terra.

Then we had reached Tom and Joe Kivelson. Oscar grabbed Joe by the arm.

"Come on, Joe; let's get moving," he said. "Hallstock's Gestapo are on the way. They have orders to get you dead or alive."

"Like blazes!" Joe told him. "I never chickened out on a fight yet, and—"

That's what I'd been afraid of. Joe is like a Zarathustra veldtbeest; the only tactics he knows is a headlong attack.

"You want to get your crew and your son killed, and yourself along with them?" Oscar asked him. "That's what'll happen if the cops catch you. Now are you coming, or will I have to knock you senseless and drag you out?"

Fortunately, at that moment somebody took a swing at Joe and grazed his cheek. It was a good thing that was all he did; he was wearing brass knuckles. Joe went down a couple of feet, bending at the knees, and caught this fellow around the hips with both hands, straightening and lifting him over his head. Then he threw him over the heads of the people in front of him. There were yells where the human missile landed.

"That's the stuff, Joe!" Oscar shouted. "Come on, we got them on the run!"

That, of course, converted a strategic retreat into an attack. We got Joe aimed toward the doors and before he knew it, we were out in the hall by the elevators. There were a couple of Ravick's men, with sergeant-at-arms arm bands, and two city cops. One of the latter got in Joe's way. Joe punched him in the face and knocked him back about ten feet in a sliding stagger before he dropped. The other cop grabbed me by the left arm.

I slugged him under the jaw with my ten-sol right and knocked him out, and I felt the wrapping on the coin roll break and the quarters come loose in my hand. Before I could drop them into my jacket pocket and get out the other roll, one of the sergeants at arms drew a gun. I just hurled the handful of coins at him. He dropped the pistol and put both hands to his face, howling in pain.

I gave a small mental howl myself when I thought of all the nice things I could have bought for ten sols. One of Joe Kivelson's followers stooped and scooped up the fallen pistol, firing a couple of times with it. Then we all rushed Joe into one of the elevators and crowded in behind him, and as I turned to start it down I could hear police sirens from the street and also from the landing stage above. In the hall outside the meeting room, four or five of Ravick's free-drink mercenaries were down on all fours scrabbling for coins, and the rest of the pursuers from the meeting room were stumbling and tripping over them. I wished I'd brought a camera along, too. The public would have loved a shot of that. I lifted the radio and spoke into it:

"This is Walter Boyd, returning you now to the regular entertainment program."

A second later, the thing whistled at me. As the car started down and the doors closed I lifted the handphone. It was Bish Ware again.

"We're going down in the elevator to Second Level Down," I said. "I have Joe and Tom and Oscar Fujisawa and a few of the *Javelin* crew with me. The place is crawling with cops now."

"Go to Third Level Down and get up on the catwalk on the right," Bish said. "I'll be along to pick you up."

"Roger. We'll be looking for you."

The car stopped at Second Level Down. I punched a button and sent it down another level. Joe Kivelson, who was dabbing at his cheek with a piece of handkerchief tissue, wanted to know what was up.

"We're getting a pickup," I told him. "Vehicle from the *Times*."

I thought it would save arguments if I didn't mention who was bringing it.

6

ELEMENTARY, MY DEAR KIVELSON

BEFORE WE left the lighted elevator car, we took a quick nose count. Besides the Kivelsons, there were five *Javelin* men—Ramón Llewellyn, Abdullah Monnahan, Abe Clifford, Cesário Vieira, and a whitebeard named Piet Dumont. Al Devis had been with us when we crashed the door out of the meeting room, but he'd fallen by the way. We had a couple of flashlights, so, after sending the car down to Bottom Level, we picked our way up the zigzag iron stairs to the catwalk, under the seventy-foot ceiling, and sat down in the dark.

Joe Kivelson was fretting about what would happen to the rest of his men.

"Fine captain I am, running out and leaving them!"

"If they couldn't keep up, that's their tough luck," Oscar Fujisawa told him. "You brought out all you could. If you'd waited any longer, none of us would have gotten out."

"They won't bother with them," I added. "You and Tom and Oscar, here, are the ones they want."

Joe was still letting himself be argued into thinking he had done the right thing when we saw the lights of a lorry coming from uptown at ceiling level. A moment later, it backed to the catwalk, and Bish Ware stuck his head out from the pilot's seat.

"Where do you gentlemen wish to go?" he asked.

"To the *Javelin*," Joe said instantly.

"Huh-uh," Oscar disagreed. "That's the first place they'll look. That'll be all right for Ramón and the others, but if they catch you and Tom, they'll shoot you and call it self-defense, or take you in and beat both of you to a jelly. This'll blow over in fifteen or twenty hours, but I'm not going anywhere near my ship, now."

"Drop us off on Second Level Down, about Eighth Street and a couple of blocks from the docks," the mate, Llewellyn, said. "We'll borrow some weapons from Patel the Pawnbroker and then circulate around and see what's going on. But you and Joe and Oscar had better go underground for a while."

"The *Times*," I said. "We have a whole pillar-building to ourselves; we could hide half the population."

That was decided upon. We all piled into the lorry, and Bish took it to an inconspicuous place on the Second Level and let down. Ramón Llewellyn and the others got out. Then we went up to Main City Level. We passed within a few blocks of Hunters' Hall. There was a lot of noise, but no shooting.

Joe Kivelson didn't have anything to say, on the trip, but he kept looking at the pilot's seat in perplexity and apprehension. I think he expected Bish to try to ram the lorry through every building we passed by or over.

We found Dad in the editorial department on the top floor, feeding voice-tape to Julio while the latter made master sheets for teleprinting. I gave him a quick rundown on what had happened that he hadn't gotten from my radio. Dad cluck-clucked in disapproval, either at my getting into a fight, assaulting an officer, or, literally, throwing money away.

Bish Ware seemed a little troubled. "I think," he said, "that I shall make a circuit of my diocese, and see what can be learned from my devoted flock. Should I turn up anything significant, I will call it in."

With that, he went tottering over to the elevator, stumbling on the way and making an unepiscopal remark. I watched him, and then turned to Dad.

"Did he have anything to drink after I left?" I asked.

"Nothing but about five cups of coffee."

I mentally marked that: *Add oddities, Bish Ware.* He'd been at least four hours without liquor, and he was walking as unsteadily as when I'd first seen him at the spaceport. I didn't know any kind of liquor that would persist like that.

Julio had at least an hour's tape to transcribe, so Dad and Joe and Tom and Oscar and I went to the living room on the floor below. Joe was still being bewildered about Bish Ware.

"How'd he manage to come for us?" he wanted to know.

"Why, he was here with me all evening," Dad said. "He came from the spaceport with Walt and

Tom, and had dinner with us. He called a few people from here, and found out about the fake riot and police raid Ravick had cooked up. You'd be surprised at how much information he can pick up around town."

Joe looked at his son, alarmed.

"Hey! You let him see—" he began.

"The wax on Bottom Level, in the Fourth Ward?" I asked. "He won't blab about that. He doesn't blab things where they oughtn't be blabbed."

"That's right," Dad backed me up. He was beginning to think of Bish as one of the *Times* staff, now. "We got a lot of tips from him, but nothing we give him gets out." He got his pipe lit again. "What about that wax, Joe?" he asked. "Were you serious when you made that motion about a price of seventy-five centisols?"

"I sure was!" Joe declared. "That's the real price, and always has been, and that's what we get or Kapstaad doesn't get any more wax."

"If Murell can top it, maybe Kapstaad won't get any more wax, period," I said. "Who's he with— Interstellar Import-Export?"

Anybody would have thought a barbwire worm had crawled onto Joe Kivelson's chair seat under him.

"Where'd you hear that?" he demanded, which is the Galaxy's silliest question to ask any newsman. "Tom, if you've been talking—"

"He hasn't," I said. "He didn't need to. It sticks out a parsec in all directions." I mentioned some of the things I'd noticed while interviewing Murell, and his behavior after leaving the ship. "Even before I'd talked to him, I wondered why

Tom was so anxious to get aboard with me. He didn't know we'd arranged to put Murell up here; he was going to take him to see that wax, and then take him to the *Javelin*. You were going to produce him at the meeting and have him bid against Belsher, only that tread-snail fouled your lines for you. So then you thought you had to stall off a new contract till he got out of the hospital.''

The two Kivelsons and Oscar Fujisawa were looking at one another; Joe and Tom in consternation, and Oscar in derision of both of them. I was feeling pretty good. Brother, I thought, Sherlock Holmes never did better, himself.

That, all of a sudden, reminded me of Dr. John Watson, whom Bish perceived to have been in Afghanistan. That was one thing Sherlock H. Boyd hadn't deduced any answers for. Well, give me a little more time. And more data.

"You got it all figured out, haven't you?" Joe was asking sarcastically. The sarcasm was as hollow as an empty oil drum.

"The *Times*," Dad was saying, trying not to sound too proud, "has a very sharp reportorial staff, Joe."

"It isn't Interstellar," Oscar told me, grinning. "It's Argentine Exotic Organics. You know, everybody thought Joe, here, was getting pretty high-toned, sending his daughter to school on Terra. School wasn't the only thing she went for. We got a letter from her, the last time the *Cape Canaveral* was in, saying that she'd contacted Argentine Organics and that a man was coming out on the *Peenemünde*, posing as a travel-book author. Well, he's here, now."

"You'd better keep an eye on him," I advised.

"If Steve Ravick gets to him, he won't be much use to you."

"You think Ravick would really harm Murell?" Dad asked.

He thought so, too. He was just trying to comfort himself by pretending he didn't.

"What do you think, Ralph?" Oscar asked him. "If we get competitive wax buying, again, seventy-five a pound will be the starting price. I'm not spending the money till I get it, but I wouldn't be surprised to see wax go to a sol a pound on the loading floor here. And you know what that would mean."

"Thirty for Steve Ravick," Dad said. That puzzled Oscar, till I explained that "thirty" is newsese for "the end." "I guess Walt's right. Ravick would do anything to prevent that." He thought for a moment. "Joe, you were using the wrong strategy. You should have let Ravick get that thirty-five centisol price established for the Co-operative, and then had Murell offer seventy-five or something like that."

"You crazy?" Joe demanded. "Why, then the Co-op would have been stuck with it."

"That's right. And as soon as Murell's price was announced, everybody would drop out of the Co-operative and reclaim their wax, even the captains who owe Ravick money. He'd have nobody left but a handful of thugs and barflies."

"But that would smash the Co-operative," Joe Kivelson objected. "Listen, Ralph; I've been in the Co-operative all my life, since before Steve Ravick was heard of on this planet. I've worked hard for the Co-operative, and—"

You didn't work hard enough, I thought. You

let Steve Ravick take it away from you. Dad told Joe pretty much the same thing:

"You don't have a Co-operative, Joe. Steve Ravick has a racket. The only thing you can do with this organization is smash it, and then rebuild it with Ravick and his gang left out."

Joe puzzled over that silently. He'd been thinking that it was the same Co-operative his father and Simon MacGregor and the other old hunters had organized, and that getting rid of Ravick was simply a matter of voting him out. He was beginning to see, now, that parliamentary procedure wasn't any weapon against Ravick's force and fraud and intimidation.

"I think Walt has something," Oscar Fujisawa said. "As long as Murell's in the hospital at the spaceport, he's safe, but as soon as he gets out of Odin Dock & Shipyard territory, he's going to be a clay pigeon."

Tom hadn't been saying anything. Now he cleared his throat.

"On the *Peenemünde*, I was talking about taking Mr. Murell for a trip in the *Javelin*," he said. "That was while we were still pretending he'd come here to write a book. Maybe that would be a good idea, anyhow."

"It's a cinch we can't let him get killed on us," his father said. "I doubt if Exotic Organics would send anybody else out, if he was."

"Here," Dad said. "We'll run the story we have on him in the morning edition, and then correct it and apologize to the public for misleading them and explain in the evening edition. And before he goes, we can have him make an audiovisual for the 'cast, telling everybody who he is and announcing the price he's offering. We'll put that on the air. Get enough publicity, and Steve Ravick won't dare do anything to him."

Publicity, I thought, is the only weapon Dad knows how to use. He thinks it's invincible. Me, I wouldn't bet on what Steve Ravick wouldn't dare do if you gave me a hundred to one. Ravick had been in power too long, and he was drunker on it than Bish Ware ever got on Baldur honey-rum. As an intoxicant, rum is practically a soft drink beside power.

"Well, do you think Ravick's gotten onto Murell yet?" Oscar said. "We kept that a pretty close secret. Joe and I knew about him, and so did the Mahatma and Nip Spazoni and Corkscrew Finnegan, and that was all."

"I didn't even tell Tom, here, till the Peenemünde got into radio range," Joe Kivelson said. "Then I only told him and Ramón and Abdullah and Abe and Hans Cronje."

"And Al Devis," Tom added. "He came into the conning tower while you were telling the rest of us."

The communication screen began buzzing, and I went and put it on. It was Bish Ware, calling from a pay booth somewhere.

"I have some early returns," he said. "The cops cleared everybody out of Hunters' Hall except the Ravick gang. Then Ravick reconvened the meeting, with nobody but his gang. They were very careful to make sure they had enough for a legal quorum under the bylaws, and then they voted to accept the new price of thirty-five centisols a pound."

"That's what I was afraid of," Joe Kivelson said. "Did they arrest any of my crew?"

"Not that I know of," Bish said. "They made a few arrests, but turned everybody loose later. They're still looking for you and your son. As far as I know, they aren't interested in anybody else." He glanced hastily over his shoulder, as though to make sure the door of the booth was secure. "I'm with some people, now. I'll call you back later."

"Well, that's that, Joe," Oscar said, after Bish blanked the screen. "The Ravick Co-op's stuck with the price cut. The only thing left to do is get everybody out of it we can, and organize a new one."

"I guess that's so," Joe agreed. "I wonder, though if Ravick has really got wise to Murell."

"Walt figured it out since the ship got in," Oscar said. "Belsher's been on the ship with Murell for six months. Well, call it three; everything speeds up about double in hyperspace. But in three months he ought to see as much as Walt saw in a couple of hours."

"Well, maybe Belsher doesn't know what's suspicious, the way Walt does," Tom said.

"I'm sure he doesn't," I said. "But he and Murell are both in the wax business. I'll bet he noticed dozens of things I never even saw."

"Then we'd better take awfully good care of Mr. Murell," Tom said. "Get him aboard as fast as we can, and get out of here with him. Walt, you're coming along, aren't you?"

That was what we'd agreed, while Glenn Murell was still the famous travel-book author. I wanted to get out of it, now. There wouldn't be anything happening aboard the *Javelin*, and a lot happening here in Port Sandor. Dad had the same idea, only he was one hundred per cent for my going with Murell. I think he wanted me out of Port Sandor, where I wouldn't get in the way of any small high-velocity particles of lead that might be whizzing around.

7

ABOARD THE *JAVELIN*

WE HEARD NOTHING more from Bish Ware that evening. Joe and Tom Kivelson and Oscar Fujisawa slept at the *Times* Building, and after breakfast Dad called the spaceport hospital about Murell. He had passed a good night and seemed to have thrown off all the poison he had absorbed through his skin. Dad talked to him, and advised him not to leave until somebody came for him. Tom and I took a car—and a pistol apiece and a submachine gun—and went to get him. Remembering, at the last moment, what I had done to his trousers, I unpacked his luggage and got another suit for him.

He was grateful for that, and he didn't lift an eyebrow when he saw the artillery we had with us. He knew, already, what the score was, and the rules, or absence thereof, of the game, and accepted us as members of his team. We dropped to the Bottom Level and went, avoiding traffic, to where the wax was stored. There were close to a dozen guards there now, all heavily armed.

We got out of the car, I carrying the chopper,

and one of the gang there produced a probe rod and microscope and a testing kit and a microray scanner. Murell took his time going over the wax, jabbing the probe rod in and pulling samples out of the big plastic-skinned sausages at random, making chemical tests, examining them under the microscope, and scanning other cylinders to make sure there was no foreign matter in them. He might not know what a literary agent was, but he knew tallow-wax.

I found out from the guards that there hadn't been any really serious trouble after we left Hunter's Hall. The city police had beaten a few men up, natch, and run out all the anti-Ravick hunters, and then Ravick had reconvened the meeting and acceptance of the thirty-five centisol price had been voted unanimously. The police were still looking for the Kivelsons. Ravick seemed to have gotten the idea that Joe Kivelson was the mastermind of the hunters' cabal against him. I know if I'd found that Joe Kivelson and Oscar Fujisawa were in any kind of a conspiracy together, I wouldn't pick Joe for the mastermind. It was just possible, I thought, that Oscar had been fostering this himself, in case anything went wrong. After all, self-preservation is the first law, and Oscar is a self-preserving type.

After Murell had finished his inspection and we'd gotten back in the car and were lifting, I asked him what he was going to offer, just as though I were the skipper of the biggest ship out of Port Sandor. Well, it meant as much to us as it did to the hunters. The more wax sold for, the more advertising we'd sell to the merchants, and the more people would rent teleprinters from us.

"Eighty centisols a pound," he said. Nice and

definite; quite a difference from the way he stumbled around over listing his previous publications. "Seventy-five's the Kapstaad price, regardless of what you people here have been getting from that crook of a Belsher. We'll have to go far enough beyond that to make him have to run like blazes to catch up. You can put it in the *Times* that the day of monopolistic marketing on Fenris is over."

When we got back to the *Times*, I asked Dad if he'd heard anything more from Bish.

"Yes," he said unhappily. "He didn't call in, this morning, so I called his apartment and didn't get an answer. Then I called Harry Wong's. Harry said Bish had been in there till after midnight, with some other people." He named three disreputables, two female and one male. "They were drinking quite a lot. Harry said Bish was plastered to the ears. They finally went out, around 0130. He said the police were in and out checking the crowd, but they didn't make any trouble."

I nodded, feeling very badly. Four and a half hours had been his limit. Well, sometimes a ninety per cent failure is really a triumph; after all, it's a ten per cent success. Bish had gone four and a half hours without taking a drink. Maybe the percentage would be a little better the next time. I was surely old enough to stop expecting miracles.

The mate of the *Pequod* called in, around noon, and said it was safe for Oscar to come back to the ship. The mate of the *Javelin*, Ramón Llewellyn, called in with the same report, that along the waterfront, at least, the heat was off. However, he had started an ambitious-looking overhaul operation, which looked as though it was good for a hundred hours but which could be dropped on a minute's notice, and under cover of this he had been taking on supplies and ammunition.

We made a long audiovisual of Murell announcing his price of eighty centisols a pound for wax on behalf of Argentine Exotic Organics, Ltd. As soon as that was finished, we loaded the boat-clothes we'd picked up for him and his travel kit and mine into a car, with Julio Kubanoff to bring it back to the Times, and went to the waterfront. When we arrived, Ramón Llewellyn had gotten things cleared up, and the Javelin was ready to move as soon as we came aboard.

On the Main City Level, the waterfront is a hundred feet above the ship pools; the ships load from and discharge onto the First Level Down. The city roof curves down all along the south side of the city into the water and about fifty feet below it. That way, even in the post-sunset and post-dawn storms, ships can come in submerged around the outer breakwater and under the roof, and we don't get any wind or heavy seas along the docks.

Murell was interested in everything he saw, in the brief time while we were going down along the docks to where the Javelin was berthed. I knew he'd never actually seen it before, but he must have been studying pictures of it, because from some of the remarks he made, I could tell that he was familiar with it.

Most of the ships had lifted out of the water and were resting on the wide concrete docks, but the Javelin was afloat in the pool, her contragravity on at specific-gravity weight reduction. She was a typical hunter-ship, a hundred feet long by thirty abeam, with a squat conning tower amidships, and turrets for 50-mm guns and launchers for harpoon rockets fore and aft. The only thing open about her was the air-and-water lock under the conning tower. Julio, who was piloting the car, set it down on the top of the aft gun turret. A couple of the crewmen who were on deck grabbed our bags and hurried them inside. We followed, and as soon as Julio lifted away, the lock was sealed.

Immediately, as the contragravity field dropped below the specific gravity of the ship, she began submerging. I got up into the conning tower in time to see the water of the boat pool come up over the armor-glass windows and the outside lights come on. For a few minutes, the *Javelin* swung slowly and moved forward, feeling her way with fingers of radar out of the pool and down the channel behind the breakwater and under the overhang of the city roof. Then the water line went slowly down across the windows as she surfaced. A moment later she was on full contragravity, and the ship which had been a submarine was now an aircraft.

Murell, who was accustomed to the relatively drab sunsets of Terra, simply couldn't take his eyes from the spectacle that covered the whole western half of the sky—high clouds streaming away from the daylight zone to the west and lighted from below by the sun. There were more clouds coming in at a lower level from the east. By the time the *Javelin* returned to Port Sandor, it would be full dark and rain, which would soon turn to snow, would be falling. Then we'd be in for it again for another thousand hours.

Ramón Llewellyn was saying to Joe Kivelson: "We're one man short; Devis, Abdullah's helper. Hospital."

"Get hurt in the fight, last night? He was right with us till we got out to the elevators, and then I missed him."

"No. He made it back to the ship about the same time we did, and he was all right then. Didn't even have a scratch. Strained his back at work, this morning, trying to lift a power-unit cartridge by hand."

I could believe that. Those things weighed a couple of hundred pounds. Joe Kivelson swore.

"What's he think this is, the First Century Pre-Atomic? Aren't there any lifters on the ship?"

Llewellyn shrugged. "Probably didn't want to bother taking a couple of steps to get one. The doctor told him to take treatment and observation for a day or so."

"That's Al Devis?" I asked. "What hospital?" Al Devis's strained back would be good for a two-line item; he'd feel hurt if we didn't mention it.

"Co-op hospital."

That was all right. They always sent in their patient lists to the Times. Tom was griping because he'd have to do Devis's work and his own.

"You know anything about engines, Walt?" he asked me.

"I know they generate a magnetic current and convert rotary magnetic current into one-directional repulsion fields, and violate the daylights out of all the old Newtonian laws of motion and attraction," I said. "I read that in a book. That was as far as I got. The math got a little complicated after that, and I started reading another book."

"You'd be a big help. Think you could hit anything with a 50-mm?" Tom asked. "I know you're pretty sharp with a pistol or a chopper, but a cannon's different."

"I could try. If you want to heave over an empty packing case or something, I could waste a few rounds seeing if I could come anywhere close to it."

"We'll do that," he said. "Ordinarily, I handle the after gun when we sight a monster, but somebody'll have to help Abdullah with the engines."

He spoke to his father about it. Joe Kivelson nodded.

"Walt's made some awful lucky shots with that target pistol of his, I know that," he said, "and I saw him make hamburger out of a slasher, once, with a chopper. Have somebody blow a couple of wax skins full of air for targets, and when we get a little farther southeast, we'll go down to the surface and have some shooting."

I convinced Murell that the sunset would still be there in a couple of hours, and we took our luggage down and found the cubbyhole he and I would share with Tom for sleeping quarters. A hunter-ship looks big on the outside, but there's very little room for the crew. The engines are much bigger than would be needed on an ordinary contragravity craft, because a hunter-ship operates under water as well as in the air. Then, there's a lot of cargo space for the wax, and the boat berth aft for the scout boat, so they're not exactly built for comfort. They don't really need to be; a ship's rarely out more than a hundred and fifty hours on any cruise.

Murell had done a lot of reading about every phase of the wax business, and he wanted to learn everything he could by actual observation. He said that Argentine Exotic Organics was going to keep him here on Fenris as a resident buyer and his job was going to be to deal with the hunters, either individually or through their co-operative organization, if they could get rid of Ravick and set up something he could do business with, and he wanted to be able to talk the hunters' language and understand their problems.

So I took him around over the boat, showing him everything and conscripting any crew members I came across to explain what I couldn't. I showed him the scout boat in its berth, and we climbed into it and looked around. I showed him the machine that packed the wax into skins, and the cargo holds, and the electrolytic gills that extracted oxygen from sea water while we were submerged, and the ship's armament. Finally, we got to the engine room, forward. He whistled when he saw the engines.

"Why, those things are big enough for a five-thousand-ton freighter," he said.

"They have to be," I said. "Running submerged isn't the same as running in atmosphere. You ever done any swimming?"

He shook his head. "I was born in Antarctica, on Terra. The water's a little too cold to do much swimming there. And I've spent most of my time since then in central Argentine, in the pampas country. The sports there are horseback riding and polo and things like that."

Well, whattaya know! Here was a man who had not only seen a horse, but actually ridden one. That in itself was worth a story in the *Times*.

Tom and Abdullah, who were fussing around

the engines, heard that. They knocked off what they were doing and began asking him questions—I suppose he thought they were awfully silly, but he answered all of them patiently—about horses and riding. I was looking at a couple of spare power-unit cartridges, like the one Al Devis had strained his back on, clamped to the deck out of the way.

They were only as big as a one-liter jar, rounded at one end and flat at the other where the power cable was connected, but they weighed close to two hundred pounds apiece. Most of the weight was on the outside; a dazzlingly bright plating of collapsium—collapsed matter, the electron shell collapsed onto the nucleus and the atoms in actual physical contact—and absolutely nothing but nothing could get through it. Inside was about a kilogram of strontium-90; it would keep on emitting electrons for twenty-five years, normally, but there was a miniature plutonium reactor, itself shielded with collapsium, which, among other things, speeded that process up considerably. A cartridge was good for about five years; two of them kept the engines in operation.

The engines themselves converted the electric current from the power cartridges into magnetic current, and lifted the ship and propelled it. Abdullah was explaining that to Murell and Murell seemed to be getting it satisfactorily.

Finally, we left them; Murell wanted to see the sunset some more and went up to the conning tower where Joe and Ramón were, and I decided to take a nap while I had a chance.

8

PRACTICE, 50-MM GUN

IT SEEMED AS though I had barely fallen asleep before I was wakened by the ship changing direction and losing altitude. I knew there were clouds coming in from the east, now, on the lower air currents, and I supposed that Joe was taking the *Javelin* below them to have a look at the surface of the sea. So I ran up to the conning tower, and when I got there I found that the lower clouds were solid over us, it was growing dark, and another huntership was approaching with her lights on.

"Who is she?" I asked.

"*Bulldog*, Nip Spazoni," Joe told me. "Nip's bringing my saloon fighter aboard, and he wants to meet Mr. Murell."

I remembered that the man who had roughed up the Ravick goon in Martian Joe's had made his getaway from town in the *Bulldog*. As I watched, the other ship's boat dropped out from her stern, went end-over-end for an instant, and then straightened out and came circling around astern of us, matching our speed and ejecting a magnetic grapple.

Nip Spazoni and another man climbed out with life lines fast to their belts and crawled along our upper deck, catching life lines that were thrown out to them and snapping onto them before casting loose the ones from their boat. Somebody at the lock under the conning tower hauled them in.

Nip Spazoni's name was Old Terran Italian, but he had slanted Mongoloid eyes and a sparse little chin-beard, which accounted for his nickname. The amount of intermarriage that's gone on since the First Century, any resemblance between people's names and their appearances is purely coincidental. Oscar Fujisawa, who looks as though his name ought to be Lief Ericsson, for example.

"Here's your prodigal, Joe," he was saying, peeling out of his parka as he came up the ladder. "I owe him a second gunner's share on a monster, fifteen tons of wax."

"Hey, that was a good one. You heading home, now?" Then he turned to the other man, who had followed Nip up the ladder. "You didn't do a very good job, Bill," he said. "The so-and-so's out of the hospital by now."

"Well, you know who takes care of his own," the crewman said. "Give me something for effort; I tried hard enough."

"No, I'm not going home yet," Nip was answering. "I have hold-room for the wax of another one, if he isn't bigger than ordinary. I'm going to go down on the bottom when the winds start and sit it out, and then try to get a second one." Then he saw me. "Well, hey, Walt; when did you turn into a monster-hunter?"

Then he was introduced to Murell, and he and Joe and the man from Argentine Exotic Organics sat down at the chart table and Joe yelled for a pot of coffee, and they started talking prices and quantities of wax. I sat in, listening. This was part of what was going to be the big story of the year. Finally they got that talked out, and Joe asked Nip how the monsters were running.

"Why, good; you oughtn't to have any trouble finding one," Nip said. "There must have been a Nifflheim of a big storm off to the east, beyond the Lava Islands. I got mine north of Cape Terror. There's huge patches of sea-spaghetti drifting west, all along the coast of Hermann Reuch's Land. Here." He pulled out a map. "You'll find it all along here."

Murell asked me if sea-spaghetti was something the monsters ate. His reading-up still had a few gaps, here and there.

"No, it's seaweed; the name describes it. Screwfish eat it; big schools of them follow it. Gulpers and funnelmouths and bag-bellies eat screwfish, and monsters eat them. So wherever you find spaghetti, you can count on finding a monster or two."

"How's the weather?" Joe was asking.

"Good enough, now. It was almost full dark when we finished the cutting-up. It was raining; in fifty or sixty hours it ought to be getting pretty bad." Spazoni pointed on the map. "Here's about where I think you ought to try, Joe."

I screened the *Times*, after Nip went back to his

own ship. Dad said that Bish Ware had called in, with nothing to report but a vague suspicion that something nasty was cooking. Steve Ravick and Leo Belsher were taking things, even the announcement of the Argentine Exotic Organics price, too calmly.

"I think so, myself," he added. "That gang has some kind of a knife up their sleeve. Bish is trying to find out just what it is."

"Is he drinking much?" I asked.

"Well, he isn't on the wagon, I can tell you that," Dad said. "I'm beginning to think that he isn't really sober till he's half plastered."

There might be something to that, I thought. There are all kinds of weird individualities about human metabolism; for all I knew, alcohol might actually be a food for Bish. Or he might have built up some kind of immunity, with antibodies that were themselves harmful if he didn't have alcohol to neutralize them.

The fugitive from what I couldn't bring myself to call justice proved to know just a little, but not much, more about engines than I did. That meant that Tom would still have to take Al Devis's place, and I'd have to take his with the after 50-mm. So the ship went down to almost sea surface, and Tom and I went to the stern turret.

The gun I was to handle was an old-model Terran Federation Army infantry-platoon accompanying gun. The mount, however, was power-driven, like the mount for a 90-mm contragravity tank gun. Reconciling the firing mechanism of the former with the elevating and traversing gear of the latter had produced one of the craziest pieces of machinery that ever gave an ordnance engineer nightmares. It was a local job, of course. An ordnance engineer in Port Sandor doesn't really have to be a raving maniac, but it's a help.

Externally, the firing mechanism consisted of a pistol grip and trigger, which looked all right to me. The sight was a standard binocular light-gun sight, with a spongeplastic mask to save the gunner from a pair of black eyes every time he fired it. The elevating and traversing gear was combined in one lever on a ball-and-socket joint. You could move the gun diagonally in any direction in one motion, but you had to push or pull the opposite way. Something would go plonk when the trigger was pulled on an empty chamber, so I did some dry practice at the crests of waves.

"Now, mind," Tom was telling me, "this is a lot different from a pistol."

"So I notice," I replied. I had also noticed that every time I got the cross hairs on anything and squeezed the trigger, they were on something else when the trigger went plonk. "All this gun needs is another lever, to control the motion of the ship."

"Oh, that only makes it more fun," Tom told me.

Then he loaded in a clip of five rounds, big expensive-looking cartridges a foot long, with bottle-neck cases and pointed shells.

The targets were regular tallow-wax skins, blown up and weighted at one end so that they would float upright. He yelled into the intercom, and one was chucked overboard ahead. A moment later, I saw it bobbing away astern of us. I put my face into the sight-mask, caught it, centered the cross hairs, and squeezed. The gun gave a thunderclap and recoiled past me, and when I pulled my face out of the mask, I saw a column of water and spray about fifty feet left and a hundred yards over.

"You won't put any wax in the hold with that kind of shooting," Tom told me.

I fired again. This time, there was no effect at all that I could see. The shell must have gone away over and hit the water a couple of miles astern. Before Tom could make any comment on that shot, I let off another, and this time I hit the water directly in front of the bobbing wax skin. Good line shot, but away short.

"Well, you scared him, anyhow," Tom said, in mock commendation.

I remembered some of the comments I'd made when I'd been trying to teach him to hit something smaller than the target frame with a pistol, and humbled myself. The next two shots were reasonably close, but neither would have done any damage if the rapidly vanishing skin had really been a monster. Tom clucked sadly and slapped in another clip.

"Heave over another one," he called. "That monster got away."

The trouble was, there were a lot of tricky air currents along the surface of the water. The engines were running on lift to match exactly the weight of the ship, which meant that she had no weight at all, and a lot of wind resistance. The drive was supposed to match the wind speed, and the ship was supposed to be kept nosed into the wind. A lot of that is automatic, but it can't be made fully so, which means that the pilot has to do considerable manual correcting, and no human alive can do that perfectly. Joe Kivelson or Ramón Llewellyn or whoever was at the controls was doing a masterly job, but that fell away short of giving me a stable gun platform.

I caught the second target as soon as it bobbed into sight and slammed a shell at it. The explosion was half a mile away, but the shell hadn't missed the target by more than a few yards. Heartened, I fired again, and that shot was simply dreadful.

"I know what you're doing wrong," Tom said. "You're squeezing the trigger."

"Huh?"

I pulled my face out of the sight-mask and looked at him to see if he were exhibiting any other signs of idiocy. That was like criticizing somebody for using a fork instead of eating with his fingers.

"You're not shooting a pistol," he continued. "You don't have to hold the gun on the target with the hand you shoot with. The mount control, in your other hand, does that. As soon as the cross hairs touch the target, just grab the trigger as though it was a million sols getting away from you. Well, sixteen thousand; that's what a monster's worth now, Murell prices. Jerking won't have the least effect on your hold whatever."

So *that* was why I'd had so much trouble making a pistol shot out of Tom, and why it would take a special act of God to make one out of his father. And that was why monster-hunters caused so few casualties in barroom shootings around Port Sandor, outside of bystanders and back-bar mirrors. I felt like Newton after he'd figured out why the apple bopped him on the head.

"You mean like this?" I asked innocently, as

soon as I had the hairs on the target again, violating everything I held most sacredly true about shooting.

The shell must have passed within inches of the target; it bobbed over flat and the weight pulled it up again into the backwave from the shell and it bobbed like crazy.

"That would have been a dead monster," Tom said. "Let's see you do it again."

I didn't; the next shot was terrible. Overconfidence. I had one more shot, and I didn't want to use up another clip of the *Javelin's* ammo. They cost like crazy, even if they were Army rejects. The sea current was taking the target farther away every second, but I took my time on the next one, bringing the horizontal hair level with the bottom of the inflated target and traversing quickly, grabbing the trigger as soon as the vertical hair touched it. There was a water-spout, and the target shot straight up for fifty feet; the shell must have exploded directly under it. There was a sound of cheering from the intercom. Tom asked if I wanted to fire another clip. I told him I thought I had the hang of it now, and screwed a swab onto the ramrod and opened the breech to clean the gun.

Joe Kivelson grinned at me when I went up to the conning tower.

"That wasn't bad, Walt," he said. "You never manned a 50-mm before, did you?"

"No, and it's all backward from anything I ever learned about shooting," I said. "Now, suppose I get a shot at a monster; where do I try to hit him?"

"Here, I'll show you." He got a block of lucite, a foot square on the end by two and a half feet long, out of a closet under the chart table. In it was a little figure of a Jarvis's sea-monster; long body tapering to a three-fluked tail, wide horizontal flippers like the wings of an old pre-contragravity aircraft, and a long neck with a little head and a wide tusked mouth.

"Always get him from in front," he said. "Aim right here, where his chest makes a kind of V at the base of the neck. A 50-mm will go six or eight feet into him before it explodes, and it'll explode among his heart and lungs and things. If it goes straight along his body, it'll open him up and make the cutting-up easier, and it won't spoil much wax. That's where I always shoot."

"Suppose I get a broadside shot?"

"Why, then put your shell right under the flukes at the end of the tail. That'll turn him and position him for a second shot from in front. But mostly, you'll get a shot from in front, if the ship's down near the surface. Monsters will usually try to attack the ship. They attack anything around their own size that they see," he told me. "But don't ever make a body shot broadside-to. You'll kill the monster, but you'll blow about five thousand sols' worth of wax to Nifflheim doing it."

It had been getting dusky while I had been shooting; it was almost full dark now, and the *Javelin's* lights were on. We were making close to Mach 3, headed east now, and running away from the remaining daylight.

We began running into squalls of rain, and then rain mixed with wet snow. The underside lights came on, and the lookout below began reporting patches of sea-spaghetti. Finally, the boat was dropped out and went circling away ahead, swinging its light back and forth over the water, and radioing back reports. Spaghetti. Spaghetti with a big school of screwfish working on it. Funnel-mouths working on the screwfish. Finally the speaker gave a shrill whistle.

"*Monster ho!*" the voice yelled. "About ten points off your port bow. We're circling over it now."

"Monster ho!" Kivelson yelled into the intercom, in case anybody hadn't heard. "All hands to killing stations." Then he saw me standing there, wondering what was going to happen next. "Well, mister, didn't you hear me?" he bellowed. "Get to your gun!"

Gee! I thought. I'm one of the crew, now.

"Yes sir!" I grabbed the handrail of the ladder and slid down, then raced aft to the gun turret.

9

MONSTER KILLING

THERE WAS A man in the turret, waiting to help me. He had a clip of five rounds in the gun, the searchlight on, and the viewscreen tuned to the forward pickup. After checking the gun and loading the chamber, I looked in that, and in the distance, lighted by the boat above and the searchlight of the *Javelin*, I saw a long neck with a little head on the end of it weaving about. We were making straight for it, losing altitude and speed as we went.

Then the neck dipped under the water and a little later reappeared, coming straight for the advancing light. The forward gun went off, shaking the ship with its recoil, and the head ducked under again. There was a spout from the shell behind it.

I took my eyes from the forward screen and looked out the rear window, ready to shove my face into the sight-mask. An instant later, the head and neck reappeared astern of us. I fired, without too much hope of hitting anything, and then the ship was rising and circling.

As soon as I'd fired, the monster had sounded,

headfirst. I fired a second shot at his tail, in hope of crippling his steering gear, but that was a clean miss, too, and then the ship was up to about five thousand feet. My helper pulled out the partly empty clip and replaced it with a full one, giving me five and one in the chamber.

If I'd been that monster, I thought, I'd have kept on going till I was a couple of hundred miles away from this place; but evidently that wasn't the way monsters thought, if thinking is what goes on inside a brain cavity the size of a quart bottle in a head the size of two oil drums on a body as big as the ship that was hunting him. He'd found a lot of gulpers and funnelmouths, and he wasn't going to be chased away from his dinner by somebody shooting at him.

I wondered why they didn't eat screwfish, instead of the things that preyed on them. Maybe they did and we didn't know it. Or maybe they just didn't like screwfish. There were a lot of things we didn't know about sea-monsters.

For that matter, I wondered why we didn't grow tallow-wax by carniculture. We could grow any other animal matter we wanted. I'd often thought of that.

The monster wasn't showing any inclination to come to the surface again, and finally Joe Kivelson's voice came out of the intercom:

"Run in the guns and seal ports. Secure for submersion. We're going down and chase him up."

My helper threw the switch that retracted the gun and sealed the gun port. I checked that and reported, "After gun secure." Hans Cronje's voice, a moment later, said, "Forward gun secure," and then Ramón Llewellyn said, "Ship secure; ready to submerge."

Then the *Javelin* began to settle, and the water came up over the window. I didn't know what the radar was picking up. All I could see was the screen and the window; water lighted for about fifty feet in front and behind. I saw a cloud of screwfish pass over and around us, spinning rapidly as they swam as though on lengthwise axis—they always spin counterclockwise, never clockwise. A couple of funnelmouths were swimming after them, overtaking and engulfing them.

Then the captain yelled, "Get set for torpedo," and my helper and I each grabbed a stanchion. A couple of seconds later it seemed as though King Neptune himself had given the ship a poke in the nose; my hands were almost jerked loose from their hold. Then she swung slowly, nosing up and down, and finally Joe Kivelson spoke again:

"We're going to surface. Get set to run the guns out and start shooting as soon as we're out of the water."

"What happened?" I asked my helper.

"Must have put the torp right under him and lifted him," he said. "He could be dead or stunned. Or he could be live and active and spoiling for a fight."

That last could be trouble. The *Times* had run quite a few stories, some with black borders, about ships that had gotten into trouble with monsters. A hunter-ship is heavy and it is well-armored—install hyperdrive engines in one, and you could take her from here to Terra—but a monster is a tough brute, and he has armor of his own, scales an inch or so thick and tougher than sole leather. A lot of chair seats around Port Sandor are made of single monster scales. A monster strikes with its head, like a snake. They can smash a ship's boat, and they've been known to punch armor-glass windows out of their frames. I didn't want the window in front of me coming in at me with a monster head the size of a couple of oil drums and full of big tusks following it.

The *Javelin* came up fast, but not as fast as the monster, which seemed to have been injured only in his disposition. He was on the surface already, about fifty yards astern of us, threshing with his forty-foot wing-fins, his neck arched back to strike. I started to swing my gun for the chest shot Joe Kivelson had recommended as soon as it was run out, and then the ship was swung around and tilted up forward by a sudden gust of wind. While I was struggling to get the sights back on the monster, the ship gave another lurch and the cross hairs were right on its neck, about six feet below the head. I grabbed the trigger, and as soon as the shot was off, took my eyes from the sights. I was just a second too late to see the burst, but not too late to see the monster's neck jerk one way out of the smoke puff and its head fly another. A second later, the window in front of me was splashed with blood as the headless neck came down on our fantail.

Immediately, two rockets jumped from the launcher over the gun turret, planting a couple of harpoons, and the boat, which had been circling around since we had submerged, dived into the water and passed under the monster, coming up on the other side dragging another harpoon line.

The monster was still threshing its wings and flogging with its headless neck. It takes a monster quite a few minutes to tumble to the fact that it's been killed. My helper was pounding my back black and blue with one hand and trying to pump mine off with the other, and I was getting an ovation from all over the ship. At the same time, a couple more harpoons went into the thing from the ship, and the boat put another one in from behind.

I gathered that shooting monsters' heads off wasn't at all usual, and hastened to pass it off as pure luck, so that everybody would hurry up and deny it before they got the same idea themselves.

We hadn't much time for ovations, though. We had a very slowly dying monster, and before he finally discovered that he was dead, a couple of harpoons got pulled out and had to be replaced. Finally, however, he quieted down, and the boat swung him around, bringing the tail past our bow, and the ship cut contragravity to specific-gravity level and settled to float on top of the water. The boat dived again, and payed out a line that it brought up and around and up again, lashing the monster fast alongside.

"All right," Kivelson was saying, out of the intercom. "Shooting's over. All hands for cutting-up."

I pulled on a parka and zipped it up and went out onto the deck. Everybody who wasn't needed at engines or controls was there, and equipment was coming up from below—power saws and sonocutters and even a solenoid jackhammer. There were half a dozen floodlights, on small contragravity lifters; they were run up on lines fifty feet above the ship's deck. By this time it was completely dark and fine snow was blowing. I could see that Joe Kivelson was anxious to get the cutting-up finished before the wind got any worse.

"Walt, can you use a machine gun?" he asked me.

I told him I could. I was sure of it; a machine gun is fired in a rational and decent manner.

"Well, all right. Suppose you cover for us from the boat," he said. "Mr. Murell can pilot for you. You never worked at cutting-up before, and neither did he. You'd be more of a hindrance than a help and so would he. But we do need a good machine gunner. As soon as we start throwing out waste, we'll have all the slashers and halberd fish for miles around. You just shoot them as fast as you see them."

He was courteous enough not to add: "And don't shoot any of the crew."

The boat came in and passed out the lines of its harpoons, and Murell and I took the places of Cesário Vieira and the other man. We went up to the nose, and Murell took his place at the controls, and I got back of the 7-mm machine gun and made sure that there were plenty of extra belts of ammo. Then, as we rose, I pulled the goggles down from my hood, swung the gun away from the ship, and hammered off a one-second burst to make sure it was working, after which I settled down, glad I had a comfortable seat and wasn't climbing around on that monster.

They began knocking scales loose with the jackhammer and cutting into the leathery skin underneath with sonocutters. The sea was getting heavy, and the ship and the attached monster had begun to roll.

"That's pretty dangerous work," Murell said. "If a man using one of those cutters slipped . . ."

"It's happened," I told him. "You met our peg-legged compositor, Julio. That was how he lost his leg."

"I don't blame them for wanting all they can get for tallow-wax."

They had the monster opened down the belly, and were beginning to cut loose big chunks of the yellow tallow-wax and throw them into cargo nets and swing them aboard with lifters, to be chucked down the cargo hatches. I was only able to watch that for a minute or so and tell Murell what was going on, and then the first halberd fish, with a spearlike nose and sharp ridges of the nearest thing to bone you find on Fenris, came swimming up. I swung the gun on the leader and gave him a second of fire, and then a two-second burst on the ones behind. Then I waited for a few seconds until the survivors converged on their dead and injured companions and gave them another burst, which wiped out the lot of them.

It was only a couple of seconds after that that the first slasher came in, shiny as heat-blued steel and waving four clawed tentacles that grew around its neck. It took me a second or so to get the sights on him. He stopped slashing immediately. Slashers are smart; you kill them and they find it out right away.

Before long, the water around the ship and the monster was polluted with things like that. I had to keep them away from the men, now working up to their knees in water, and at the same time avoid massacring the crew I was trying to protect, and Murell had to keep the boat in position, in spite of a steadily rising wind, and every time I had to change belts, there'd be a new rush of things that had to be shot in a hurry. The ammunition bill for covering a cutting-up operation is one of the things that runs up expenses for a huntership. The ocean bottom around here must be carpeted with machine-gun brass.

Finally, they got the job done, and everybody went below and sealed ship. We sealed the boat and went down after her. The last I saw, the remains of the monster, now stripped of wax, had been cast off, and the water around it was rioting with slashers and clawbeaks and halberd fish and similar marine unpleasantnesses.

10

MAYDAY, MAYDAY

GETTING A SHIP'S boat berthed inside the ship in the air is tricky work under the best of conditions; the way the wind was blowing by now, it would have been like trying to thread a needle inside a concrete mixer. We submerged after the ship and went in underwater. Then we had to wait in the boat until the ship rose above the surface and emptied the water out of the boat berth. When that was done and the boat berth was sealed again, the ship went down seventy fathoms and came to rest on the bottom, and we unsealed the boat and got out.

There was still the job of packing the wax into skins, but that could wait. Everybody was tired and dirty and hungry. We took turns washing up, three at a time, in the little ship's latrine which, for some reason going back to sailing-ship days on Terra, was called the "head." Finally the whole sixteen of us gathered in the relatively comfortable wardroom under the after gun turret.

Comfortable, that is, to the extent that everybody could find a place to sit down, or could move about without tripping over somebody else. There was a big pot of coffee, and everybody had a plate or bowl of hot food. There's always plenty of hot food to hand on a hunter-ship; no regular meal-times, and everybody eats, as he sleeps, when he has time. This is the only time when a whole hunter crew gets together, after a monster has been killed and cut up and the ship is resting on the bottom and nobody has to stand watch.

Everybody was talking about the killing, of course, and the wax we had in the hold, and counting the money they were going to get for it, at the new eighty-centisol price.

"Well, I make it about fourteen tons," Ramón Llewellyn, who had been checking the wax as it went into the hold, said. He figured mentally for a moment, and added, "Call it twenty-two thousand sols." Then he had to fall back on a pencil and paper to figure shares.

I was surprised to find that he was reckoning shares for both Murell and myself.

"Hey, do we want to let them do that?" I whispered to Murell. "We just came along for the ride."

"I don't want the money," he said. "These people need every cent they can get.

So did I, for that matter, and I didn't have salary and expense account from a big company on Terra. However, I hadn't come along in the expectation of making anything out of it, and a newsman has to be careful about the outside money he picks up. It wouldn't do any harm in the present instance, but as a practice it can lead to all kinds of things, like playing favorites, coloring news, killing stories that shouldn't be killed. We do enough of that as it is, like playing down the tread-snail business for Bish Ware and the spaceport people, and never killing anybody except in a "local bar." It's hard to draw a line on that sort of thing.

"We're just guests," I said. "We don't work here."

"The dickens you are," Joe Kivelson contradicted. "Maybe you came aboard as guests, but you're both part of the crew now. I never saw a prettier shot on a monster than Walt made—took that thing's head off like a chicken on a chopping block—and he did a swell job of covering for the cutting-up. And he couldn't have done that if Murell hadn't handled the boat the way he did, and that was no easy job."

"Well, let's talk about that when we get to port," I said. "Are we going right back, or are we going to try for another monster?"

"I don't know," Joe said. "We could stow the wax, if we didn't get too much, but if we stay out, we'll have to wait out the wind and by then it'll be pretty cold."

"The longer we stay out, the more the cruise'll cost," Abdullah Monnahan, the engineer, said, "and the expenses'll cut into the shares."

"Tell the truth, I'm sort of antsy to get back," Joe Kivelson said. "I want to see what's going on in Port Sandor."

"So am I," Murell said. "I want to get some kind of office opened, and get into business. What time will the *Cape Canaveral* be getting in? I want a big cargo, for the first time."

"Oh, not for four hundred hours, at the least," I said. "The spaceships always try to miss the early-dark and early-daylight storms. It's hard to get a big ship down in a high wind."

"That'll be plenty of time, I suppose," Murell said. "There's all that wax you have stored, and what I can get out of the Co-operative stores from crews that reclaim it. But I'm going to have a lot to do."

"Yes," I agreed. "Dodging bullets, for one."

"Oh, I don't expect any trouble," Murell said. "This fellow Ravick's shot his round."

He was going to say something else, but before he could say it there was a terrific roar forward. The whole ship bucked like a recoiling gun, throwing everybody into a heap, and heeled over to starboard. There were a lot of yells, particularly from those who had been splashed with hot coffee, and somebody was shouting something about the magazines.

"The magazines are aft, you dunderhead," Joe Kivelson told him, shoving himself to his feet. "Stay put, everybody; I'll see what it is."

He pulled open the door forward. An instant later, he had slammed it shut and was dogging it fast.

"Hull must be ruptured forward; we're making water. It's spouting up the hatch from the engine room like a geyser," he said. "Ramón, go see what it's like in the boat berth. The rest of you, follow him, and grab all the food and warm clothing you can. We're going to have to abandon."

He stood by the doorway aft, shoving people through and keeping them from jamming up, saying: "Take it easy, now; don't crowd. We'll all get out." There wasn't any panic. A couple of men

were in the doorway of the little galley when I
came past, handing out cases of food. As nothing
was coming out at the instant, I kept on, and on
the way back to the boat-berth hatch, I pulled
down as many parkas and pairs of overpants as I
could carry, squeezing past Tom, who was col-
lecting fleece-lined hip boots. Eash pair was buck-
led together at the tops; a hunter always does that,
even at home ashore.

Ramón had the hatch open, and had opened the
top hatch of the boat, below. I threw my double
armload of clothing down through it and slid
down after, getting out of the way of the load of
boots Tom dumped ahead of him. Joe Kivelson
came down last, carrying the ship's log and some
other stuff. A little water was trickling over the
edge of the hatch above.

"It's squirting up from below in a dozen
places," he said, after he'd sealed the boat. "The
whole front of the ship must be blown out."

"Well, now we know what happened to Simon
MacGregor's *Claymore*," I said, more to myself
than to anybody else.

Joe and Hans Cronje, the gunner, were getting a
rocket out of the locker, detaching the harpoon
and fitting on an explosive warhead. He stopped,
while he and Cronje were loading it into the after
launcher, and nodded at me.

"That's what I think, too," he said. "Everybody
grab onto something; we're getting the door
open."

I knew what was coming and started hugging
a stanchion as though it were a long-lost
sweetheart, and Murell, who didn't but knew
enough to imitate those who did, hugged it from

the other side. The rocket whooshed out of the launcher and went off with a deafening bang outside. For an instant, nothing happened, and I told Murell not to let go. Then the lock burst in and the water, at seventy fathoms' pressure, hit the boat. Abdullah had gotten the engines on and was backing against it. After a little, the pressure equalized and we went out the broken lock stern first.

We circled and passed over the *Javelin*, and then came back. She was lying in the ooze, a quarter over on her side, and her whole bow was blown out to port. Joe Kivelson got the square box he had brought down from the ship along with the log, fussed a little with it, and then launched it out the disposal port. It was a radio locator. Sometimes a lucky ship will get more wax than the holds' capacity; they pack it in skins and anchor it on the bottom, and drop one of those gadgets with it. It would keep on sending a directional signal and the name of the ship for a couple of years.

"Do you really think it was sabotage?" Murell was asking me. Blowing up a ship with sixteen men aboard must have seemed sort of extreme to him. Maybe that wasn't according to Terran business ethics. "Mightn't it have been a power unit?"

"No. Power units don't blow, and if one did, it would vaporize the whole ship and a quarter of a cubic mile of water around her. No, that was old fashioned country-style chemical explosive. Cataclysmite, probably."

"Ravick?" he asked, rather unnecessarily.

"You know how well he can get along without you and Joe Kivelson, and here's a chance to get along without both of you together." Everybody in the boat was listening, so I continued: "How much do you know about this fellow Devis, who strained his back at the last moment?"

"Engine room's where he could have planted something," Joe Kivelson said.

"He was in there by himself for a while, the morning after the meeting," Abdullah Monnahan added.

"And he disappeared between the meeting room and the elevator, during the fight," Tom mentioned. "And when he showed up, he hadn't been marked up any. I'd have thought he'd have been pretty badly beaten—unless they knew he was one of their own gang."

"We're going to look Devis up when we get back," somebody said pleasantly.

"If we get back," Ramón Llewellyn told him. "That's going to take some doing."

"We have the boat," Hans Cronje said. "It's a little crowded, but we can make it back to Port Sandor."

"I hope we can," Abe Clifford, the navigator, said. "Shall we take her up, Joe?"

"Yes, see what it's like on top," the skipper replied.

Going up, we passed a monster at about thirty fathoms. It stuck its neck out and started for us. Monnahan tilted the boat almost vertical and put on everything the engines had, lift and drive parallel. An instant later, we broke the surface and shot into the air.

The wind hit the boat as though it had been a ping-pong ball, and it was several seconds, and bad seconds at that, before Monnahan regained even a semblance of control. There was considerable bad language, and several of the crew had bloody noses. Monnahan tried to get the boat turned into the wind. A circuit breaker popped, and red lights blazed all over the instrument panel. He eased off and let the wind take over, and for a while we were flying in front of it like a rifle bullet. Gradually, he nosed down and submerged.

"Well, that's that." Joe Kivelson said, when we were back in the underwater calm again. "We'll have to stay under till the wind's over. Don't anybody move around or breathe any deeper than you have to. We'll have to conserve oxygen."

"Isn't the boat equipped with electrolytic gills?" Murell asked.

"Sure, to supply oxygen for a maximum of six men. We have sixteen in here."

"How long will our air last, for sixteen of us?" I asked.

"About eight hours."

It would take us fifty to get to Port Sandor, running submerged. The wind wouldn't even begin to fall in less than twenty.

"We can go south, to the coast of Hermann Reuch's Land," Abe Clifford, the navigator, said. "Let me figure something out."

He dug out a slide rule and a pencil and pad and sat down with his back to the back of the pilot's seat, under the light. Everybody watched him in a silence which Joe Kivelson broke suddenly by bellowing:

"Dumont! You light that pipe and I'll feed it to you!"

Old Piet Dumont grabbed the pipe out of his mouth with one hand and pocketed his lighter with the other.

"Gosh, Joe; I guess I just wasn't thinking . . ." he began.

"Well, give me that pipe." Joe put it in the drawer under the charts. "Now you won't have it handy the next time you don't think."

After a while, Abe Clifford looked up. "Ship's position I don't have exactly; somewhere around East 25 Longitude, South 20 Latitude. I can't work out our present position at all, except that we're somewhere around South 30 Latitude. The locator signal is almost exactly north-by-northeast of us. If we keep it dead astern, we'll come out in Sancerre Bay, on Hermann Reuch's Land. If we make that, we're all right. We'll be in the lee of the Hacksaw Mountains, and we can surface from time to time to change air, and as soon as the wind falls we can start for home."

Then he and Abdullah and Joe went into a huddle, arguing about cruising speed submerged. The results weren't so heartening.

"It looks like a ten-hour trip, submerged," Joe said. "That's two hours too long, and there's no way of getting more oxygen out of the gills than we're getting now. We'll just have to use less. Everybody lie down and breathe as shallowly as possible, and don't do anything to use energy. I'm going to get on the radio and see what I can raise."

Big chance, I thought. These boat radios were only used for communicating with the ship while scouting; they had a strain-everything range of about three hundred miles. Hunter-ships don't crowd that close together when they're working. Still, there was a chance that somebody else might be sitting it out on the bottom within hearing. So Abe took the controls and kept the signal from the wreck of the *Javelin* dead astern, and Joe Kivelson began speaking into the radio:

"Mayday, Mayday, Mayday, Mayday. Captain Kivelson, *Javelin*, calling. My ship was wrecked by an explosion; all hands now in scout boat, proceeding toward Sancerre Bay, on course south-by-southwest from the wreck. Locator signal is being broadcast from the *Javelin*. Other than that, we do not know our position. Calling all craft, calling Mayday."

He stopped talking. The radio was silent except for an occasional frying-fat crackle of static. Then he began over again.

I curled up, trying to keep my feet out of anybody's face and my face clear of anybody else's feet. Somebody began praying, and somebody else told him to belay it, he was wasting oxygen. I tried to go to sleep, which was the only practical thing to do. I must have succeeded. When I woke again, Joe Kivelson was saying, exasperatedly:

"Mayday, Mayday, Mayday, Mayday . . ."

11

DARKNESS AND COLD

THE NEXT TIME I woke, Tom Kivelson was reciting the Mayday, Mayday incantation into the radio, and his father was asleep. The man who had been praying had started again, and nobody seemed to care whether he wasted oxygen or not. It was a Theosophist prayer to the Spirit Guides, and I remembered that Cesário Vieira was a Theosophist. Well, maybe there really were Spirit Guides. If there were, we'd all be finding out before long. I found that I didn't care one hoot which way, and I set that down to oxygen deficiency.

Then Glenn Murell broke in on the monotone call for help and the prayer.

"We're done for if we stay down here another hour," he said. "Any argument on that?"

There wasn't any. Joe Kivelson opened his eyes and looked around.

"We haven't raised anything at all on the radio," Murell went on. "That means nobody's within an hour of reaching us. Am I right?"

"I guess that's about the size of it," Joe Kivelson conceded.

"How close to land are we?"

"The radar isn't getting anything but open

water and schools of fish," Abe Clifford said. "For all I know, we could be inside Sancerre Bay now."

"Well, then, why don't we surface?" Murell continued. "It's a thousand to one against us, but if we stay here our chances are precisely one hundred per cent negative."

"What do you think?" Joe asked generally. "I think Mr. Murell's stated it correctly."

"There is no death," Cesário said. "Death is only a change, and then more of life. I don't care what you do."

"What have we got to lose?" somebody else asked. "We're broke and gambling on credit now."

"All right; we surface," the skipper said. "Everybody grab onto something. We'll take the Nifflheim of a slamming around as soon as we're out of the water."

We woke up everybody who was sleeping, except the three men who had completely lost consciousness. Those we wrapped up in blankets and tarpaulins, like mummies, and lashed them down. We gathered everything that was loose and made it fast, and checked the fastenings of everything else. Then Abdullah Monnahan pointed the nose of the boat straight up and gave her everything the engines could put out. Just as we were starting upward, I heard Cesário saying:

"If anybody wants to see me in the next reincarnation, I can tell you one thing; I won't reincarnate again on Fenris!"

The headlights only penetrated fifty or sixty feet ahead of us. I could see slashers and clawbeaks and funnelmouths and gulpers and things like that getting out of our way in a hurry. Then

we were out of the water and shooting straight up
in the air.

It was the other time all over again, doubled in
spades, only this time Abdullah didn't try to fight
it; he just kept the boat rising. Then it went end-
over-end, again and again. I think most of us
blacked out; I'm sure I did, for a while. Finally,
more by good luck than good management, he got
us turned around with the wind behind us. That
lasted for a while, and then we started keyholing
again. I could see the instrument panel from
where I'd lashed myself fast; it was going completely bughouse. Once, out the window in front,
I could see jagged mountains ahead. I just shut my
eyes and waited for the Spirit Guides to come and
pick up the pieces.

When they weren't along, after a few seconds
that seemed like half an hour, I opened my eyes
again. There were more mountains ahead, and
mountains to the right. This'll do it, I thought, and
I wondered how long it would take Dad to find out
what had happened to us. Cesário had started
praying again, and so had Abdullah Monnahan,
who had just remembered that he had been
brought up a Moslem. I hoped he wasn't trying to
pray in the direction of Mecca, even allowing that
he knew which way Mecca was from Fenris generally. That made me laugh, and then I thought,
This is a fine time to be laughing at anything.
Then I realized that things were so bad that anything more that happened was funny.

I was still laughing when I discovered that the
boat had slowed to a crawl and we were backing
in between two high cliffs. Evidently Abdullah,
who had now stopped praying, had gotten

enough control of the boat to keep her into the wind and was keeping enough speed forward to yield to it gradually. That would be all right, I thought, if the force of the wind stayed constant, and as soon as I thought of that, it happened. We got into a relative calm, the boat went forward again, and then was tossed up and spun around. Then I saw a mountain slope directly behind us, out the rear window.

A moment later, I saw rocks and boulders sticking out of it in apparent defiance of gravitation, and then I realized that it was level ground and we were coming down at it backward. That lasted a few seconds, and then we hit stern-on, bounced and hit again. I was conscious up to the third time we hit.

The next thing I knew, I was hanging from my lashings from the side of the boat, which had become the top, and the headlights and the lights on the control panel were out, and Joe Kivelson was holding a flashlight while Abe Clifford and Glenn Murell were trying to get me untied and lower me. I also noticed that the air was fresh, and very cold.

"Hey, we're down!" I said, as though I were telling anybody anything they didn't know. "How many are still alive?"

"As far as I know, all of us," Joe said. "I think I have a broken arm." I noticed, then, that he was holding his left arm stiffly at his side. Murell had a big gash on top of his head, and he was mopping blood from his face with his sleeve while he worked.

When they got me down, I looked around. Somebody else was playing a flashlight around at the stern, which was completely smashed. It was a miracle the rocket locker hadn't blown up, but the main miracle was that all, or even any, of us were still alive.

We found a couple of lights that could be put on, and we got all of us picked up and the unconscious revived. One man, Dominic Silverstein, had a broken leg. Joe Kivelson's arm was, as he suspected, broken, another man had a fractured wrist, and Abdullah Monnahan thought a couple of ribs were broken. The rest of us were in one piece, but all of us were cut and bruised. I felt sore all over. We also found a nuclear-electric heater that would work, and got it on. Tom and I rigged some tarpaulins to screen off the ruptured stern and keep out the worst of the cold wind. After they got through setting and splinting the broken bones and taping up Abdullah's ribs, Cesário and Murell got some water out of one of the butts and started boiling it for coffee. I noticed that Piet Dumont had recovered his pipe and was smoking it, and Joe Kivelson had his lit.

"Well, where are we?" somebody was asking Abe Clifford.

The navigator shook his head. "The radio's smashed, so's the receiver for the locator, and so's the radio navigational equipment. I can state positively, however, that we are on the north coast of Hermann Reuch's Land."

Everybody laughed at that except Murell. I had to explain to him that Hermann Reuch's Land was the antarctic continent of Fenris, and hasn't any other coast.

"I'd say we're a good deal west of Sancerre Bay," Cesário Vieira hazarded. "We can't be east of it, the way we got blown west. I think we must be at least five hundred miles east of it."

"Don't fool yourself, Cesário," Joe Kivelson told him. "We could have gotten into a turbulent updraft and been carried to the upper, eastward winds. The altimeter was trying to keep up with the boat and just couldn't, half the time. We don't know where we went. I'll take Abe's estimate and let it go at that."

"Well, we're up some kind of a fjord," Tom said. "I think it branches like a Y, and we're up the left branch, but I won't make a point of that."

"I can't find anything like that on this map," Abe Clifford said, after a while.

Joe Kivelson swore. "You ought to know better than that, Abe; you know how thoroughly this coast hasn't been mapped."

"How much good will it do us to know where we are, right now?" I asked. "If the radio's smashed, we can't give anybody our position."

"We might be able to fix up the engines and get the boat in the air again, after the wind drops." Monnahan said. "I'll take a look at them and see how badly they've been banged up."

"With the whole stern open?" Hans Cronje asked. "We'd freeze stiffer than a gun barrel before we went a hundred miles."

"Then we can pack the stern full of wet snow and let it freeze, instead of us," I suggested. "There'll be plenty of snow before the wind goes down."

Joe Kivelson looked at me for a moment. "That would work," he said. "How soon can you get started on the engines. Abdullah?"

"Right away. I'll need somebody to help me,

though. I can't do much the way you have me bandaged up."

"I think we'd better send a couple of parties out," Ramón Llewellyn said. "We'll have to find a better place to stay than this boat. We don't all have parkas or lined boots, and we have a couple of injured men. This heater won't be enough; in about seventy hours we'd all freeze to death sitting around it."

Somebody mentioned the possibility of finding a cave.

"I doubt it," Llewellyn said. "I was on an exploring expedition down here, once. This is all igneous rock, mostly granite. There aren't many caves. But there may be some sort of natural shelter, or something we can make into a shelter, not too far away. We have two half-ton lifters; we could use them to pile up rocks and build something. Let's make up two parties. I'll take one; Abe, you take the other. One of us can go up and the other can go down."

We picked parties, trying to get men who had enough clothing and hadn't been too badly banged around in the landing. Tom wanted to go along, but Abdullah insisted that he stay and help with the inspection of the boat's engines. Finally six of us—Llewellyn, myself, Glenn Murell, Abe Clifford, old Piet Dumont, and another man—went out through the broken stern of the boat. We had two portable floodlights—a scout boat carries a lot of equipment—and Llewellyn took the one and Clifford the other. It had begun to snow already, and the wind was coming straight up the narrow ravine into which we had landed, driving it at us. There was a stream between the two walls of rock, swollen by the rains that had come just before the darkness, and the rocks in and beside it were coated with ice. We took one look at it and shook our heads. Any exploring we did would be done without trying to cross that. We stood for a few minutes trying to see through the driving snow, and then we separated, Abe Clifford, Dumont and the other man going up the stream and Ramón Llewellyn, Glenn Murell and I going down.

A few hundred yards below the boat, the stream went over a fifty-foot waterfall. We climbed down beside it, and found the ravine widening. It was a level beach, now, or what had been a beach thousands of years ago. The whole coast of Hermann Reuch's land is sinking in the Eastern Hemisphere and rising in the Western. We turned away from the stream and found that the wind was increasing in strength and coming at us from the left instead of in front. The next thing we knew, we were at the point of the mountain on our right and we could hear the sea roaring ahead and on both sides of us. Tom had been right about that V-shaped fjord, I thought.

We began running into scattered trees now, and when we got around the point of the mountain we entered another valley.

Trees, like everything else on Fenris, are considerably different from anything analogous on normal planets. They aren't tall, the biggest not more than fifteen feet high, but they are from six to eight feet thick, with all the branches at the top, sprouting out in all directions and reminding me of pictures of Medusa. The outside bark is a hard shell, which grows during the beginning of our four hot seasons a year. Under that will be more bark, soft and spongy, and this gets more and more dense toward the middle; and then comes the hardwood core, which may be as much as two feet thick.

"One thing, we have firewood," Murell said, looking at them.

"What'll we cut it with; our knives?" I wanted to know.

"Oh, we have a sonocutter on the boat," Ramón Llewellyn said. "We can chop these things into thousand-pound chunks and float them to camp with the lifters. We could soak the spongy stuff on the outside with water and let it freeze, and build a hut out of it, too." He looked around, as far as the light penetrated the driving snow. "This wouldn't be a bad place to camp."

Not if we're going to try to work on the boat, I thought. And packing Dominic, with his broken leg, down over that waterfall was something I didn't want to try, either. I didn't say anything. Wait till we got back to the boat. It was too cold and windy here to argue, and besides, we didn't know what Abe and his party might have found upstream.

12

CASTAWAYS WORKING

WE HAD BEEN away from the boat for about two hours; when we got back, I saw that Abdullah and his helpers had gotten the deck plates off the engine well and used them to build a more substantial barricade at the ruptured stern. The heater was going and the boat was warm inside, not just relatively to the outside, but actually comfortable. It was even more crowded, however, because there was a ton of collapsium shielding, in four sections, and the generator and power unit, piled in the middle. Abdullah and Tom and Hans Cronje were looking at the converters, which to my not very knowing eye seemed to be in a hopeless mess.

There was some more work going on up at the front. Cesário Vieira had found a small portable radio that wasn't in too bad condition, and had it apart. I thought he was doing about the most effective work of anybody, and waded over the pile of engine parts to see what he was doing. It wasn't much of a radio. A hundred miles was the absolute limit of its range, at least for sending.

"Is this all we have?" I asked, looking at it. It was the same type as the one I carried on the job, camouflaged in a camera case, except that it wouldn't record.

"There's the regular boat radio, but it's smashed up pretty badly. I was thinking we could do something about cannibalizing one radio out of parts from both of them."

We use a lot of radio equipment on the *Times*, and I do a good bit of work on it. I started taking the big set apart and then remembered the receiver for the locator and got at that, too. The trouble was that most of the stuff in all the sets had been miniaturized to a point where watchmaker's tools would have been pretty large for working on them, and all we had was a general-repair kit that was just about fine enough for gunsmithing.

While we were fooling around with the radios, Ramón Llewellyn was telling the others what we found up the other branch of the fjord. Joe Kivelson shook his head over it.

"That's too far from the boat. We can't trudge back and forth to work on the engines. We could cut firewood down there and float it up with the lifters, and I think that's a good idea about using slabs of the soft wood to build a hut. But let's build the hut right here."

"Well, suppose I take a party down now and start cutting?" the mate asked.

"Not yet. Wait till Abe gets back and we see what he found upstream. There may be something better up there."

Tom, who had been poking around in the converters, said:

"I think we can forget about the engines. This is a machine-shop job. We need parts, and we haven't anything to make them out of or with."

That was about what I'd thought. Tom knew

more about lift-and-drive engines than I'd ever learn, and I was willing to take his opinion as confirmation of my own.

"Tom, take a look at this mess," I said. "See if you can help us with it."

He came over, looked at what we were working on, and said, "You need a magnifier for this. Wait till I see something." Then he went over to one of the lockers, rummaged in it, and found a pair of binoculars. He came over to us again, sat down, and began to take them apart. As soon as he had the two big objective lenses out, we had two fairly good magnifying glasses.

That was a big help, but being able to see what had to be done was one thing, and having tools to do it was another. So he found a sewing kit and a piece of emery stone, and started making little screwdrivers out of needles.

After a while, Abe Clifford and Piet Dumont and the other man returned and made a beeline for the heater and the coffeepot. After Abe was warmed a little, he said:

"There's a little waterfall about half a mile up. It isn't too hard to get up over it, and above, the ground levels off into a big bowl-shaped depression that looks as if it had been a lake bottom, once. The wind isn't so bad up there, and this whole lake bottom or whatever it is is grown up with trees. It would be a good place to make a camp, if it wasn't so far from the boat."

"How hard would it be to cut wood up there and bring it down?" Joe asked, going on to explain what he had in mind.

"Why, easy. I don't think it would be nearly as hard as the place Ramón found."

"Neither do I," the mate agreed. "Climbing up

that waterfall down the stream with a half tree trunk would be a lot harder than dropping one over beside the one above." He began zipping up his parka. "Let's get the cutter and the lifters and go up now."

"Wait till I warm up a little, and I'll go with you," Abe said.

Then he came over to where Cesário and Tom and I were working, to see what we were doing. He chucked appreciatively at the midget screwdrivers and things Tom was making.

"I'll take that back, Ramón," he said. "I can do a lot more good right here. Have you taken any of the radio navigational equipment apart, yet?" he asked us.

We hadn't. We didn't know anything about it.

"Well, I think we can get some stuff out of the astrocompass that can be used. Let me in here, will you?"

I got up. "You take over for me," I said. "I'll go on the wood-chopping detail."

Tom wanted to go, too; Abe told him to keep on with his toolmaking. Piet Dumont said he'd guide us, and Glenn Murell said he'd go along. There was some swapping around of clothes and we gathered up the two lifters and the sonocutter and a floodlight and started upstream.

The waterfall above the boat was higher than the one below, but not quite so hard to climb, especially as we had the two lifters to help us. The worst difficulty, and the worst danger, was from the wind.

Once we were at the top, though, it wasn't so bad. We went a couple of hundred yards through a narrow gorge, and then we came out onto the old lake bottom Abe had spoken about. As far as our lights would shine in the snow, we could see stubby trees with snaky branches growing out of the tops.

We just started on the first one we came to, slicing the down-hanging branches away to get at the trunk and then going to work on that. We took turns using the sonocutter, and the rest of us stamped around to keep warm. The first trunk must have weighed a ton and a half, even after the branches were all off; we could barely lift one end of it with both lifters. The spongy stuff, which changed from bark to wood as it went in to the middle, was two feet thick. We cut that off in slabs, to use for building the hut. The hardwood core, once we could get it lit, would make a fine hot fire. We could cut that into burnable pieces after we got it to camp. We didn't bother with the slashings; just threw them out of the way. There was so much big stuff here that the branches weren't worth taking in.

We had eight trees down and cut into slabs and billets before we decided to knock off. We didn't realize until then how tired and cold we were. A couple of us had taken the wood to the waterfall and heaved it over at the side as fast as the others got the trees down and cut up. If we only had another cutter and a couple more lifters, I thought. If we only had an airworthy boat . . .

When we got back to camp, everybody who wasn't crippled and had enough clothes to get away from the heater came out and helped. First, we got a fire started—there was a small arc torch, and we needed that to get the dense hardwood burning—and then we began building a hut against the boat. Everybody worked on that but Dominic Silverstein. Even Abe and Cesário knocked off work on the radio, and Joe Kivelson and the man with the broken wrist gave us a little one-handed help. By this time, the wind had fallen and the snow was coming down thicker. We made snow shovels out of the hard outer bark, although they broke in use pretty often, and banked snow up against the hut. I lost track of how long we worked, but finally we had a place we could all get into, with a fireplace, and it was as warm and comfortable as the inside of the boat.

We had to keep cutting wood, though. Before long it would be too cold to work up in the woods, or even go back and forth between the woods and the camp. The snow finally stopped, and then the sky began to clear and we could see stars. That didn't make us happy at all. As long as the sky was clouded and the snow was falling, some of the heat that had been stored during the long day was being conserved. Now it was all radiating away into space.

The stream froze completely, even the waterfall. In a way, that was a help; we could slide wood down over it, and some of the billets would slide a couple of hundred yards downstream. But the cold was getting to us. We only had a few men working at woodcutting—Cesário, and old Piet Dumont, and Abe Clifford and I, because we were the smallest and could wear bigger men's parkas and overpants over our own. But as long as any of us could pile on enough clothing and waddle out of the hut, we didn't dare stop. If the firewood ran out, we'd all freeze stiff in no time at all.

Abe Clifford got the radio working, at last. It

was a peculiar job as ever was, but he thought it would have a range of about five hundred miles. Somebody kept at it all the time, calling Mayday. I think it was Bish Ware who told me that Mayday didn't have anything to do with the day after the last of April; it was Old Terran French, m'aidez, meaning "help me." I wondered how Bish was getting along, and I wasn't too optimistic about him.

Cesário and Abe and I were up at the waterfall, picking up loads of firewood—we weren't bothering, now, with anything but the hard and slow-burning cores—and had just gotten two of them hooked onto the lifters. I straightened for a moment and looked around. There wasn't a cloud in the sky, and two of Fenris's three moons were making everything as bright as day. The glisten of the snow and the frozen waterfall in the double moonlight was beautiful.

I turned to Cesário. "See what all you'll miss, if you take your next reincarnation off Fenris," I said. "This, and the long sunsets and sunrises, and—"

Before I could list any more sights unique to our planet, the 7-mm machine gun, down at the boat, began hammering; a short burst, and then another, and another and another.

13

THE BEACON LIGHT

WE ALL SAID, "Shooting!" and, "The machine gun!" as though we had to tell each other what it was.

"Something's attacking them" Cesário guessed.

"Oh, there isn't anything to attack them now," Abe said. "All the critters are dug in for the winter. I'll bet they're just using it to chop wood with."

That could be; a few short bursts would knock off all the soft wood from one of those big billets and expose the hard core. Only why didn't they use the cutter? It was at the boat now.

"We better go see what it is," Cesário insisted. "It might be trouble."

None of us was armed; we'd never thought we'd need weapons. There are quite a few Fenrisian land animals, all creepers or crawlers, that are dangerous, but they spend the extreme hot and cold periods in burrows, in almost cataleptic sleep. It occurred to me that something might have burrowed among the rocks near the camp and been roused by the heat of the fire.

We hadn't carried a floodlight with us—there was no need for one in the moonlight. Of the two at camp, one was pointed up the ravine toward us, and the other into the air. We began yelling as soon as we caught sight of them, not wanting to be dusted over lightly with 7-mm's before anybody recognized us. As soon as the men at the camp heard us, the shooting stopped and they started shouting to us. Then we could distinguish words.

"Come on in! We made contact!"

We pushed into the hut, where everybody was crowded around the underhatch of the boat, which was now the side door. Abe shoved through, and I shoved in after him. Newsman's conditioned reflex; get to where the story is. I even caught myself saying, "Press," as I shoved past Abdullah Monnahan.

"What happened?" I asked, as soon as I was inside. I saw Joe Kivelson getting up from the radio and making place for Abe. "Who did you contact?"

"The Mahatma; *Helldiver*," he said. "Signal's faint, but plain; they're trying to make a directional fix on us. There are about a dozen ships out looking for us: *Helldiver*, *Pequod*, *Bulldog*, *Dirty Gertie* . . . " He went on naming them.

"How did they find out?" I wanted to know. "Somebody pick up our Mayday while we were cruising submerged?"

Abe Clifford was swearing into the radio. "No, of course not. We don't know where in Nifflheim we are. All the instruments in the boat were smashed."

"Well, can't you shoot the stars, Abe?" The

voice—I thought it was Feinberg's—was almost as inaudible as a cat's sneeze.

"Sure we can. If you're in range of this makeshift set, the position we'd get would be practically the same as yours," Abe told him. "Look, there's a floodlight pointed straight up. Can you see that?"

"In all this moonlight? We could be half a mile away and not see it."

"We've been firing with a 7-mm," the navigator said.

"I know; I heard it. On the radio. Have you got any rockets? Maybe if you shot one of them up we could see it."

"Hey, that's an idea! Hans, have we another rocket with an explosive head?"

Cronje said we had, and he and another man got it out and carried it from the boat. I repeated my question to Joe Kivelson.

"No. Your Dad tried to call the *Javelin* by screen; that must have been after we abandoned ship. He didn't get an answer, and put out a general call. Nip Spazoni was nearest, and he cruised around and picked up the locator signal and found the wreck, with the boat berth blown open and the boat gone. Then everybody started looking for us."

Feinberg was saying that he'd call the other ships and alert them. If the *Helldiver* was the only ship we could contact by radio, the odds were that if they couldn't see the rocket from Feinberg's ship, nobody else could. The same idea must have occurred to Abe Clifford.

"You say you're all along the coast. Are the other ships west or east of you?"

"West, as far as I know."

"Then we must be way east of you. Where are you now?"

"About five hundred miles east of Sancerre Bay."

That meant we must be at least a thousand miles east of the bay. I could see how that happened. Both times the boat had surfaced, it had gone straight up, lift and drive operating together. There is a constant wind away from the sunlight zone at high level, heated air that has been lifted, and there is a wind at a lower level out of the dark zone, coming in to replace it. We'd gotten completely above the latter and into the former.

There was some yelling outside, and then I could hear Hans Cronje:

"Rocket's ready for vertical launching. Ten seconds, nine, eight, seven, six, five, four, three, two, one; rocket off!"

There was a whoosh outside. Clifford, at the radio, repeated: "Rocket off!" Then it banged, high overhead. "Did you see it? he asked.

"Didn't see a thing," Feinberg told him.

"Hey, I know what they would see!" Tom Kivelson burst out. "Say we go up and set the woods on fire?"

"Hey, that's an idea. Listen, Mahatma; we have a big forest of flowerpot trees up on a plateau above us. Say we set that on fire. Think you could see it?"

"I don't see why not, even in this moonlight. Wait a minute, till I call the other ships."

Tom was getting into warm outer garments. Cesário got out the arc torch, and he and Tom and I raced out through the hut and outdoors. We hastened up the path that had been tramped and dragged to the waterfall, got the lifters off the logs, and used them to help ourselves up over the rocks beside the waterfall.

We hadn't bothered doing anything with the slashings, except to get them out of our way, while we were working. Now we gathered them into piles among the trees, placing them to take advantage of what little wind was still blowing, and touched them off with the arc torch. Soon we had the branches of the trees burning, and then the soft outer wood of the trunks. It actually began to get uncomfortably hot, although the temperature was now down around minus 90° Fahrenheit.

Cesário was using the torch. After he got all the slashings on fire, he started setting fire to the trees themselves, going all around them and getting the soft outer wood burning. As soon as he had one tree lit, he would run on to another.

"This guy's a real pyromaniac," Tom said to me, wiping his face on the sleeve of his father's parka which he was wearing over his own.

"Sure I am," Cesário took time out to reply. "You know who I was about fifty reincarnations ago? Nero, burning Rome." Theosophists never hesitated to make fun of their religion, that way. The way they see it, a thing isn't much good if it can't stand being made fun of. "And look at the job I did on Moscow, a little later."

"Sure; I remember that. I was Napoleon then. What I'd have done to you if I'd caught you, too."

"Yes, and I know what he was in another reincarnation," Tom added. "Mrs. O'Leary's cow!"

Whether or not Cesário really had had any past astral experience, he made a good job of firebugging on this forest. We waited around for a while, far enough back for the heat to be just comfortable and pleasant, until we were sure that it was burning well on both sides of the frozen stream. It even made the double moonlight dim, and it was sending up huge clouds of fire-reddened smoke, and where the fire didn't light the smoke, it was black in the moonlight. There wouldn't be any excuse for anybody not seeing that. Finally, we started back to camp.

As soon as we got within earshot, we could hear the excitement. Everybody was jumping and yelling. "They see it! They see it!"

The boat was full of voices, too, from the radio:

"*Pequod* to *Dirty Gertie,* we see it, too, just off our port bow . . . Yes, *Bulldog,* we see your running lights; we're right behind you . . . *Slasher* to *Pequod:* we can's see you at all. Fire a flare, please . . . "

I pushed in to the radio. "This is Walter Boyd, *Times* representative with the *Javelin* castaways," I said. "Has anybody a portable audio-visual pickup that I can use to get some pictures in to my paper with?"

That started general laughter among the operators on the ships that were coming in.

"We have one, Walt," Oscar Fujisawa's voice told me. "I'm coming in ahead in the *Pequod* scout boat; I'll bring it with me."

"Thanks, Oscar," I said. Then I asked him: "Did you see Bish Ware before you left port?"

"I should say I did!" Oscar told me. "You can thank Bish Ware that we're out looking for you now. Tell you about it as soon as we get in."

14

THE RESCUE

THE SCOUT BOAT from the Pequod came in about thirty minutes later, from up the ravine where the forest fire was sending up flame and smoke. It passed over the boat and the hut beside it and the crowd of us outside, and I could see Oscar in the machine gunner's seat aiming a portable audiovisual telecast camera. After he got a view of us, cheering and waving our arms, the boat came back and let down. We ran to it, all of us except the man with the broken leg and a couple who didn't have enough clothes to leave the fire, and as the boat opened I could hear Oscar saying:

"Now I am turning you over to Walter Boyd, the *Times* correspondent with the *Javelin* castaways."

He gave me the camera when he got out, followed by his gunner, and I got a view of them, and of the boat lifting and starting west to guide the ships in. Then I shut it off and said to him:

"What's this about Bish Ware? You said he was the one who started the search."

"That's right," Oscar said. "About thirty hours after you left port, he picked up some things that made him think the *Javelin* had been sabotaged.

132

He went to your father, and he contacted me—
Mohandas Feinberg and I still had our ships in
port—and started calling the *Javelin* by screen.
When he couldn't get response, your father put
out a general call to all hunter-ships. Nip Spazoni
reported boarding the *Javelin*, and then went
searching the area where he thought you'd been
hunting, picked up your locator signal, and found
the *Javelin* on the bottom with her bow blown out
and the boat berth open and the boat gone. We all
figured you'd head south with the boat, and that's
where we went to look."

"Well, Bish Ware; he was dead drunk, last I
heard of him," Joe Kivelson said.

"Aah, just an act," Oscar said. "That was to fool
the city cops, and anybody else who needed fooling. It worked so well that he was able to crash a
party Steve Ravick was throwing at Hunters' Hall,
after the meeting. That was where he picked up
some hints that Ravick had a spy in the *Javelin*
crew. He spent the next twenty or so hours following that up, and heard about your man Devis
straining his back. He found out what Devis did
on the *Javelin*, and that gave him the idea that
whatever the sabotage was, it would be something
to the engines. What did happen, by the way?"

A couple of us told him, interrupting one
another. He nodded.

"That was what Nip Spazoni thought when he
looked at the ship. Well, after that he talked to
your father and to me, and then your father began
calling and we heard from Nip."

You could see that it absolutely hurt Joe Kivelson to have to owe his life to Bish Ware.

"Well, it's lucky anybody listened to him," he grudged. "I wouldn't have."

"No, I guess maybe you wouldn't," Oscar told him, not very cordially. "I think he did a mighty sharp piece of detective work, myself."

I nodded, and then, all of a sudden, another idea, under *Bish Ware, Reformation of*, hit me. Detective work; that was it. We could use a good private detective agency in Port Sandor. Maybe I could talk him into opening one. He could make a go of it. He had all kinds of contacts, he was handy with a gun, and if he recruited a couple of tough but honest citizens who were also handy with guns and built up a protective and investigative organization, it would fill a long-felt need and at the same time give him something beside Baldur honey-rum to take his mind off whatever he was drinking to keep from thinking about. If he only stayed sober half the time, that would be a fifty per cent success.

Ramón Llewellyn was wanting to know whether anybody'd done anything about Al Devis.

"We didn't have time to bother with any Al Devises," Oscar said. "As soon as Bish figured out what had happened aboard the *Javelin*, we knew you'd need help and need it fast. He's keeping an eye on Al for us till we get back."

"That's if he doesn't get any drunker and forget," Joe said.

Everybody, even Tom, looked at him in angry reproach.

"We better find out what he drinks and buy you a jug of it, Joe," Oscar's gunner told him.

The *Helldiver*, which had been closet to us

when our signal had been picked up, was the first ship in. She let down into the ravine, after some maneuvering around, and Mohandas Feinberg and half a dozen of his crew got off with an improvised stretcher on a lifter and a lot of blankets. We got our broken-leg case aboard, and Abdullah Monnahan, and the man with the broken wrist. There were more ships coming, so the rest of us waited. Joe Kivelson should have gone on the *Helldiver*, to have his broken arm looked at, but a captain's always the last man off, so he stayed.

Oscar said he'd take Tom and Joe, and Glenn Murrell and me, on the *Pequod*. I was glad of that. Oscar and his mate and his navigator are all bachelors, and they use the *Pequod* to throw parties on when they're not hunting, so it is more comfortably fitted than the usual hunter-ship. Joe decided not to try to take anything away from the boat. He was going to do something about raising the *Javelin*, and the salvage ship could stop here and pick everything up.

"Well, one thing," Oscar told him. "Bring that machine gun, and what small arms you have. I think things are going to get sort of rough in Port Sandor, in the next twenty or so hours."

I was beginning to think so, myself. The men who had gotten off the *Helldiver*, and the ones who got off Corkscrew Finnegan's *Dirty Gertie* and Nip Spazoni's *Bulldog* were all talking about what was going to have to be done about Steve Ravick. Bombing *Javelin* would have been a good move for Ravick, if it had worked. It hadn't, though, and now it was likely to be the thing that would finish him for good.

It wasn't going to be any picnic, either. He had

his gang of hoodlums, and he could count on
Morton Hallstock's twenty or thirty city police;
they'd put up a fight, and a hard one. And they
were all together, and the hunter fleet was coming
in one ship at a time. I wondered if the Ravick-
Hallstock gang would try to stop them at the water
front, or concentrate at Hunters' Hall or the
Municipal Building to stand siege. I knew one
thing, though. However things turned out, there
was going to be an awful lot of shooting in Port
Sandor before it was over.

Finally, everybody had been gotten onto one
ship or another but Oscar and his gunner and the
Kivelsons and Murell and myself. Then the
Pequod, which had been circling around at five
thousand feet, let down and we went aboard. The
conning tower was twice as long as usual on a
hunter-ship, and furnished with a lot of easy
chairs and a couple of couches. There was a big
combination view and communication screen,
and I hurried to that and called the *Times*.

Dad came on, as soon as I finished punching the
wavelength combination. He was in his shirt
sleeves, and he was wearing a gun. I guess we
made kind of a show of ourselves, but, after all,
he'd come within an ace of being all out of family,
and I'd come within an ace of being all out,
period. After we got through with the happy re-
union, I asked him what was the situation in Port
Sandor. He shook his head.

"Not good, Walt. The word's gotten around that
there was a bomb planted aboard the *Javelin*, and
everybody's taking just one guess who did it. We
haven't expressed any opinions one way or

another, yet. We've been waiting for confirmation."

"Set for recording," I said. "I'll give you the story as far as we know it."

He nodded, reached one hand forward out of the picture, and then nodded again. I began with our killing the monster and going down to the bottom after the cutting-up, and the explosion. I told him what we had seen after leaving the ship and circling around it in the boat.

"The condition of the hull looked very much like the effect of a charge of high explosive exploding in the engine room," I finished.

"We got some views of it, transmitted in by Captain Spazoni, of the *Bulldog*," he said. "Captain Courtland, of the Spaceport Police, has expressed the opinion that it could hardly be anything but a small demolition bomb. Would you say accident can be ruled out?"

"I would. There was nobody in the engine room at the time; we were resting on the bottom, and all hands were in the wardroom."

"That's good enough," Dad said. "We'll run it as 'very convincing and almost conclusive' evidence of sabotage." He'd shut off the recorder for that. "Can I get the story of how you abandoned ship and landed, now?"

His hand moved forward, and the recorder went on again. I gave a brief account of our experiences in the boat, the landing and wreck, and our camp, and the firewood cutting, and how we had repaired the radio. Joe Kivelson talked for a while, and so did Tom and Glenn Murell. I was going to say something when they finished, and I sat down

on one of the couches. I distinctly remember leaning back and relaxing.

The next thing I knew, Oscar Fujisawa's mate
was shaking me awake.

"We're in sight of Port Sandor," he was telling
me.

I mumbled something, and then sat up and
found that I had been lying down and that somebody had thrown a blanket over me. Tom Kivelson was still asleep under a blanket on the other
couch, across from me. The clock over the instrument panel had moved eight G.S. hours. Joe
Kivelson wasn't in sight, but Glenn Murell and
Oscar were drinking coffee. I went to the front
window, and there was a scarlet glow on the horizon ahead of me.

That's another sight Cesário Vieria will miss, if
he takes his next reincarnation off Fenris. Really,
it's nothing but damp, warm air, blown up from
the exhaust of the city's main ventilation plant,
condensing and freezing as it hits the cold air
outside, and floodlighted from below. I looked at
it for a while, and then got myself a cup of coffee
and when I had finished it I went to the screen.

It was still tuned to the Times, and Mohandas
Feinberg was sitting in front of it, smoking one of
his twisted black cigars. He had a big 10-mm
Sterberg stuffed into the waistband of his trousers.

"You guys poked along," he said. "I always
thought the Pequod was fast. We got in three
hours ago."

"Who else is in?"

"Corkscrew and some of his gang are here at the
Times, now. Bulldog and Slasher just got in a

while ago. Some of the ships that were farthest west and didn't go to your camp have been in quite a while. We're having a meeting here. We are organizing the Port Sandor Vigilance Committee and Renegade Hunters' Co-operative."

15

VIGILANTES

WHEN THE *Pequod* surfaced under the city roof, I saw what was cooking. There were twenty or more ships, either on the concrete docks or afloat in the pools. The waterfront was crowded with men in boat clothes, forming little knots and breaking up to join other groups, all milling about talking excitedly. Most of them were armed; not just knives and pistols, which is normal costume, but heavy rifles or submachine guns. Down to the left, there was a commotion and people were getting out of the way as a dozen men come pushing through, towing a contragravity skid with a 50-mm ship's gun on it. I began not liking the looks of things, and Glenn Murell, who had come up from his nap below, was liking it even less. He'd come to Fenris to buy tallow-wax, not to fight a civil war. I didn't want any of that stuff, either. Getting rid of Ravick, Hallstock and Belsher would come under the head of civic improvements, but towns are rarely improved by having battles fought in them.

Maybe I should have played dumb and waited till I'd talked to Dad face to face, before making any statements about what had happened on the

Javelin, I thought. Then I shrugged that off. From the minute the *Javelin* had failed to respond to Dad's screen-call and the general call had gone out to the hunter-fleet, everybody had been positive of what had happened. It was too much like the loss of the *Claymore,* which had made Ravick president of the Co-op.

Port Sandor had just gotten all of Steve Ravick that anybody could take. They weren't going to have any more of him, and that was all there was to it.

Joe Kivelson was grumbling about his broken arm; that meant that when a fight started, he could only go in swinging with one fist, and that would cut the fun in half. Another reason why Joe is a wretched shot is that he doesn't like pistols. They're a little too impersonal to suit him. They weren't for Oscar Fujisawa; he had gotten a Mars-Consolidated Police Special out of the chart-table drawer and put it on, and he was loading cartridges into a couple of spare clips. Down on the main deck, the gunner was serving out small arms, and there was an acrimonious argument because everybody wanted a chopper and there weren't enough choppers to go around. Oscar went over to the ladder head and shouted down at them.

"Knock off the argument, down there; you people are all going to stay on the ship. I'm going up to the *Times;* as soon as I'm off, float her out into the inner channel and keep her afloat, and don't let anybody aboard you're not sure of."

"That where we're going?" Joe Kivelson asked.

"Sure. That's the safest place in town for Mr.

Murell and I want to find out exactly what's going on here."

"Well, here; you don't need to put me in storage," Murell protested. "I can take care of myself."

Add, Famous Last Words, I thought.

"I'm sure of it, but we can't take any chances," Oscar told him. "Right now, you are Fenris's Indispensable Man. If you're not around to buy tallow-wax, Ravick's won the war."

Oscar and Murell and Joe and Tom Kivelson and I went down into the boat; somebody opened the port and we floated out and lifted onto the Second Level Down. There was a fringe of bars and cafés and dance halls and outfitters and ship chandlers for a couple of blocks back, and then we ran into the warehouse district. Oscar ran up town to a vehicle shaft above the Times Building, careful to avoid the neighborhood of Hunters' Hall or the Municipal Building.

There was a big crowd around the Times, mostly business district people and quite a few women. They were mostly out on the street and inside the street-floor vehicle port. Not a disorderly crowd, but I noticed quite a few rifles and submachine guns. As we slipped into the vehicle port, they recognized the Pequod's boat, and there was a rush after it. We had trouble getting down without setting it on anybody, and more trouble getting out of it. They were all friendly—too friendly for comfort. They began cheering us as soon as they saw us.

Oscar got Joe Kivelson, with his arm in a sling, out in front where he could be seen, and began shouting: "Please make way; this man's been injured. Please don't crowd; we have an injured man here." The crowd began shoving back, and in the rear I could hear them taking it up: "Joe Kivelson; he's been hurt. They're carrying Joe Kivelson off." That made Joe curse a blue streak, and somebody said, "Oh, he's been hurt real bad; just listen to him!"

When we got up to the editorial floor, Dad and Bish Ware and a few others were waiting at the elevator for us. Bish was dressed as he always was, in his conservative black suit, with the organic opal glowing in his neckcloth. Dad had put a coat on over his gun. Julio was wearing two pistols and a knife a foot long. There was a big crowd in the editorial office—ships' officers, merchants, professional people. I noticed Sigurd Ngozori, the banker, and Professor Hartzenbosch—he was wearing a pistol, too, rather self-consciously—and the Zen Buddhist priest, who evidently had something under his kimono. They all greeted us enthusiastically and shook hands with us. I noticed that Joe Kivelson was something less than comfortable about shaking hands with Bish Ware. The fact that Bish had started the search for the *Javelin* that had saved our lives didn't alter the opinion Joe had formed long ago that Bish was just a worthless old souse. Joe's opinions are all collapsium-plated and impervious to outside influence.

I got Bish off to one side as we were going into the editorial room.

"How did you get onto it?" I asked.

He chuckled deprecatingly. "No trick at all," he said. "I just circulated and bought drinks for people. The trouble with Ravick's gang, it's an army of mercenaries. They'll do anything for the price of a drink, and as long as my rich uncle stays solvent, I always have the price of a drink. In the five years I've spent in this Garden Spot of the Galaxy, I've learned some pretty surprising things about Steve Ravick's operations."

"Well, surely, nobody was going around places like Martian Joe's or One Eye Swanson's boasting that they'd put a time bomb aboard the *Javelin*," I said.

"It came to pretty nearly that," Bish said. "You'd be amazed at how careless people who've had their own way for a long time can get. For instance, I've known for some time that Ravick has spies among the crews of a lot of hunterships. I tried, a few times, to warn some of these captains, but except for Oscar Fujisawa and Corkscrew Finnegan, none of them would listen to me. It wasn't that they had any doubt that Ravick would do that; they just wouldn't believe that any of *their* crew were traitors.

"I've suspected this Devis for a long time, and I've spoken to Ramón Llewellyn about him, but he just let it go in one ear and out the other. For one thing, Devis always has more money to spend than his share of the *Javelin* take would justify. He's the showoff type; always buying drinks for everybody and playing the big shot. Claims to win it gambling, but all the times I've ever seen him gambling, he's been losing.

"I knew about this hoard of wax we saw the day Murell came in for some time. I always thought it was being held out to squeeze a better price out of Belsher and Ravick. Then this friend of mine with whom I was talking aboard the *Peenemünde* mentioned that Murell seemed to know more about the tallow-wax business than about literary matters, and after what happened at the meeting and afterward, I began putting two and two together. When I crashed that party at Hunters' Hall, I heard a few things, and they all added up.

"And then, about thirty hours after the *Javelin* left port, I was in the Happy Haven, and who should I see, buying drinks for the house, but Al Devis. I let him buy me one, and he told me he'd strained his back hand-lifting a power-unit cartridge. A square dance got started a little later, and he got into it. His back didn't look very strained to me. And then I heard a couple of characters in One Eye Swanson's betting that the *Javelin* would never make port again."

I knew what had happened from then on. If it hadn't been for Bish Ware, we'd still be squatting around a fire down on the coast of Hermann Reuch's Land till it got too cold to cut wood, and then we'd freeze. I mentioned that, but Bish just shrugged it off and suggested we go on in and see what was happening inside.

"Where is Al Devis?" I asked. "A lot of people want to talk to him."

"I know they do. I want to get to him first, while he's still in condition to do some talking of his own. But he just dropped out of sight, about the time your father started calling the *Javelin*."

"Ah!" I drew a finger across under my chin, and mentioned the class of people who tell no tales. Bish shook his head slowly.

"I doubt it," he said. "Not unless it was absolutely necessary. That sort of thing would have a discouraging effect the next time Ravick wanted a

special job done. I'm pretty sure he isn't at Hunters' Hall, but he's hiding somewhere."

Joe Kivelson had finished telling what had
happened aboard the *Javelin* when we joined the
main crowd, and everybody was talking about
what ought to be done with Steve Ravick. Oddly
enough, the most bloodthirsty were the banker
and the professor. Well, maybe it wasn't so odd.
They were smart enough to know what Steve
Ravick was really doing to Port Sandor, and it hurt
them as much as it did the hunters. Dad and Bish
seemed to be the only ones present who weren't in
favor of going down to Hunters' Hall right away
and massacring everybody in it, and then doing
the same at the Municipal Building.

"That's what I say!" Joe Kivelson was shouting.
"Let's go clean out both rats' nests. Why, there
must be a thousand hunter-ship men at the waterfront, and look how many people in town who
want to help. We got enough men to eat Hunters'
Hall whole."

"You'll find it slightly inedible, Joe," Bish told
him. "Ravick has about thirty men of his own and
fifteen to twenty city police. He has at least four
50-mm's on the landing stage above, and he has
half a dozen heavy machine guns and twice that
many light 7-mm's."

"Bish is right," somebody else said. "They have
the vehicle port on the street level barricaded, and
they have the two floors on the level below sealed
off. We got men all around it and nobody can get
out, but if we try to blast our way in, it's going to
cost us like Nifflheim."

"You mean you're just going to sit here and talk
about it and not do anything?" Joe demanded.

"We're going to do something, Joe," Dad told him. "But we've got to talk about what we're going to do, and how we're going to do it, or it'll be us who'll get wiped out."

"Well, we'll have to decide on what it'll be, pretty quick," Mohandas Gandhi Feinberg said.

"What are things like at the Municipal Building?" Oscar Fujisawa asked. "You say Ravick has fifteen to twenty city cops at Hunters' Hall. Where are the rest of them? That would only be five to ten."

"At the Municipal Building," Bish said. "Hallstock's holed up there, trying to pretend that nothing out of the ordinary is happening."

"Good. Let's go to the Municipal Building, first," Oscar said. "Take a couple of hundred men, make a lot of noise, shoot out a few windows and all yell, 'Hang Mort Hallstock!' loud enough, and he'll recall the cops he has at Hunters' Hall to save his own neck. Then the rest of us can make a quick rush and take Hunters' Hall."

"We'll have to keep our main force around Hunters' Hall while we're demonstrating at the Municipal Building," Corkscrew Finnegan said. "We can't take a chance on Ravick's getting away."

"I couldn't care less whether he gets away or not," Oscar said. "I don't want Steve Ravick's blood. I just want him out of the Co-operative, and if he runs out from it now, he'll never get back in."

"You want him, and you want him alive," Bish Ware said. "Ravick has close to four million sols banked on Terra. Every millisol of that's money he's stolen from the monster-hunters of this planet, through the Co-operative. If you just take him out and string him up, you'll have the Nifflheim of a time getting hold of any of it."

That made sense to all the ship captains, even Joe Kivelson, after Dad reminded him of how much the salvage job on the *Javelin* was going to cost. It took Sigurd Ngozori a couple of minutes to see the point, but then, hanging Steve Ravick wasn't going to cost the Fidelity & Trust Company anything.

"Well, this isn't my party," Glenn Murell said, "but I'm too much of a businessman to see how watching somebody kick on the end of a rope is worth four million sols."

"Four million sols," Bish said, "and wondering, the rest of your lives, whether it was justice or just murder."

The Buddhist priest looked at him, a trifle startled. After all, he was the only clergyman in the crowd; he ought to have thought of that, instead of this outrageous mock-bishop.

"I think it's a good scheme," Dad said. "Don't mass any more men around Hunters' Hall than necessary. You don't want the police to be afraid to leave when Hallstock calls them in to help him at Municipal Building."

Bish Ware rose. "I think I'll see what I can do at Hunters' Hall, in the meantime," he said. "I'm going to see if there's some way in from the First or Second Level Down. Walt, do you still have that sleep-gas gadget of yours?"

I nodded. It was, ostensibly, nothing but an oversized pocket lighter, just the sort of a thing a gadget-happy kid would carry around. It worked perfectly as a lighter, too, till you pushed in on a little gismo on the side. Then, instead of producing a flame, it squirted out a small jet of sleep gas. It would knock out a man; it would almost knock out a Zarathustra veldtbeest. I'd bought it from a spaceman on the *Cape Canaveral*. I'd always suspected that he'd stolen it on Terra, because it was an expensive little piece of work, but was I going to ride a bicycle six hundred and fifty light-years to find out who it belonged to? One of the chemists' shops at Port Sandor made me up some fills for it, and while I had never had to use it, it was a handy thing to have in some of the places I had to follow stories into, and it wouldn't do anybody any permanent damage, the way a gun would.

"Yes; it's down in my room. I'll get it for you," I said.

"Be careful, Bish," Dad said. "That gang would kill you sooner than look at you."

"Who, me?" Bish staggered into a table and caught hold of it. "Who'd wanna hurt me? I'm just good ol' Bish Ware. *Good* ol' Bish! nobody hurt him; he'sh everybody's friend." He let go of the table and staggered into a chair, upsetting it. Then he began to sing:

"Come all ye hardy spacemen, and harken while I tell
Of fluorine-tainted Nifflheim,
the Planetary Hell."

Involuntarily, I began clapping my hands. It was a superb piece of acting—Bish Ware sober playing Bish Ware drunk, and that's not an easy role for anybody to play. Then he picked up the chair and sat down on it.

"Who do you have around Hunters' Hall, and

how do I get past them?" he asked. "I don't want a clipful from somebody on my own side."

Nip Spazoni got a pencil and a pad of paper and began drawing a plan.

"This is Second Level Down," he said. "We have a car here, with a couple of men in it. It's watching this approach here. And we have a ship's boat, over here, with three men in it, and a 7-mm machine gun. And another car—no, a jeep, here. Now, up on the First Level Down, we have two ships' boats, one here, and one here. The password is 'Exotic,' and the countersign is 'Organics.' " He grinned at Murell. "Compliment to your company."

"Good enough. I'll want a bottle of liquor. My breath needs a little touching up, and I may want to offer somebody a drink. If I could get inside that place, there's no telling what I might be able to do. If one man can get in and put a couple of guards to sleep, an army can get in after him."

Brother, I thought, if he pulls this one off, he's in. Nobody around Port Sandor will ever look down on Bish Ware again, not even Joe Kivelson. I began thinking about the detective agency idea again, and wondered if he'd want a junior partner. Ware & Boyd, Planetwide Detective Agency.

I went down to the floor below with him and got him my lighter gas-projector and a couple of spare fills for it, and found the bottle of Baldur honey-rum that Dad had been sure was around somewhere. I was kind of doubtful about that, and he noticed my hesitation in giving it to him and laughed.

"Don't worry, Walt," he said. "This is strictly for protective coloration—and odoration. I shall be quite sparing with it, I assure you."

I shook hands with him, trying not to be too solemn about it, and he went down in the elevator and I went up the stairs to the floor above. By this time, the Port Sandor Vigilance Committee had gotten itself sorted out. The rank-and-file Vigilantes were standing around yacking at one another, and a smaller group—Dad and Sigurd Ngozori and the Reverend Sugitsuma and Oscar and Joe and Corkscrew and Nip and the Mahatma—were in a huddle around Dad's editorial table, discussing strategy and tactics.

"Well, we'd better get back to the docks before it starts," Corkscrew was saying. "No hunter crew will follow anybody but their own ships' officers."

"We'll have to have somebody the uptown people will follow," Oscar said. "These people won't take orders from a woolly-pants hunter captain. How about you, Sigurd?"

The banker shook his head. "Ralph Boyd's the man for that," he said.

"Ralph's needed right here; this is G.H.Q.," Oscar said. "This is a job that's going to have to be run from one central command. We've got to make sure the demonstration against Hallstock and the operation against Hunters' Hall are synchronized."

"I have about a hundred and fifty workmen, and they all have or can get something to shoot with," another man said. I looked around, and saw that it was Casmir Oughourlian, of Rodriguez & Oughourlian Shipyards. "They'll follow me, but I'm not too well known uptown."

"Hey, Professor Hartzenbosch," Mohandas Feinberg said. "You're a respectable-looking

duck; you ever have any experience leading a
lynch mob?"

Everybody laughed. So, to his credit, did the
professor.

"I've had a lot of experience with children," the
professor said. "Children are all savages. So are
lynch mobs. Things that are equal to the same
thing are equal to one another. Yes, I'd say so."

"All right," Dad said. "Say I'm Chief of Staff, or
something. Oscar, you and Joe and Corkscrew and
the rest of you decide who's going to take over-all
command of the hunters. Casmir, you'll command your workmen, and anybody else from the
shipyards and engine works and repair shops and
so on. Sigurd, you and the Reverend, here, and
Professor Hartzenbosch gather up all the uptown
people you can. Now, we'll have to decide on how
much force we need to scare Mort Hallstock, and
how we're going to place the main force that will
attack Hunters' Hall."

"I think we ought to wait till we see what Bish
Ware can do," Oscar said. "Get our gangs together, and find out where we're going to put
who, but hold off the attack for a while. If he can
get inside Hunters' Hall, we may not even need
this demonstration at the Municipal Building."

Joe Kivelson started to say something. The rest
of his fellow ship captains looked at him severely,
and he shut up. Dad kept on jotting down figures
of men and 50-mm guns and vehicles and auto
weapons we had available.

He was still doing it when the fire alarm started.

16

CIVIL WAR POSTPONED

THE MOANER WENT on for thirty seconds, like a banshee mourning its nearest and dearest. It was everywhere, Main City Level and the four levels below. What we have in Port Sandor is a volunteer fire organization—or disorganization, rather—of six independent companies, each of which cherishes enmity for all the rest. It's the best we can do, though; if we depended on the city government, we'd have no fire protection at all. They do have a central alarm system, though, and the *Times* is connected with that.

Then the moaner stopped, and there were four deep whistle blasts for Fourth Ward, and four more shrill ones for Bottom Level. There was an instant's silence, and then a bedlam of shouts from the hunter-boat captains. That was where the tallow-wax that was being held out from the Cooperative was stored.

"Shut up!" Dad roared, the loudest I'd ever heard him speak. "Shut up and listen!"

"Fourth Ward, Bottom Level," a voice from the fire-alarm speaker said. "This is a tallow-wax fire. It is not the Co-op wax; it is wax stored in an otherwise disused area. It is dangerously close to stored 50-mm cannon ammunition, and it is directly under the pulpwood lumber plant, on the Third Level Down, and if the fire spreads up to that, it will endanger some of the growing vats at the carniculture plant on the Second Level Down. I repeat, this is a tallow-wax fire. Do not use water or chemical extinguishers."

About half of the Vigilantes, businessmen who belonged to one or another of the volunteer companies had bugged out for their fire stations already. The Buddhist priest and a couple of doctors were also leaving. The rest, mostly hunter-ship men, were standing around looking at one another.

Oscar Fujisawa gave a sour laugh. "That diversion idea of mine was all right," he said. "The only trouble was that Steve Ravick thought of it first."

"You think he started the fire?" Dad began, and then gave a sourer laugh than Oscar's. "Am I dumb enough to ask that?"

I had started assembling equipment as soon as the feint on the Municipal Building and the attack on Hunters' Hall had gotten into the discussion stage. I would use a jeep that had a heavy-duty audiovisual recording and transmitting outfit on it, and for situations where I'd have to leave the jeep and go on foot, I had a lighter outfit like the one Oscar had brought with him in the *Pequod's* boat. Then I had my radio for two-way conversation with the office. And, because this wasn't likely to be the sort of war in which the rights of noncombatants like war correspondents would be

taken very seriously, I had gotten out my Sterberg
7.7-mm.

Dad saw me buckling it on, and seemed rather
distressed.

"Better leave that, Walt," he said. "You don't
want to get into any shooting."

Logical, I thought. If you aren't prepared for
something, it just won't happen. There's an awful
lot of that sort of thinking going on. As I remember
my Old Terran history, it was even indulged in by
governments, at one time. None of them exists
now.

"You know what all crawls into the Bottom
Level," I reminded him. "If you don't, ask Mr.
Murell, here. One sent him to the hospital."

Dad nodded; I had a point there. The abandoned sections of Bottom Level are full of tread-
snails and other assorted little nasties, and the
heat of the fire would stir them all up and start
them moving around. Even aside from the possibility that, having started the fire, Steve Ravick's
gang would try to take steps to keep it from being
put out too soon, a gun was going to be a comfort-
ing companion, down there.

"Well, stay out of any fighting. Your job's to get
the news, not play hero in gun fights. I'm no hero;
that's why I'm sixty years old. I never knew many
heroes that got that old."

It was my turn to nod. On that, Dad had a point. I
said something about getting the news, not making it, and checked the chamber and magazine of
the Sterberg, and then slung my radio and picked
up the audiovisual outfit.

Tom and Joe Kivelson had left already, to round

up the scattered *Javelin* crew for fire fighting. The attack on the Municipal Building and on Hunters' Hall had been postponed, but it wasn't going to be abandoned. Oscar and Professor Hartzenbosch and Dad and a couple of others were planning some sort of an observation force of a few men for each place, until the fire had been gotten out or under control. Glenn Murell decided he'd go out with me, at least as far as the fire, so we went down to the vehicle port and got the jeep out. Main City Level Broadway was almost deserted; everybody had gone down below where the excitement was. We started down the nearest vehicle shaft and immediately got into a jam, above a lot of stuff that was going into the shaft from the First Level Down, mostly manipulators and that sort of thing. There were no police around, natch, and a lot of volunteers were trying to direct traffic and getting in each other's way. I got some views with the jeep camera, just to remind any of the public who needed reminding what our city administration wasn't doing in an emergency. A couple of pieces of apparatus, a chemical tank and a pumper marked SALAMANDER VOLUNTEER FIRE COMPANY NO. 3 came along, veered out of the jam, and continued uptown.

"If they know another way down, maybe we'd better follow them," Murell suggested.

"They're not going down. They're going to the lumber plant, in case the fire spreads upward," I said. "They wouldn't be taking that sort of equipment to a wax fire."

"Why not?"

I looked at him. "I thought you were in the wax business," I said.

"I am, but I'm no chemist. I don't know anything about how wax burns. All I know is what it's
used for, roughly, and who's in the market for it."

"Well, you know about those jumbo molecules,
don't you?" I asked. "They have everything but
the kitchen sink in them, including enough oxygen to sustain combustion even under water or in
a vacuum. Not enough oxygen to make wax
explode, like powder, but enough to keep it burning. Chemical extinguishers are all smothering
agents, and you just can't smother a wax fire. And
water's worse than useless."

He wanted to know why.

"Burning wax is a liquid. The melting point is
around 250 degrees Centigrade. Wax ignites at
750. It has no boiling point, unless that's the burning point. Throw water on a wax fire and you get a
steam explosion, just as you would if you threw it
on molten metal, and that throws the fire around
and spreads it."

"If it melts that far below the ignition point,
wouldn't it run away before it caught fire?"

"Normally, it would. That's why I'm sure this
fire was a touch-off. I think somebody planted a
thermoconcentrate bomb. A thermoconcentrate
flame is around 850 Centigrade; the wax would
start melting and burning almost instantaneous-
ly. In any case, the fire will be at the bottom of the
stacks. If it started there, melted wax would run
down from above and keep the fire going, and if it
started at the top, burning wax would run down
and ignite what's below."

"Well, how in blazes do you put a wax fire
out?" he wanted to know.

"You don't. You just pull away all the wax that

hasn't caught fire yet, and then try to scatter the fire and let it burn itself out . . . Here's our chance!"

All this conversation we had been screaming into each other's ears, in the midst of a pandemonium of yelling, cursing, siren howling and bell clanging; just then I saw a hole in the vertical traffic jam and edged the jeep into it, at the same time remembering that the jeep carried, and I was entitled to use, a fire siren. I added its howls to the general uproar and dropped down one level. Here a string of big manipulators were trying to get in from below, sprouting claw hooks and grapples and pusher arms in all directions. I made my siren imitate a tail-tramped tomcat a couple of times, and got in among them.

Bottom Level Broadway was a frightful mess, and I realized that we had come down right between two units of the city power plant, big mass-energy converters. The street was narrower than above, and ran for a thousand yards between ceiling-high walls, and everything was bottlenecked together. I took the jeep up till we were almost scraping the ceiling, and Murell, who had seen how the audiovisual was used, took over with it while I concentrated on inching forward. The noise was even worse down here than it had been above; we didn't attempt to talk.

Finally, by impudence and plain foolhardiness, I got the jeep forward a few hundred yards, and found myself looking down on a big derrick with a fifty-foot steel boom tipped with a four-clawed grapple, shielded in front with sheet steel like a gun shield. It was painted with the emblem of the Hunters' Co-operative, but the three men on it looked like shipyard workers. I didn't get that, at all. The thing had been built to handle burning wax, and was one of three kept on the Second Level Down under Hunters' Hall. I wondered if Bish Ware had found a way for a gang to get in at the bottom of Hunters' Hall. I simply couldn't see Steve Ravick releasing equipment to fight the fire his goons had started for him in the first place.

I let down a few feet, gave a polite little scream with my siren, and then yelled down to the men on it:

"Where'd that thing come from?"

"Hunters' Hall; Steve Ravick sent it. The other two are up at the fire already, and if this mess ahead doesn't get straightened out . . ." From there on, his remarks were not suitable for publication in a family journal like the *Times*.

I looked up ahead, rising to the ceiling again, and saw what was the matter. It was one of the dredgers from the waterfront, really a submarine scoop shovel, that they used to keep the pools and the inner channel from sanding up. I wasn't surprised it was jammed; I couldn't see how they'd gotten this far uptown with it. I got a few shots of that, and then unhooked the handphone of my radio. Julio Kubanoff answered.

"You getting everything I'm sending in?" I asked.

"Yes. What's that two-em-dashed thing up ahead, one of the harbor dredgers?"

"That's right. Hey, look at this, once." I turned the audiovisual down on the claw derrick. "The men on it look like Rodriguez & Oughourlian's people, but they say Steve Ravick sent it. What do you know about it?"

"Hey, Ralph! What's this Walt's picked up about Ravick sending equipment to fight the fire?" he yelled.

Dad came over, and nodded. "It wasn't Ravick, it was Mort Hallstock. He commandeered the Co-op equipment and sent it up," he said. "He called me and wanted to know whom to send for it that Ravick's gang wouldn't start shooting at right away. Casmir Oughourlian sent some of his men."

Up front, something seemed to have given way. The dredger went lurching forward, and everything moved off after it.

"I get it," I said. "Hallstock's getting ready to dump Ravick out the airlock. He sees, now, that Ravick's a dead turkey; he doesn't want to go into the oven along with him."

"Walt, can't you ever give anybody credit with trying to do something decent, once in a while?" Dad asked.

"Sure I can. Decent people. There are a lot of them around, but Mort Hallstock isn't one of them. There was an Old Terran politician named Al Smith, once. He had a little saying he used in that kind of case: 'Let's look at the record.' "

"Well, Mort's record isn't very impressive, I'll give you that," Dad admitted. "I understand Mort's up at the fire now. Don't spit in his eye if you run into him."

"I won't," I promised. "I'm kind of particular where I spit."

Things must be looking pretty rough around Municipal Building, I thought. Maybe Mort's afraid the people will start running Fenris again, after this. He might even be afraid there'd be an election.

By this time, I'd gotten the jeep around the dredger—we'd come to the end of the nuclear-power plant buildings—and cut off into open country. That is to say, nothing but pillar-buildings two hundred yards apart and piles of bagged mineral nutrients for the hydroponic farms. We could see a blaze of electric lights ahead where the fire must be, and after a while we began to run into lorries and lifter-skids hauling ammunition away from the area. Then I could see a big mushroom of greasy black smoke spreading out close to the ceiling. The electric lights were brighter ahead, and there was a confused roar of voices and sirens and machines.

And there was a stink.

There are a lot of stinks around Port Sandor, though the ventilation system carries most of them off before they can spread out of their own areas. The plant that reprocesses sewage to get organic nutrients for the hydroponic farms, and the plant that digests hydroponic vegetation to make nutrients for the carniculture vats. The carniculture vats themselves aren't any flower gardens. And the pulp plant where our synthetic lumber is made. But the worst stink there is on Fenris is a tallow-wax fire. Fortunately, they don't happen often.

17

TALLOW-WAX FIRE

Now THAT WE were out of the traffic jam, I could poke along and use the camera myself. The wax was stacked in piles twenty feet high, which gave thirty feet of clear space above them, but the section where they had been piled was badly cut up by walls and full of small extra columns to support the weight of the pulp plant above and the carniculture vats on the level over that. However, the piles themselves weren't separated by any walls, and the fire could spread to the whole stock of wax. There were more men and vehicles on the job than room for them to work. I passed over the heads of the crowd around the edges and got onto a comparatively unobstructed side where I could watch and get views of the fire fighters pulling down the big skins of wax and loading them onto contragravity skids to be hauled away. It still wasn't too hot to work unshielded, and they weren't anywhere near the burning stacks, but the fire seemed to be spreading rapidly. The dredger and the three shielded derricks hadn't gotten into action yet.

I circled around clockwise, dodging over, under and around the skids and lorries hauling wax out of danger. They were taking them into the section through which I had brought the jeep a few minutes before, and just dumping them on top of the piles of mineral nutrients.

The operation seemed to be directed from an improvised headquarters in the area that had been cleared of ammunition. There were a couple of view screens and a radio, operated by women. I saw one of the teachers I'd gone to school to a few years ago, and Joe Kivelson's wife, and Oscar Fujisawa's current girl friend, and Sigurd Ngozori's secretary, and farther off there was an equally improvised coffee-and-sandwich stand. I grounded the jeep, and Murell and I got out and went over to the headquarters. Joe Kivelson seemed to be in charge.

I have, I believe, indicated here and there that Joe isn't one of our mightier intellects. There are a lot of better heads, but Joe can be relied upon to keep his, no matter what is happening or how bad it gets. He was sitting on an empty box, his arm in a now-filthy sling, and one of Mohandas Feinberg's crooked black cigars in his mouth. Usually, Joe smokes a pipe, but a cigar's less bother for a temporarily one-armed man. Standing in front of him, like a schoolboy in front of the teacher, was Mayor Morton Hallstock.

"But, Joe, they simply won't!" His Honor was wailing. "I did talk to Mr. Fieschi; he says he knows this is an emergency, but there's a strict company directive against using the spaceport area for storage of anything but cargo that has either just come in or is being shipped out on the next ship."

"What's this all about?" Murell asked.

"Fieschi, at the spaceport, won't let us store this wax in the spaceport area," Joe said. "We got to get it stored somewhere; we need a lot of floor space to spread this fire out on, once we get into it. We have to knock the burning wax cylinders apart, and get them separated enough so that burning wax won't run from one to another."

"Well, why can't we store it in the spaceport area?" Murrell wanted to know. "It is going out on the next ship. I'm consigning it to Exotic Organics, in Buenos Aires." He turned to Joe. "Are those skins all marked to indicate who owns them?"

"That's right. And any we gather up loose, from busted skins, we can figure some way of settling how much anybody's entitled to from them."

"All right. Get me a car and run me to the spaceport. Call them and tell them I'm on the way. I'll talk to Fieschi myself."

"Martha!" Joe yelled to his wife. "Car and driver, quick. And then call the spaceport for me; get Mr. Fieschi or Mr. Mansour on screen."

Inside two minutes, a car came in and picked Murell up. By that time, Joe was talking to somebody at the spaceport. I called the paper, and told Dad that Murell was buying the wax for his company as fast as it was being pulled off the fire, at eighty centisols a pound. He said that would go out as a special bulletin right away. Then I talked to Morton Hallstock, and this time he wasn't giving me any of the run-along-sonny routine. I told him, rather hypocritically, what a fine thing he'd done, getting that equipment from Hunters' Hall. I suspect I sounded as though I were mayor of Port Sandor and Hallstock, just seventeen years old, had done something the grownups thought was real smart for a kid. If so, he didn't seem to notice. Sombody connected with the press was being nice to him. I asked him where Steve Ravick was.

"Mr. Ravick is at Hunters' Hall," he said. "He thought it would be unwise to make a public appearance just now." Oh, brother, what an understatement! "There seems to be a lot of public feeling against him, due to some misconception that he was responsible for what happened to Captain Kivelson's ship. Of course, that is absolutely false. Mr. Ravick had absolutely nothing to do with that. He wasn't anywhere near the *Javelin*."

"Where's Al Devis?" I asked.

"Who? I don't believe I know him."

After Hallstock got into his big black air-limousine and took off, Joe Kivelson gave a short laugh.

"I could have told him where Al Devis is," he said. "No, I couldn't, either," he corrected himself. "That's a religious question, and I don't discuss religion."

I shut off my radio in a hurry. "Who got him?" I asked.

Joe named a couple of men from one of the hunter-ships.

"Here's what happened. There were six men on guard here; they had a jeep with a 7-mm machine gun. About an hour ago, a lorry pulled in, with two men in boat-clothes on it. They said that Pierre Karolyi's *Corinne* had just come in with a hold full of wax, and they were bringing it up from the docks, and where should they put it? Well, the men on guard believed that; Pierre'd gone off into the twilight zone after the *Helldiver* contacted us, and he could have gotten a monster in the meantime.

"Well, they told these fellows that there was more room over on the other side of the stacks, and the lorry went up above the stacks and started across, and when they were about the middle, one of the men in it threw out a thermoconcentrate bomb. The lorry took off, right away. The only thing was that there were two men in the jeep, and one of them was at the machine gun. They'd lifted to follow the lorry over and show them where to put this wax, and as soon as the bomb went off, the man at the gun grabbed it and caught the lorry in his sights and let go. This fellow hadn't been covering for cutting-up work for years for nothing. He got one burst right in the control cabin, and the lorry slammed into the next column foundation. After they called in an alarm on the fire the bomb had started, a couple of them went to see who'd been in the lorry. The two men in it were both dead, and one of them was Al Devis."

"Pity," I said. "I'd been looking forward to putting a recording of his confession on the air. Where is this lorry now?"

Joe pointed toward the burning wax piles. "Almost directly on the other side. We have a couple of men guarding it. The bodies are still in it. We don't want any tampering with it till it can be properly examined; we want to have the facts straight, in case Hallstock tries to make trouble for the men who did the shooting."

I didn't know how he could. Under any kind of Federation law at all, a man killed committing a felony—and bombing and arson ought to qualify for that—is simply bought and paid for; his blood is on nobody's head but his own. Of course, a small matter like legality was always the least of Mort Hallstock's worries.

"I'll go get some shots of it," I said, and then I snapped on my radio and called the story in.

Dad had already gotten it, from fire-alarm center, but he hadn't heard that Devis was one of the deceased arsonists. Like me, he was very sorry to hear about it. Devis as Devis was no loss, but alive and talking he'd have helped us pin both the wax fire and the bombing of the *Javelin* on Steve Ravick. Then I went back and got in the jeep.

They were beginning to get in closer to the middle of the stacks where the fire had been started. There was no chance of getting over the top of it, and on the right there were at least five hundred men and a hundred vehicles, all working like crazy to pull out unburned wax. Big manipulators were coming up and grabbing as many of the half-ton sausages as they could, and lurching away to dump them onto skids or into lorries or just drop them on top of the bags of nutrient stacked beyond. Jeeps and cars would dart in, throw grapnels on the end of lines, and then pull away all the wax they could and return to throw their grapnels again. As fast as they pulled the big skins down, men with hand-lifters like the ones we had used at our camp to handle firewood would pick them up and float them away.

That seemed to be where the major effort was being made, at present, and I could see lifter-skids coming in with big blower fans on them. I knew what the strategy was, now; they were going to pull the wax away to where it was burning on one

side, and then set up the blowers and blow the
heat and smoke away on that side. That way, on
the other side more men could work closer to the
fire, and in the long run they'd save more wax.

I started around the wax piles to the left,
clockwise, to avoid the activity on the other side,
and before long I realized that I'd have done better
not to have. There was a long wall, ceiling-high,
that stretched off uptown in the direction of the
spaceport, part of the support for the weight of the
pulpwood plant on the level above, and piled
against it was a lot of junk machinery of different
kinds that had been hauled in here and dumped
long ago and then forgotten. The wax was piled
almost against this, and the heat and smoke forced
me down.

I looked at the junk pile and decided that I could
get through it on foot. I had been keeping up a
running narration into my radio, and I commented on all this salvageable metal lying in here
forgotten, with our perennial metal shortages.
Then I started picking my way through it, my
portable audiovisual camera slung over my
shoulder and a flashlight in my hand. My left
hand, of course; it's never smart to carry a light in
your right, unless you're left-handed.

The going wasn't too bad. Most of the time, I
could get between things without climbing over
them. I was going between a broken-down press
from the lumber plant and a leaky 500-gallon
pressure cooker from the carniculture nutrient
plant when I heard something moving behind me,
and I was suddenly very glad that I hadn't let
myself be talked into leaving my pistol behind.

It was a thing the size of a ten-gallon keg, with a

thick tail and flippers on which it crawled, and six tentacles like small elephants' trunks around a circular mouth filled with jagged teeth halfway down the throat. There are a dozen or so names for it, but mostly it is called a meat-grinder.

The things are always hungry and try to eat anything that moves. The mere fact that I would be as poisonous to it as any of the local flora or fauna would be to me made no difference; this meat-grinder was no biochemist. It was coming straight for me, all its tentacles writhing.

I had had my Sterberg out as soon as I'd heard the noise. I also remembered that my radio was on, and that I was supposed to comment on anything of interest that took place around me.

"Here's a meat-grinder, coming right for me," I commented in a voice not altogether steady, and slammed three shots down its tooth-studded gullet. Then I scored my target, at the same time keeping out of the way of the tentacles. He began twitching a little. I fired again. The meat-grinder jerked slightly, and that was all.

"Now I'm going out and take a look at that lorry." I was certain now that the voice was shaky.

The lorry—and Al Devis and his companion—had come to an end against one of the two-hundred-foot masonry and concrete foundations the columns rest on. It had hit about halfway up and folded almost like an accordion, sliding down to the floor. With one thing and another, there is a lot of violent death around Port Sandor. I don't like to look at the results. It's part of the job, however, and this time it wasn't a pleasant job at all.

The two men who were guarding the wreck and

contents were sitting on a couple of boxes, smoking and watching the fire-fighting operation.

I took the partly empty clip out of my pistol and put in a full one on the way back, and kept my flashlight moving its circle of light ahead and on both sides of me. That was foolish, or at least unnecessary. If there'd been one meat-grinder in that junk pile, it was a safe bet there wasn't anything else. Meat-grinders aren't popular neighbors, even for tread-snails. As I approached the carcass of the grinder I had shot I found a ten-foot length of steel rod and poked it a few times. When it didn't even twitch, I felt safe in walking past it.

I got back in the jeep and returned to where Joe Kivelson was keeping track of what was going on in five screens, including one from a pickup on a lifter at the ceiling, and shouting orders that were being reshouted out of loudspeakers all over the place. The Odin Dock & Shipyard equipment had begun coming out; lorries picking up the wax that had been dumped back from the fire and wax that was being pulled off the piles, and material-handling equipment. They had a lot of small fork-lifters that were helping close to the fire.

A lot of the wax was getting so soft that it was hard to handle, and quite a few of the plastic skins had begun to split from the heat. Here and there I saw that outside piles had begun to burn at the bottom, from burning wax that had run out underneath. I had moved around to the right and was getting views of the big claw-derricks at work picking the big sausages off the tops of piles, and while I was swinging the camera back and forth, I was trying to figure just how much wax there had been to start with, and how much was being saved. Each of those plastic-covered cylinders was a thousand pounds; one of the claw-derricks was picking up two or three of them at a grab. . . .

I was still figuring when shouts of alarm on my right drew my head around. There was an uprush of flame, and somebody began screaming, and I could see an ambulance moving toward the center of excitement and firemen in asbestos suits converging on a run. One of the piles must have collapsed and sombody must have been splashed. I gave an involuntary shudder. Burning wax was hotter than melted lead, and it stuck to anything it touched, worse than napalm. I saw a man being dragged out of further danger, his clothes on fire, and asbestos-suited firemen crowding around to tear the burning garments from him. Before I could get to where it had happened, though, they had him in the ambulance and were taking him away. I hoped they'd get him to the hospital before he died.

Then more shouting started around at the right as a couple more piles began collapsing. I was able to get all of that—the wax sausages sliding forward, the men who had been working on foot running out of danger, the flames shooting up, and the gush of liquid fire from below. All three derricks moved in at once and began grabbing wax cylinders away on either side of it.

Then I saw Guido Fieschi, the Odin Dock & Shipyard's superintendent, and caught him in my camera, moving the jeep toward him.

"Mr. Fieschi!" I called. "Give me a few seconds and say something."

He saw me and grinned.

"I just came out to see how much more could be saved," he said. "We have close to a thousand tons on the shipping floor or out of danger here and on the way in, and it looks as though you'll be able to save that much more. That'll be a million and a half sols we can be sure of, and a possible three million, at the new price. And I want to take this occasion, on behalf of my company and of Terra-Odin Spacelines, to welcome a new freight shipper."

"Well, that's wonderful news for everybody on Fenris," I said, and added mentally, "with a few exceptions." Then I asked if he'd heard who had gotten splashed.

"No. I know it happened; I passed the ambulance on the way out. I certainly hope they get to work on him in time."

Then more wax started sliding off the piles, and more fire came running out at the bottom. Joe Kivelson's voice, out of the loudspeakers all around, was yelling:

"Everybody away from the front! Get the blowers in; start in on the other side!"

18

THE TREASON OF BISH WARE

I WANTED TO find out who had been splashed, but
Joe Kivelson was too busy directing the new
phase of the fight to hand out casualty reports to
the press, and besides, there were too many things
happening all at once that I had to get. I went
around to the other side where the incendiaries
had met their end, moving slowly as close to the
face of the fire as I could get and shooting the
burning wax flowing out from it. A lot of equipment, including two of the three claw-derricks
and a dredger—they'd brought a second one up
from the waterfront—were moving to that side. By
the time I had gotten around, the blowers had
been maneuvered into place and were ready to
start. There was a lot of back-and-forth yelling to
make sure that everybody was out from in front,
and then the blowers started.

It looked like a horizontal volcanic eruption;
burning wax blowing away from the fire for close
to a hundred feet into the clear space beyond. The
derricks and manipulators and the cars and jeeps
with grapnels went in on both sides, snatching
and dragging wax away. Because they had the
wind from the blowers behind them, the men

could work a lot closer, and the fire wasn't spreading as rapidly. They were saving a lot of wax; each one of those big sausages that the lifters picked up and floated away weighed a thousand pounds, and was worth, at the new price, eight hundred sols.

Finally, they got everything away that they could, and then the blowers were shut down and the two dredge shovels moved in, scooping up the burning sludge and carrying it away, scattering it on the concrete. I would have judged that there had been six or seven million sols' worth of wax in the piles to start with, and that a little more than half of it had been saved before they pulled the last cylinder away.

The work slacked off; finally, there was nothing but the two dredges doing anything, and then they backed away and let down, and it was all over but standing around and watching the scattered fire burn itself out. I looked at my watch. It was two hours since the first alarm had come in. I took a last swing around, got the spaceport people gathering up wax and hauling it away, and the broken lake of fire that extended downtown from where the stacks had been, and then I floated my jeep over to the sandwich-and-coffee stand and let down, getting out. Maybe, I thought, I could make some kind of deal with somebody like Interworld News on this. It would make a nice thrilling feature-program item. Just a little slice of life from Fenris, the Garden Spot of the Galaxy.

I got myself a big zhoumy-loin sandwich with hot sauce and a cup of coffee, made sure that my portable radio was on, and circulated among the fire fighters, getting comments. Everybody had been a hero, natch, and they were all very unbashful about admitting it. There was a great deal of wisecracking about Al Devis buying himself a ringside seat for the fire he'd started. Then I saw Cesário Vieira and joined him.

"Have all the fire you want, for a while?" I asked him.

"Brother, and how! We could have used a little of this over on Hermann Reuch's Land, though. Have you seen Tom around anywhere?"

"No. Have you?"

"I saw him over there, about an hour ago. I guess he stayed on this side. After they started blowing it, I was over on Al Devis's side." He whistled softly. "Was that a mess!"

There was still a crowd at the fire, but they seemed all to be townspeople. The hunters had gathered where Joe Kivelson had been directing operations. We finished our sandwiches and went over to join them. As soon as we got within earshot, I found that they were all in a very ugly mood.

"Don't fool around," one man was saying as we came up. "Don't even bother looking for a rope. Just shoot them as soon as you see them."

Well, I thought, a couple of million sols' worth of tallow-wax, in which they all owned shares, was something to get mean about. I said something like that.

"It's not that," another man said. "It's Tom Kivelson."

"What about him?" I asked, alarmed.

"Didn't you hear? He got splashed with burning wax," the hunter said. "His whole back was on fire; I don't know whether he's alive now or not."

So that was who I'd seen screaming in agony while the firemen tore his burning clothes away. I pushed through, with Cesário behind me, and found Joe Kivelson and Mohandas Feinberg and Corkscrew Finnegan and Oscar Fujisawa and a dozen other captains and ships' officers in a huddle.

"Joe," I said, "I just heard about Tom. Do you know anything yet?"

Joe turned. "Oh, Walt. Why, as far as we know, he's alive. He was alive when they got him to the hospital."

"That's at the spaceport?" I unhooked my handphone and got Dad. He'd heard about a man being splashed, but didn't know who it was. He said he'd call the hospital at once. A few minutes later, he was calling me back.

"He's been badly burned, all over the back. They're preparing to do a deep graft on him. They said his condition was serious, but he was alive five minutes ago."

I thanked him and hung up, relaying the information to the others. They all looked worried. When the screen girl at a hospital tells you somebody's serious, instead of giving you the well-as-can-be-expected routine, you know it is serious. Anybody who makes it alive to a hospital, these days, has an excellent chance, but injury cases do die, now and then, after they've been brought in. They are the "serious" cases.

"Well, I don't suppose there's anything we can do," Joe said heavily.

"We can clean up on the gang that started this fire," Oscar Fujisawa said. "Do it now; then if Tom doesn't make it, he's paid for in advance."

Oscar, I recalled, was the one who had been the most impressed with Bish Ware's argument that lynching Steve Ravick would cost the hunters the four million sols they might otherwise be able to recover, after a few years' interstellar litigation, from his bank account on Terra. That reminded me that I hadn't even thought of Bish since I'd left the *Times*. I called back. Dad hadn't heard a word from him.

"What's the situation at Hunters' Hall?" I asked.

"Everything's quiet there. The police left when Hallstock commandeered that fire-fighting equipment. They helped the shipyard men get it out, and then they all went to the Municipal Building. As far as I know, both Ravick and Belsher are still in Hunters' Hall. I'm in contact with the vehicles on guard at the approaches; I'll call them now."

I relayed that. The others nodded.

"Nip Spazoni and a few others are bringing men and guns up from the docks and putting a cordon around the place on the Main City Level," Oscar said. "Your father will probably be hearing that they're moving into position now."

He had. He also said that he had called all the vehicles on the First and Second Levels Down; they all reported no activity in Hunters' Hall except one jeep on Second Level Down, which did not report at all.

Everybody was puzzled about that.

"That's the jeep that reported Bish Ware going

in on the bottom," Mohandas Feinberg said. "I wonder if somebody inside mightn't have gotten both the man on the jeep and Bish."

"He could have left the jeep," Joe said. "Maybe he went inside after Bish."

"Funny he didn't call in and say so." somebody said.

"No, it isn't," I contradicted. "Manufacturers' claims to the contrary, there is no such thing as a tap-proof radio. Maybe he wasn't supposed to leave his post, but if he did, he used his head not advertising it."

"That makes sense," Oscar agreed. "Well, whatever happened, we're not doing anything standing around up here. Let's get it started."

He walked away, raising his voice and calling, "Pequod! Pequod! All hands on deck!"

The others broke away from the group, shouting the names of their ships to rally their crews. I hurried over to the jeep and checked my equipment. There wasn't too much film left in the big audiovisual, so I replaced it with a fresh sound-and-vision reel, good for another couple of hours, and then lifted to the ceiling. Worrying about Tom wouldn't help Tom, and worrying about Bish wouldn't help Bish, and I had a job to do.

What I was getting now, and I was glad I was starting a fresh reel for it, was the beginning of the First Fenris Civil War. A long time from now, when Fenris was an important planet in the Federation, maybe they'd make today a holiday, like Bastille Day or the Fourth of July or Federation Day. Maybe historians, a couple of centuries from now, would call me an important primary source, and if Cesário's religion was right, maybe I'd be one of them, saying, "Well, after all, is Boyd such a reliable source? He was only seventeen years old at the time."

Finally, after a lot of yelling and confusion, the Rebel Army got moving. We all went up to Main City Level and went down Broadway, spreading out side streets when we began running into the cordon that had been thrown around Hunters' Hall. They were mostly men from the waterfront who hadn't gotten to the wax fire, and they must have stripped the guns off half the ships in the harbor and mounted them on lorries or cargo skids.

Nobody, not even Joe Kivelson, wanted to begin with any massed frontal attack on Hunters' Hall.

"We'll have to bombard the place," he was saying. "We try to rush it and we'll lose half our gang before we get in. One man with good cover and a machine gun's good for a couple of hundred in the open."

"Bish may be inside," I mentioned.

"Yes," Oscar said, "and even aside from that, that building was built with our money. Let's don't burn the house down to get rid of the cockroaches."

"Well, how are you going to do it, then?" Joe wanted to know. Rule out frontal attack and Joe's at the end of his tactics.

"You stay up here. Keep them amused with a little smallarms fire at the windows and so on. I'll take about a dozen men and go down to Second Level. If we can't do anything else, we can bring a couple of skins of tallow-wax down and set fire to it and smoke them out."

That sounded like a pretty expensive sort of

smudge, but seeing how much wax Ravick had burned uptown, it was only fair to let him in on some of the smoke. I mentioned that if we got into the building and up to Main City Level, we'd need some way of signaling to avoid being shot by our own gang, and got the wave-length combination of the *Pequod* scout boat, which Joe and Oscar were using for a command car. Oscar picked ten or twelve men, and they got into a lorry and went uptown and down a vehicle shaft to Second Level. I followed in my jeep, even after Oscar and his crowd let down and got out, and hovered behind them as they advanced on foot to Hunters' Hall.

The Second Level Down was the vehicle storage, where the derricks and other equipment had been kept. It was empty now except for a workbench, a hand forge and some other things like that, a few drums of lubricant, and several piles of sheet metal. Oscar and his men got inside and I followed, going up to the ceiling. I was the one who saw the man lying back of a pile of sheet metal, and called their attention.

He wore boat-clothes and had black whiskers, and he had a knife and a pistol on his belt. At first I thought he was dead. A couple of Oscar's followers, dragging him out, said:

"He's been sleep-gassed."

Somebody else recognized him. He was the lone man who had been on guard in the jeep. The jeep was nowhere in sight.

I began to be really worried. My lighter gadget could have been what had gassed him. It probably was; there weren't many sleep-gas weapons on Fenris. I had to get fills made up specially for mine. So it looked to me as though somebody had

gotten mine off Bish, and then used it to knock out
our guard. Taken if off his body, I guessed. That
crowd wasn't any more interested in taking prisoners alive than we were.

We laid the man on a workbench and put a
rolled-up sack under his head for a pillow. Then
we started up the enclosed stairway. I didn't think
we were going to run into any trouble, though I
kept my hand close to my gun. If they'd knocked
out the guard, they had a way out, and none of
them wanted to stay in that building any longer
than they had to.

The First Level Down was mostly storerooms,
with nobody in any of them. As we went up the
stairway to the Main City Level, we could hear
firing outside. Nobody inside was shooting back. I
unhooked my handphone.

"We're in," I said when Joe Kivelson answered.
"Stop the shooting; we're coming up to the vehicle port."

"Might as well. Nobody's paying any attention
to it," he said.

The firing slacked off as the word was passed
around the perimeter, and finally it stopped entirely. We went up into the open arched vehicle
port. It was barricaded all around, and there were
half a dozen machine guns set up, but not a living
thing.

"We're going up," I said. "They've all lammed
out. The place is empty."

"You don't know that," Oscar chided. "It might
be bulging with Ravick's thugs, waiting for us to
come walking up and be mowed down."

Possible. Highly improbable, though, I thought.
The escalators weren't running, and we weren't

going to alert any hypothetical ambush by starting them. We tiptoed up, and I even drew my
pistol to show that I wasn't being foolhardy. The
big social room was empty. A couple of us went
over and looked behind the bar, which was the
only hiding place in it. Then we went back to the
rear and tiptoed to the third floor.

The meeting room was empty. So were the offices behind it. I looked in all of them, expecting
to find Bish Ware's body. Maybe a couple of other
bodies, too. I'd seen him shoot the tread-snail, and
I didn't think he'd die unpaid for. In Steve
Ravick's office, the safe was open and a lot of
papers had been thrown out. I pointed that out to
Oscar, and he nodded. After seeing that, he
seemed to relax, as though he wasn't expecting to
find anybody any more. We went to the third
floor. Ravick's living quarters were there, and
they were magnificiently luxurious. The hunters,
whose money had paid for all that magnificence
and luxury, cursed.

There were no bodies there, either, or on the
landing stage above. I unhooked the radio again.

"You can come in, now," I said. "The place is
empty. Nobody here but us Vigilantes."

"Huh?" Joe couldn't believe that. "How'd they
get out?"

"They got out on the Second Level Down." I
told him about the sleep-gassed guard.

"Did you bring him to? What did he say?"

"Nothing; we didn't. We can't. You get sleep-
gassed, you sleep till you wake up. That ought to
be two to four hours for this fellow."

"Well, hold everything; we're coming in."

We were all in the social room; a couple of the

men had poured drinks or drawn themselves beers at the bar and rung up NO SALE on the cash register. Somebody else had a box of cigars he'd picked up in Ravick's quarters on the fourth floor and was passing them around. Joe and about two or three hundred other hunters came crowding up the escalator, which they had turned on below.

"You didn't find Bish Ware, either, I'll bet," Joe was saying.

"I'm afraid they took him along for a hostage," Oscar said. "The guard was knocked out with Walt's gas gadget, that Bish was carrying."

"Ha!" Joe cried. "Bet you it was the other way round; Bish took them out."

That started an argument. While it was going on, I went to the communication screen and got the *Times*, and told Dad what had happened.

"Yes," he said. "That was what I was afraid you'd find. Glenn Murell called in from the spaceport a few minutes ago. He says Mort Hallstock came in with his car, and he heard from some of the workmen that Bish Ware, Steve Ravick and Leo Belsher came in on the Main City Level in a jeep. They claimed protection from a mob, and Captain Courtland's police are protecting them."

19

MASKS OFF

THERE WAS dead silence for two or three seconds. If a kitten had sneezed, everybody would have heard it. Then it started, first an inarticulate roar, and then a babel of unprintabilities. I thought I'd heard some bad language from these same men in this room when Leo Belsher's announcement of the price cut had been telecast, but that was prayer meeting to this. Dad was still talking. At least, I saw his lips move in the screen.

"Say that again, Ralph," Oscar Fujisawa shouted.

Dad must have heard him. At least, his lips moved again, but I wasn't a lip reader and neither was Oscar. Oscar turned to the mob—by now, it was that, pure and simple—and roared, in a voice like a foghorn, *"Shut up and listen!"* A few of those closest to him heard him. The rest kept on shouting curses. Oscar waited a second, and then pointed his submachine gun at the ceiling and hammered off the whole clip.

"Shut up, a couple of hundred of you, and listen!" he commanded, on the heels of the blast. Then he turned to the screen again. "Now, Ralph; what was it you were saying?"

"Hallstock got to the spaceport about half an hour ago," Dad said. "He bought a ticket to Terra. Sigurd Ngozori's here; he called the bank and one of the clerks there told him that Hallstock had checked out his whole account, around three hundred thousand sols. Took some of it in cash and the rest in Banking Cartel drafts. Murell says that his information is that Bish Ware, Steve Ravick and Leo Belsher arrived earlier, about an hour ago. He didn't see them himself, but he talked with spaceport workmen who did."

The men who had crowded up to the screen seemed to have run out of oaths and obscenities now. Oscar was fitting another clip into his submachine gun.

"Well, we'll have to go to the spaceport and get them," he said. "And take four ropes instead of three."

"You'll have to fight your way in," Dad told him. "Odin Dock & Shipyard won't let you take people out of their spaceport without a fight. They've all bought tickets by now, and Fieschi will have to protect them."

"Then we'll kick the blankety-blank spaceport apart," somebody shouted.

That started it up again. Oscar wondered if getting silence was worth another clip of cartridges, and decided it wasn't. He managed to make himself heard without it.

"We'll do nothing of the kind. We need that spaceport to stay alive. But we will take Ravick and Belsher and Hallstock—"

"And that etaoin shrdlu traitor of a Ware!" Joe Kivelson added.

"And Bish Ware," Oscar agreed. "They only

have fifty police; we have three or four thousand men."

Three or four thousand undisciplined hunters, against fifty trained, disciplined and organized soldiers, because that was what the spaceport police were. I knew their captain, and the lieutenants. They were old Regular Army, and they ran the police force like a military unit.

"I'll bet Ware was working for Ravick all along," Joe was saying.

That wasn't good thinking even for Joe Kivelson. I said:

"If he was working for Ravick all along, why did he tip Dad and Oscar and the Mahatma on the bomb aboard the *Javelin*? That wasn't any help to Ravick."

"I get it," Oscar said. "He never was working for anybody but Bish Ware. When Ravick got into a jam, he saw a way to make something for himself by getting Ravick out of it. I'll bet, ever since he came here, he was planning to cut in on Ravick somehow. You notice, he knew just how much money Ravick had stashed away on Terra? When he saw the spot Ravick was in, Bish just thought he had a chance to develop himself another rich uncle."

I'd been worse stunned than anybody by Dad's news. The worst of it was that Oscar could be right. I hadn't thought of that before. I'd just thought that Ravick and Belsher had gotten Bish drunk and found out about the way the men were posted around Hunters' Hall and the lone man in the jeep on Second Level Down.

Then it occurred to me that Bish might have seen a way of getting Fenris rid of Ravick and at the same time save everybody the guilt of lynching him. Maybe he'd turned traitor to save the rest of us from ourselves.

I turned to Oscar. "Why get excited about it?" I asked. "You have what you wanted. You said yourself that you couldn't care less whether Ravick got away or not, as long as you got him out of the Co-op. Well, he's out for good now."

"That was before the fire," Oscar said. "We didn't have a couple of million sols' worth of wax burned. And Tom Kivelson wasn't in the hospital with half the skin burned off his back, and a coin toss whether he lives or not."

"Yes. I thought you were Tom's friend," Joe Kivelson reproached me.

I wondered how much skin hanging Steve Ravick would grow on Tom's back. I didn't see much percentage in asking him, though. I did turn to Oscar Fujisawa with a quotation I remembered from *Moby Dick*, the book he'd named his ship from.

"How many barrels will thy vengeance yield thee, even if thou gettest it, Captain Ahab?" I asked. *"It will not fetch thee much in our Nantucket market."*

He looked at me angrily and started to say something. Then he shrugged.

"I know, Walt," he said. "But you can't measure everything in barrels of whale oil. Or skins of tallow-wax."

Which was one of those perfectly true statements which are also perfectly meaningless. I gave up. My job's to get the news, not to make it. I wondered if that meant anything, either.

They finally got the mob sorted out, after a lot of

time wasted in pillaging Ravick's living quarters on the fourth floor. *However, the troops stopped to loot the enemy's camp.* I'd come across that line fifty to a hundred times in history books. Usually, it had been expensive looting; if the enemy didn't counterattack, they managed, at least, to escape. More to the point, they gathered up all the cannon and machine guns around the place and got them onto contragravity in the street. There must have been close to five thousand men, by now, and those who couldn't crowd onto vehicles marched on foot, and the whole mass, looking a little more like an army than a mob, started up Broadway.

Since it is not proper for reporters to loot on the job, I had gotten outside in my jeep early and was going ahead, swinging my camera back to get the parade behind me. Might furnish a still-shot illustration for somebody's History of Fenris in a century or so.

Broadway was empty until we came to the gateway to the spaceport area. There was a single medium combat car there, on contragravity halfway to the ceiling, with a pair of 50-mm guns and a rocket launcher pointed at us, and under it, on the roadway, a solitary man in an olive-green uniform stood.

I knew him; Lieutenant Ranjit Singh, Captain Courtland's second-in-command. He was a Sikh. Instead of a steel helmet, he wore a striped turban, and he had a black beard that made Joe Kivelson's blond one look like Tom Kivelson's chin-fuzz. On his belt, along with his pistol, he wore the little *kirpan*, the dagger all Sikhs carry. He also carried a belt radio, and as we approached he lifted the phone to his mouth and a loudspeaker on the combat car threw his voice at us:

"All right, that's far enough, now. The first vehicle that comes within a hundred yards of this gate will be shot down."

One man, and one combat car, against five thousand, with twenty-odd guns and close to a hundred machine guns. He'd last about as long as a pint of trade gin at a Sheshan funeral. The only thing was, before he and the crew of the combat car were killed, they'd wipe out about ten or fifteen of our vehicles and a couple of hundred men, and they would be the men and vehicles in the lead.

Mobs are a little different from soldiers, and our Rebel Army was still a mob. Mobs don't like to advance into certain death, and they don't like to advance over the bodies and wreckage of their own forward elements. Neither do soldiers, but soldiers will do it. Soldiers realize, when they put on the uniform, that some day they may face death in battle, and if this is it, this is it.

I got the combat car and the lone soldier in the turban—that would look good in anybody's history book—and moved forward, taking care that he saw the *Times* lettering on the jeep and taking care to stay well short of the deadline. I let down to the street and got out, taking off my gun belt and hanging it on the control handle of the jeep. Then I walked forward.

"Lieutenant Ranjit," I said, "I'm representing the *Times*. I have business inside the spaceport. I want to get the facts about this. It may be that when I get this story, these people will be satisfied."

"We will, like Nifflheim!" I heard Joe Kivelson bawling, above and behind me. "We want the men who started the fire my son got burned in."

"Is that the Kivelson boy's father?" the Sikh asked me, and when I nodded, he lifted the phone to his lips again. "Captain Kivelson," the loudspeaker said, "your son is alive and under skin-grafting treatment here at the spaceport hospital. His life is not, repeat not, in danger. The men you are after are here, under guard. If any of them are guilty of any crimes, and if you can show any better authority than an armed mob to deal with them, they may, may, I said, be turned over for trial. But they will not be taken from this spaceport by force, as long as I or one of my men remains alive."

"That's easy. We'll get them afterward," Joe Kivelson shouted.

"Somebody may. You won't," Ranjit Singh told him. "Van Steen, hit that ship's boat first, and hit it at the first hostile move anybody in this mob makes."

"Yes, sir. With pleasure," another voice replied.

Nobody in the Rebel Army, if that was what it still was, had any comment to make on that. Lieutenant Ranjit turned to me.

"Mr. Boyd," he said. None of this sonny-boy stuff; Ranjit Singh was a man of dignity, and he respected the dignity of others. "If I admit you to the spaceport, will you give these people the facts exactly as you learn them?"

"That's what the Times always does, Lieutenant." Well, almost all the facts almost always.

"Will you people accept what this Times reporter tells you he has learned?"

"Yes, of course." That was Oscar Fujisawa.

"I won't!" That was Joe Kivelson. "He's always taking the part of that old rumpot of a Bish Ware."

"Lieutenant, that remark was a slur on my paper, as well as myself," I said. "Will you permit Captain Kivelson to come in along with me? And somebody else," I couldn't resist adding, "so that people will believe him?"

Ranjit Singh considered that briefly. He wasn't afraid to die—I believe he was honestly puzzled when he heard people talking about fear—but his job was to protect some fugitives from a mob, not to die a useless hero's death. If letting in a small delegation would prevent an attack on the spaceport without loss of life and ammunition— or maybe he reversed the order of importance—he was obliged to try it.

"Yes. You may choose five men to accompany Mr. Boyd," he said. "They may not bring weapons in with them. Sidearms," he added, "will not count as weapons."

After all, a *kirpan* was a sidearm, and his religion required him to carry that. The decision didn't make me particularly happy. Respect for the dignity of others is a fine thing in an officer, but like journalistic respect for facts, it can be carried past the point of being a virtue. I thought he was over-estimating Joe Kivelson's self-control.

Vehicles in front began grounding, and men got out and bunched together on the street. Finally, they picked their delegation: Joe Kivelson, Oscar Fujisawa, Casmir Oughourlian the shipyard man, one of the engineers at the nutrient plant, and the Reverend Hiram Zilker, the Orthodox-Monophysite preacher. They all had pistols, even the Reverend Zilker, so I went back to the jeep and put mine on. Ranjit Singh had switched his radio off the speaker and was talking to somebody else.

After a while, an olive-green limousine piloted by a policeman in uniform and helmet floated in and grounded. The six of us got into it, and it lifted again.

The car let down in a vehicle hall in the administrative area, and the police second lieutenant, Chris Xantos, was waiting alone, armed only with the pistol that was part of his uniform and wearing a beret instead of a helmet. He spoke to us, and ushered us down a hallway toward Guido Fieschi's office.

I get into the spaceport administrative area about once in twenty or so hours. Oughourlian is a somewhat less frequent visitor. The others had never been there, and they were visibly awed by all the gleaming glass and brightwork, and the soft lights and the thick carpets. All Port Sandor ought to look like this, I thought. It could, and maybe now it might, after a while.

There were six chairs in a semicircle facing Guido Fieschi's desk, and three men sitting behind it. Fieschi, who had changed clothes and washed since the last time I saw him, sat on the extreme right. Captain Courtland, with his tight mouth under a gray mustache and the quadruple row of medal ribbons on his breast, was on the left. In the middle, the seat of honor, was Bish Ware, looking as though he were presiding over a church council to try some rural curate for heresy.

As soon as Joe Kivelson saw him, he roared angrily:

"There's the dirty traitor who sold us out! He's the worst of the lot; I wouldn't be surprised if—"

Bish looked at him like a bishop who has just been contradicted on a point of doctrine by a choirboy.

"Be quiet!" he ordered. "I did not follow this man you call Ravick here to this . . . this running-hot-and-cold Paradise planet, and I did not spend five years fraternizing with its unwashed citizenry and creating for myself the role of town drunkard of Port Sandor, to have him taken from me and lynched after I have arrested him. People do not lynch my prisoners."

"And who in blazes are you?" Joe demanded.

Bish took cognizance of the question, if not the questioner.

"Tell them, if you please, Mr. Fieschi," he said.

"Well, Mr. Ware is a Terran Federation Executive Special Agent," Fieschi said. "Captain Courtland and I have known that for the past five years. As far as I know, nobody else was informed of Mr. Ware's position."

After that, you could have heard a gnat sneeze.

Everybody knows about Executive Special Agents. There are all kinds of secret agents operating in the Federation—Army and Navy Intelligence, police of different sorts, Colonial Office agents, private detectives, Chartered Company agents. But there are fewer Executive Specials than there are inhabited planets in the Federation. They rank, ex officio, as Army generals and Space Navy admirals; they have the privilege of the floor in Parliament, they take orders from nobody but the President of the Federation. But very few people have ever seen one, or talked to anybody who has.

And Bish Ware—*good ol' Bish; he'sh everybodysh frien'*—was one of them. And I had been trying to make a man of him and reform him. I'd even thought, if he stopped drinking, he might make a success as a private detective—at Port

Sandor, on Fenris! I wondered what color my face had gotten now, and I started looking around for a crack in the floor, to trickle gently and unobtrusively into.

And it should have been obvious to me, maybe not that he was an Executive Special, but that he was certainly no drunken barfly. The way he'd gone four hours without a drink, and seemed to be just as drunk as ever. That was right—just as drunk as he'd ever been; which was to say, cold sober. There was the time I'd seen him catch that falling bottle and set it up. No drunken man could have done that; a man's reflexes are the first thing to be affected by alcohol. And the way he shot that tread-snail. I've seen men who could shoot well on liquor, but not quick-draw stuff. That calls for perfect co-ordination. And the way he went into his tipsy act at the *Times*—veteran actor slipping into a well-learned role.

He drank, sure. He did a lot of drinking. But there are men whose systems resist the effects of alcohol better than others, and he must have been an exceptional example of the type, or he'd never have adopted the sort of cover personality he did. It would have been fairly easy for him. Space his drinks widely, and never take a drink unless he had to, to maintain the act. When he was at the *Times* with just Dad and me, what did he have? A fruit fizz.

Well, at least I could see it after I had my nose rubbed in it. Joe Kivelson was simply gaping at him. The Reverend Zilker seemed to be having trouble adjusting, too. The shipyard man and the chemical engineer weren't saying anything, but it had kicked them for a loss, too. Oscar Fujisawa

was making a noble effort to be completely un-
surprised. Oscar is one of our better poker players.

"I thought it might be something like that," he
lied brazenly. "But, Bish . . . Excuse me, I mean,
Mr. Ware . . ."

"Bish, if you please, Oscar."

"Bish, what I'd like to know is what you wanted
with Ravick," he said. "They didn't send any
Executive Special Agent here for five years to
investigate this tallow-wax racket of his."

"No. We have been looking for him for a long
time. Fifteen years, and I've been working on it
that long. You might say, I have made a career of
him. Steve Ravick is really Anton Gerrit."

Maybe he was expecting us to leap from our
chairs and cry out, "Aha! The infamous Anton
Gerrit! Brought to book at last!" We didn't. We
just looked at one another, trying to connect some
meaning to the name. It was Joe Kivelson, of all
people, who caught the first gleam.

"I know that name," he said. "Something on
Loki, wasn't it?"

Yes; that was it. Now that my nose was rubbed
in it again, I got it.

"The Loki enslavements. Was that it?" I asked.
"I read about it, but I never seem to have heard of
Gerrit."

"He was the mastermind. The ones who were
caught, fifteen years ago, were the underlings, but
Ravick was the real Number One. He was responsible for the enslavement of from twenty to thirty
thousand Lokian natives, gentle, harmless,
friendly people, most of whom were worked to
death in the mines."

No wonder an Executive Special would put in

fifteen years looking for him. You murder your
grandmother, or rob a bank, or burn down an
orphanage with the orphans all in bed upstairs, or
something trivial like that, and if you make an
off-planet getaway, you're reasonably safe. Of
course there's such a thing as extradition, but who
bothers? Distances are too great, and communication is too slow, and the Federation depends on
every planet to do its own policing.

But enslavement's something different. The
Terran Federation is a government of and for—if
occasionally not by—all sapient peoples of all
races. The Federation Constitution guarantees
equal rights to all. Making slaves of people,
human or otherwise, is a direct blow at everything
the Federation stands for. No wonder they kept
hunting fifteen years for the man responsible for
the Loki enslavements.

"Gerrit got away, with a month's start. By the
time we had traced him to Baldur, he had a year's
start on us. He was five years ahead of us when we
found out that he'd gone from Baldur to Odin. Six
years ago, nine years after we'd started hunting
for him, we decided, from the best information we
could get, that he had left Odin on one of the
local-stop ships for Terra, and dropped off along
the way. There are six planets at which those
Terra-Odin ships stop. We sent a man to each of
them. I drew this prize out of the hat.

"When I landed here, I contacted Mr. Fieschi,
and we found that a man answering to Gerrit's
description had come in on the *Peenemünde* from
Odin seven years before, about the time Gerrit had
left Odin. The man who called himself Steve
Ravick. Of course, he didn't look anything like

the pictures of Gerrit, but facial surgery was something we'd taken for granted he'd have done. I finally managed to get his fingerprints."

Special Agent Ware took out a cigar, inspected it with the drunken oversolemnity he'd been drilling himself into for five years, and lit it. Then he saw what he was using and rose, holding it out, and I went to the desk and took back my lighter-weapon.

"Thank you, Walt. I wouldn't have been able to do this if I hadn't had that. Where was I? Oh, yes. I got Gerrit-alias-Ravick's fingerprints, which did not match the ones we had on file for Gerrit, and sent them in. It was eighteen months later that I got a reply on them. According to his fingerprints, Steve Ravick was really a woman named Ernestine Coyón, who had died of acute alcoholism in the free public ward of a hospital at Paris-on-Baldur fourteen years ago."

"Why, that's incredible!" the Reverend Zilker burst out, and Joe Kivelson was saying: "Steve Ravick isn't any woman . . ."

"Least of all one who died fourteen years ago," Bish agreed. "But the fingerprints were hers. A pauper, dying in a public ward of a big hospital. And a man who has to change his identity, and who has small, woman-sized hands. And a crooked hospital staff surgeon. You get the picture now?"

"They're doing the same thing on Tom's back, right here," I told Joe. "Only you can't grow fingerprints by carniculture, the way you can human tissue for grafting. They had to have palm and finger surfaces from a pair of real human hands. A pauper, dying in a free-treatment ward,

her body shoved into a mass-energy converter."
Then I thought of something else. "That show-off
trick of his, crushing out cigarettes in his palm," I
said.

Bish nodded commendingly. "Exactly. He'd
have about as much sensation in his palms as I'd
have wearing thick leather gloves. I'd noticed
that.

"Well, six months going, and a couple of
months waiting on reports from other planets,
and six months coming, and so on, it wasn't until
the Peenemünde got in from Terra, the last time,
that I got final confirmation. Dr. Watson, you'll
recall."

"Who, you perceived, had been in Afghanis-
tan," I mentioned, trying to salvage something.
Showing off. The one I was trying to impress was
Walt Boyd.

"You caught that? Careless of me," Bish chided
himself. "What he gave me was a report that they
had finally located a man who had been a staff
surgeon at this hospital on Baldur at the time. He's
now doing a stretch for another piece of malprac-
tice he was unlucky enough to get caught at later.
We will not admit making deals with any crimi-
nals, in jail or out, but he is willing to testify, and
is on his way to Terra now. He can identify pictures of Anton Gerrit as those of the man he operated on fourteen years ago, and his testimony and
Ernestine Coyon's fingerprints will identify Ravick as that man. With all the Colonial Constabulary and Army Intelligence people got on Gerrit on
Loki, simple identification will be enough. Gerrit
was proven guilty long ago, and it won't be any
trouble, now, to prove that Ravick is Gerrit."

"Why didn't you arrest him as soon as you got the word from your friend from Afghanistan?" I wanted to know.

"Good question; I've been asking myself that," Bish said, a trifle wryly. "If I had, the *Javelin* wouldn't have been bombed, that wax wouldn't have been burned, and Tom Kivelson wouldn't have been injured. What I did was send my friend, who is a Colonial Constabulary detective, to Gimli, the next planet out. There's a Navy base there, and always at least a couple of destroyers available. He's coming back with one of them to pick Gerrit up and take him to Terra. They ought to be in in about two hundred and fifty hours. I thought it would be safer all around to let Gerrit run loose till then. There's no place he could go.

"What I didn't realize, at the time, was what a human H-bomb this man Murell would turn into. Then everything blew up at once. Finally, I was left with the choice of helping Gerrit escape from Hunters' Hall or having him lynched before I could arrest him." He turned to Kivelson. "In the light of what you knew, I don't blame you for calling me a dirty traitor."

"But how did I know . . ." Kivelson began.

"That's right. You weren't supposed to. That was before you found out. You ought to have heard what Gerrit and Belsher—as far as I know, that is his real name—called me *after* they found out, when they got out of that jeep and Captain Courtland's men snapped the handcuffs on them. It even shocked a hardened sinner like me."

There was a lot more of it. Bish had managed to get into Hunters' Hall just about the time Al Devis and his companion were starting the fire

Ravick—Gerrit—had ordered for a diversion. The whole gang was going to crash out as soon as the fire had attracted everybody away. Bish led them out onto the Second Level Down, sleep-gassed the lone man in the jeep, and took them to the spaceport, where the police were waiting for them.

As soon as I'd gotten everything, I called the *Times*. I'd had my radio on all the time, and it had been coming in perfectly. Dad, I was happy to observe, was every bit as flabbergasted as I had been at who and what Bish Ware was. He might throw my campaign to reform Bish up at me later on, but at the moment he wasn't disposed to, and I was praising Allah silently that I hadn't had a chance to mention the detective agency idea to him. That would have been a little too much.

"What are they doing about Belsher and Hallstock?" he asked.

"Belsher goes back to Terra with Ravick. Gerrit, I mean. That's where he collected his cut on the tallow-wax, so that is where he'd have to be tried. Bish is convinced that somebody in Kapstaad Chemical must have been involved, too. Hallstock is strictly a local matter."

"That's about what I thought. With all this interstellar back-and-forth, it'll be a long time before we'll be able to write thirty under the story."

"Well, we can put thirty under the Steve Ravick story," I said.

Then it hit me. The Steve Ravick story was finished; that is, the local story of racketeer rule in the Hunters' Co-operative. But the Anton Gerrit story was something else. That was Federation-wide news; the end of a fifteen-year manhunt for the most wanted criminal in the known Galaxy. And who had that story, right in his hot little hand? Walter Boyd, the ace—and only—reporter for the mighty Port Sandor *Times*.

"Yes," I continued. "The Ravick story's finished. But we still have the Anton Gerrit story, and I'm going to work on it right now."

20

FINALE

THEY HAD TOM KIVELSON in a private room at the hospital; he was sitting up in a chair, with a lot of pneumatic cushions around him, and a lunch tray on his lap. He looked white and thin. He could move one arm completely, but the bandages they had loaded him with seemed to have left the other free only at the elbow. He was concentrating on his lunch, and must have thought I was one of the nurses, or a doctor, or something of the sort.

"Are you going to let me have a cigarette and a cup of coffee, when I'm through with this?" he asked.

"Well, I don't have any coffee, but you can have one of my cigarettes," I said.

Then he looked up and gave a whoop. "Walt! How'd you get in here? I thought they weren't going to let anybody in to see me till this afternoon."

"Power of the press," I told him. "Bluff, blarney, and blackmail. How are they treating you?"

"Awful. Look what they gave me for lunch. I thought we were on short rations down on Hermann Reuch's Land. How's Father?"

"He's all right. They took the splint off, but he still has to carry his arm in a sling."

"Lucky guy; he can get around on his feet, and I'll bet he isn't starving, either. You know, speaking about food, I'm going to feel like a cannibal eating carniculture meat, now. My whole back's carniculture." He filled his mouth with whatever it was they were feeding him and asked, through it: "Did I miss Steve Ravick's hanging?"

I was horrified. "Haven't these people told you anything?" I demanded.

"Nah; they wouldn't even tell me the right time. Afraid it would excite me."

So I told him; first who Bish Ware really was, and then who Ravick really was. He gaped for a moment, and then shoveled in more food.

"Go on; what happened?"

I told him how Bish had smuggled Gerrit and Leo Belsher out on Second Level Down and gotten them to the spaceport, where Courtland's men had been waiting for them.

"Gerrit's going to Terra, and from there to Loki. They want the natives to see what happens to a Terran who breaks Terran law; teach them that our law isn't just to protect us. Belsher's going to Terra, too. There was a big ship captains' meeting; they voted to reclaim their wax and sell it individually to Murell, but to retain membership in the Co-op. They think they'll have to stay in the Co-op to get anything that's gettable out of Gerrit's and Belsher's money. Oscar Fujisawa and Cesário Vieira are going to Terra on the *Cape Canaveral* to start suit to recover anything they can, and also to petition for reclassification of Fenris. Oscar's coming back on the next ship, but Cesário's going to stay on as the Co-op representative. I suppose he and Linda will be getting married."

"Natch. They'll both stay on Terra, I suppose. Hey, whattaya know! Cesário's getting off Fenris without having to die and reincarnate."

He finished his lunch, such as it was and what there was of it, and I relieved him of the tray and set it on the floor beyond his chair. I found an ashtray and lit a cigarette for him and one for myself, using the big lighter. Tom looked at it dubiously, predicting that sometime I'd push the wrong thing and send myself bye-byes for a couple of hours. I told him how Bish had used it.

"Bet a lot of people wanted to hang him, too, before they found out who he was and what he'd really done. What's my father think of Bish, now?"

"Bish Ware is a great and good man, and the savior of Fenris," I said. "And he was real smart, to keep an act like that up for five years. Your father modestly admits that it even fooled *him*."

"Bet Oscar Fujisawa knew it all along."

"Well, Oscar modestly admits that he suspected something of the sort, but he didn't feel it was his place to say anything."

Tom laughed, and then wanted to know if they were going to hang Mort Hallstock. "I hope they wait till I can get out of here."

"No, Odin Dock & Shipyard claim he's a political refugee and they won't give him up. They did loan us a couple of accountants to go over the city books, to see if we could find any real evidence of misappropriation, and whattaya know, there were no city books. The city of Port Sandor didn't keep books. We can't even take that three hundred thousand sols away from him; for all we can prove, he saved them out of his five-thousand-sol-a-year salary. He's shipping out on the *Cape Canaveral*, too."

"Then we don't have any government at all!"

"Are you fooling yourself we ever had one?"

"No, but—"

"Well, we have one now. A temporary dictatorship; Bish Ware is dictator. Fieschi loaned him Ranjit Singh and some of his men. The first thing he did was gather up the city treasurer and the chief of police and march them to the spaceport; Fieschi made Hallstock buy them tickets, too. But there aren't going to be any unofficial hangings. This is a law-abiding planet, now."

A nurse came in, and disapproved of Tom smoking and of me being in the room at all.

"Haven't you had your lunch yet?" she asked Tom.

He looked at her guilelessly and said, "No; I was waiting for it."

"Well, I'll get it," she said. "I thought the other nurse had brought it." She started out, and then she came back and had to fuss with his cushions, and then she saw the tray on the floor.

"You did so have your lunch!" she accused.

Tom looked at her as innocently as ever. "Oh, you mean these samples? Why, they were good; I'll take all of them. And a big slab of roast beef, and brown gravy, and mashed potatoes. And how about some ice cream?"

It was a good try; too bad it didn't work.

"Don't worry, Tom," I told him. "I'll get my lawyer to spring you out of this jug, and then we'll take you to my place and fill you up on Mrs. Laden's cooking."

The nurse sniffed. She suspected, quite correctly, that whoever Mrs. Laden was, she didn't know anything about scientific dietetics.

When I got back to the *Times*, Dad and Julio had had their lunch and were going over the teleprint edition. Julio was printing corrections on blank sheets of plastic and Dad was cutting them out and cementing them over things that needed correcting on the master sheets. I gave Julio a short item to the effect that Tom Kivelson, son of Captain and Mrs. Joe Kivelson, one of the *Javelin* survivors who had been burned in the tallow-wax fire, was now out of all danger, and recovering. Dad was able to scrounge that onto the first page.

There was a lot of other news. The T.F.N. destroyer *Simón Bolivar*, en route from Gimli to pick up the notorious Anton Gerrit, alias Steve Ravick, had come out of hyperspace and into radio range. Dad had talked to the skipper by screen and gotten interviews, which would be telecast, both with him and Detective-Major Mac-Bride of the Colonial Constabulary. The *Simón Bolivar* would not make landing, but go into orbit and send down a boat. Detective-Major MacBride (alias Dr. John Watson) would remain on Fenris to take over local police activities.

More evidence had been unearthed at Hunters' Hall on the frauds practiced by Leo Belsher and Gerrit-alias-Ravick; it looked as though a substantial sum of money might be recovered, eventually, from the bank accounts and other holdings of both men on Terra. Acting Resident-Agent Gonzalo Ware—Ware, it seemed, really was his right name, but look what he had in front of it—had promulgated more regulations and edicts, and a crackdown on the worst waterfront dives was in progress. I'll bet the devoted flock was horrified at what their beloved bishop had turned into. Bish would leave his diocese in a lot healthier condition than he'd found it, that was one thing for sure. And most of the gang of thugs and plug-uglies who had been used to intimidate and control the Hunters' Co-operative had been gathered up and jailed on vagrancy charges; prisoners were being put to work cleaning up the city.

And there was a lot about plans for a registration of voters, and organization of election boards, and a local electronics-engineering firm had been awarded a contract for voting machines. I didn't think there had ever been a voting machine on Fenris before.

"The commander of the *Bolivar* says he'll take your story to Terra with him, and see that it gets to Interworld News," Dad told me as we were sorting the corrected master sheets and loading them into the photoprint machine, to be sent out on the air. "The *Bolivar*'ll make Terra at least two hundred hours ahead of the *Cape Canaveral*. Interworld will be glad to have it. It isn't often they get a story like that with the first news of anything, and this'll be a big story."

"You shouldn't have given me the exclusive by-line," I said. "You did as much work on it as I did."

"No, I didn't, either," he contradicted, "and I knew what I was doing."

With the work done, I remembered that I hadn't had anything to eat since breakfast, and I went down to take inventory of the refrigerator. Dad went along with me, and after I had assembled a

lunch and sat down to it, he decided that his pipe
needed refilling, lit it, poured a cup of coffee and
sat down with me.

"You know, Walt, I've been thinking, lately,"
he began.

Oh-oh, I thought. When Dad makes that remark,
in just that tone, it's all hands to secure ship for
diving.

"We've all had to do a lot of thinking, lately," I
agreed.

"Yes. You know, they want me to be mayor of
Port Sandor."

I nodded and waited till I got my mouth empty.
I could see a lot of sense in that. Dad is honest and
scrupulous and public-spirited; too much so,
sometimes, for his own good. There wasn't any
question of his ability, and while there had always
been antagonism between the hunter-ship crews
and waterfront people and the uptown business
crowd, Dad was well liked and trusted by both
parties.

"Are you going to take it?" I asked.

"I suppose I'll have to, if they really want me. Be
a sort of obligation."

That would throw a lot more work on me. Dad
could give some attention to the paper as mayor,
but not as much as now.

"What do you want me to try to handle for
you?" I asked.

"Well, Walt, that's what I've been thinking
about," he said. "I've been thinking about it for
a long time, and particularly since things got
changed around here. I think you ought to go to
school some more."

That made me laugh. "What, back to Hartzenbosch?" I asked. "I could teach him more than he could teach me, now."

"I doubt that, Walt. Professor Hartzenbosch may be an old maid in trousers, but he's really a very sound scholar. But I wasn't thinking about that. I was thinking about your going to Terra to school."

"*Huh?*" I forgot to eat, for a moment. "Let's stop kidding."

"I didn't start kidding; I meant it."

"Well, think again, Dad. It costs money to go to school on Terra. It even costs money to go to Terra."

"We have a little money, Walt. Maybe more than you think we do. And with things getting better, we'll lease more teleprinters and get more advertising. You're likely to get better than the price of your passage out of that story we're sending off on the *Bolivar,* and that won't be the end of it, either. Fenris is going to be in the news for a while. You may make some more money writing. That's why I was careful to give you the by-line on that Gerrit story." His pipe had gone out again; he took time out to relight it, and then added: "Anything I spend on this is an investment. The *Times* will get it back."

"Yes, that's another thing; the paper," I said. "If you're going to be mayor, you won't be able to do everything you're doing on the paper now, and then do all my work too."

"Well, shocking as the idea may be, I think we can find somebody to replace you."

"Name one," I challenged.

"Well, Lillian Arnaz, at the Library, has always been interested in newspaper work," he began.

"A girl!" I hooted. "You have any idea of some of the places I have to go to get stories?"

"Yes. I have always deplored the necessity. But a great many of them have been closed lately, and the rest are being run in a much more seemly manner. And she wouldn't be the only reporter. I hesitate to give you any better opinion of yourself than you have already, but it would take at least three people to do the work you've been doing. When you get back from Terra, you'll find the *Times* will have a very respectable reportorial staff."

"What'll I be, then?" I wondered.

"Editor," Dad told me. "I'll retire and go into politics full time. And if Fenris is going to develop the way I believe it will, the editor of the *Times* will need a much better education than I have."

I kept on eating, to give myself an excuse for silence. He was right, I knew that. But college on Terra; why, that would be at least four years, maybe five, and then a year for the round trip . . .

"Walt, this doesn't have to be settled right away," Dad said. "You won't be going on the *Simón Bolivar*, along with Ravick and Belsher. And that reminds me. Have you talked to Bish lately? He'd be hurt if you didn't see him before he left."

The truth was, I'd been avoiding Bish, and not just because I knew how busy he was. My face felt like a tallow-wax fire every time I thought of how I'd been trying to reform him, and I didn't quite know what I'd be able to say to him if I met him again. And he seemed to me to be an entirely different person, as though the old Bish Ware, whom I had liked in spite of what I'd thought he was, had died, and some total stranger had taken his place.

But I went down to the Municipal Building. It didn't look like the same place. The walls had been scrubbed; the floors were free from litter. All the drove of loafers and hangers-on had been run out, or maybe jailed and put to work. I looked into a couple of offices; everybody in them was busy. A few of the old police force were still there, but their uniforms had been cleaned and pressed, they had all shaved recently, and one or two looked as though they liked being able to respect themselves, for a change.

The girl at the desk in the mayor's outside office told me Bish had a delegation of uptown merchants, who seemed to think that reform was all right in its place but it oughtn't to be carried more than a few blocks above the waterfront. They were protesting the new sanitary regulations. Then she buzzed Bish on the handphone, and told me he'd see me in a few minutes. After a while, I heard the delegation going down the hall from the private office door. One of them was saying:

"Well, this is what we've always been screaming our heads off for. Now we've got it good and hard; we'll just have to get used to it."

When I went in, Bish rose from his desk and came to meet me, shaking my hand. He looked and was dressed like the old Bish Ware I'd always known.

"Glad you dropped in, Walt. Find a seat. How are things on the *Times*?"

"You ought to know. You're making things busy for us."

"Yes. There's so much to do, and so little time to

do it. Seems as though I've heard somebody say that before."

"Are you going back to Terra on the *Simón Bolívar?*"

"Oh, Allah forbid! I made a trip on a destroyer, once, and once is enough for a lifetime. I won't even be able to go on the *Cape Canaveral;* I'll take the *Peenemünde* when she gets in. I'm glad MacBride—Dr. Watson—is going to stop off. He'll be a big help. Don't know what I'd have done without Ranjit Singh."

"That won't be till after the *Cape Canaveral* gets back from Terra."

"No. That's why I'm waiting. Don't publish this, Walt, I don't want to start any premature rumors that might end in disappointments, but I've recommended immediate reclassification to Class III, and there may be a Colonial Office man on the *Cape Canaveral* when she gets in. Resident-Agent, permanent. I hope so; he'll need a little breaking in."

"I saw Tom Kivelson this morning," I said. "He seems to be getting along pretty well."

"Didn't anybody at the hospital tell you about him?" Bish asked.

I shook my head. He cursed all hospital staffs.

"I wish military security was half as good. Why, Tom's permanently injured. He won't be crippled, or anything like that, but there was considerable unrepairable damage to his back muscles. He'll be able to get around, but I doubt it he'll ever be able to work on a hunter-ship again."

I was really horrified. Monster-hunting was Tom's whole life. I said something like that.

"He'll just have to make a new life for himself.

Joe says he's going to send him to school on Terra. He thinks that was his own idea, but I suggested it to him."

"Dad wants me to go to school on Terra."

"Well, that's a fine idea. Tom's going on the Peenemünde, along with me. Why don't you come with us?"

"That would be great, Bish. I'd like it. But I just can't."

"Why not?"

"Well, they want Dad to be mayor, and if he runs, they'll all vote for him. He can't handle this and the paper both alone."

"He can get help on both jobs."

"Yes, but . . . Why, it would be years till I got back. I can't sacrifice the time. Not now."

"I'd say six years. You can spend your voyage time from here cramming for entrance qualifications. Schools don't bother about academic credits any more; they're only interested in how much you know. You take four years' regular college, and a year postgrading, and you'll have all the formal education you'll need."

"But, Bish, I can get that here, at the Library," I said. "We have every book on film that's been published since the Year Zero."

"Yes. And you'd die of old age before you got a quarter through the first film bank, and you still wouldn't have an education. Do you know which books to study, and which ones not to bother with? Or which ones to read first, so that what you read in the others will be comprehensible to you? That's what they'll give you on Terra. The tools, which you don't have now, for educating yourself."

I thought that over. It made sense. I'd had a lot of the very sort of trouble he'd spoken of, trying to get information for myself in proper order, and I'd read a lot of books that duplicated other books I'd read, and books I had trouble understanding because I hadn't read some other book first. Bish had something there. I was sure he had. But six years!

I said that aloud, and added: "I can't take the time. I have to be *doing* things."

"You'll do things. You'll do them a lot better for waiting those six years. You aren't eighteen yet. Six years is a whole third of your past life. No wonder it seems long to you. But you're thinking the wrong way; you're relating those six years to what has passed. Relate them to what's ahead of you, and see how little time they are. You take ordinary care of yourself and keep out of any more civil wars, and you have sixty more years, at least. Your six years at school are only one-tenth of that. I was fifty when I came here to this Creator's blunder of a planet. Say I had only twenty more years; I spent a quarter of them playing town drunk here. I'm the one who ought to be in a rush and howling about lost time, not you. I ought to be in such a hurry I'd take the *Simón Bolivar* to Terra and let this place go to—to anywhere you might imagine to be worse."

"You know, I don't think you like Fenris."

"I don't. If I were a drinking man, this planet would have made a drunkard of me. Now, you forget about these six years chopped out of your busy life. When you get back here, with an education, you'll be a kid of twenty-four, with a big long life ahead of you and your mind stocked with things you don't have now that will help you make something—and more important, something enjoyable—out of it."

There was a huge crowd at the spaceport to see us off, Tom and Bish Ware and me. Mostly, it was for Bish. If I don't find a monument to him when I get back, I'll know there is no such thing as gratitude. There had been a big banquet for us the evening before, and I think Bish actually got a little tipsy. Nobody can be sure, though; it might have been just the old actor back in his role. Now they were all crowding around us, as many as could jam in, in the main lounge of the Peenemünde. Joe Kivelson and his wife. Dad and Julio and Mrs. Laden, who was actually being cordial to Bish, and who had a bundle for us that we weren't to open till we were in hyperspace. Lillian Arnaz, the girl who was to take my place as star reporter. We were going to send each other audiovisuals; advice from me on the job, and news from the Times from her. Glenn Murell, who had his office open by now and was grumbling that there had been a man from Interstellar Import-Export out on the Cape Canaveral, and if the competition got any stiffer the price of tallow-wax would be forced up on him to a sol a pound. And all the Javelin hands who had been wrecked with us on Hermann Reuch's Land, and the veterans of the Civil War, all but Oscar and Cesário, who will be at the dock to meet us when we get to Terra.

I wonder what it'll be like, on a world where you go to bed every time it gets dark and get up when it gets light, and can go outdoors all the time. I wonder how I'll like college, and meeting people from all over the Federation, and swapping tall stories about our home planets.

And I wonder what I'll learn. The long years ahead, I can't imagine them now, will be spent on the *Times*, and I ought to learn things to fit me for that. But I can't get rid of the idea about carniculture growth of tallow-wax. We'll have to do something like that. The demand for the stuff is growing, and we don't know how long it'll be before the monsters are hunted out. We know how fast we're killing them, but we don't know how many there are or how fast they breed. I'll talk to Tom about that; maybe between us we can hit on something, or at least lay a foundation for somebody else who will.

The crowd pushed out and off the ship, and the three of us were alone, here in the lounge of the *Peenemünde*, where the story started and where it ends. Bish says no story ends, ever. He's wrong. Stories die, and nothing in the world is deader than a dead news story. But before they do, they hatch a flock of little ones, and some of them grow into bigger stories still. What happens after the ship lifts into the darkness, with the pre-dawn glow in the east, will be another, a new, story.

But to the story of how the hunters got an honest co-operative and Fenris got an honest government, and Bish Ware got Anton Gerrit the slaver, I can write

*

*Ed. note: "The End."

Lone Star Planet

CHAPTER I

THEY STARTED GIVING me the business as soon as I came through the door into the Secretary's outer office.

There was Ethel K'wang-Li, the Secretary's receptionist, at her desk. There was Courtlant Staynes, the assistant secretary to the Undersecretary for Economic Penetration, and Norman Gazarin, from Protocol, and Toby Lawder, from Humanoid Peoples' Affairs, and Raoul Chavier, and Hans Mannteufel, and Olga Reznik.

It was a wonder there weren't more of them watching the condemned man's march to the gibbet: the word that the Secretary had called me in must have gotten all over the Department since the offices had opened.

"Ah, Mr. Machiavelli, I presume," Ethel kicked off.

"Machiavelli, Junior." Olga picked up the ball. "At least, that's the way he signs it."

"God's gift to the Consular Service, and the Consular Service's gift to Policy Planning," Gazarin added.

"Take it easy, folks. These Hooligan Diplomats would as soon shoot you as look at you," Mannteufel warned.

"Be sure and tell the Secretary that your friends all want important posts in the Galactic Empire." Olga again.

"Well, I'm glad some of you could read it," I fired back. "Maybe even a few of you understood what it was all about."

"Don't worry, Silk," Gazarin told me. "Secretary Ghopal understands what it was all about. All too well, you'll find."

A buzzer sounded gently on Ethel K'wang-Li's desk. She snatched up the handphone and whispered into it. A deathly silence filled the room while she listened, whispered some more, then hung it up.

They were all staring at me.

"Secretary Ghopal is ready to see Mr. Stephen Silk," she said. "This way, please."

As I started across the room, Staynes began drumming on the top of the desk with his fingers, the slow reiterated rhythm to which a man marches to a military execution.

"A cigarette?" Lawder inquired tonelessly. "A glass of rum?"

There were three men in the Secretary of State's private office. Ghopal Singh, the Secretary, dark-faced, gray-haired, slender and elegant, meeting me halfway to his desk. Another slender man, in black, with a silver-threaded, black neck-scarf: Rudolf Klüng, the Secretary of the Department of Aggression.

And a huge, gross-bodied man with a fat baby-face and opaque black eyes.

When I saw him, I really began to get frightened.

The fat man was Natalenko, the Security Coördinator.

"Good morning, Mister Silk," Secretary Ghopal greeted me, his hand extended. "Gentlemen, Mr. Stephen Silk, about whom we were speaking. This way, Mr. Silk, if you please."

There was a low coffee-table at the rear of the office, and four easy chairs around it. On the round brass table-top were cups and saucers, a coffee urn, cigarettes—and a copy of the current issue of the *Galactic Statesmen's Journal*, open at an article entitled *Probable Future Courses of Solar League Diplomacy*, by somebody who had signed himself Machiavelli, Jr.

I was beginning to wish that the pseudonymous Machiavelli, Jr. had never been born, or, at least, had stayed on Theta Virgo IV and been a wineberry planter as his father had wanted him to be.

As I sat down and accepted a cup of coffee, I avoided looking at the periodical. They were probably going to hang it around my neck before they shoved me out of the airlock.

"Mr. Silk is, as you know, in our Consular Service," Ghopal was saying to the others. "Back on Luna on rotation, doing something in Mr. Halvord's section. He is the gentleman who did such a splendid job for us on Assha—Gamma Norma III.

"And, as he has just demonstrated," he added, gesturing toward the *Statesman's Journal* on the Benares-work table, "he is a student both of the diplomacy of the past and the implications of our present policies."

"A bit frank," Klüng commented dubiously.

"But judicious," Natalenko squeaked, in the high eunuchoid voice that came so incongruously from his bulk. "He aired his singularly accurate predictions in a periodical that doesn't have a circulation of more than a thousand copies outside his own department. And I don't think the public's semantic reactions to the terminology of imperialism is as bad as you imagine. They seem quite satisfied, now, with the change in the title of your department, from Defense to Aggression."

"Well, we've gone into that, gentlemen," Ghopal said. "If the article really makes trouble for us, we can always disavow it. There's no censorship of the *Journal*. And Mr. Silk won't be around to draw fire on us."

Here it comes, I thought.

"That sounds pretty ominous, doesn't it, Mr. Silk?" Natalenko tittered happily, like a ten-year-old who has just found a new beetle to pull the legs out of.

"It's really not as bad as it sounds, Mr. Silk," Ghopal hastened to reassure me. "We are going to have to banish you for a while, but I daresay that won't be so bad. The social life here on Luna has probably begun to pall, anyhow. So we're sending you to Capella IV."

"Capella IV," I repeated, trying to remember something about it. Capella was a GO-type, like Sol; that wouldn't be so bad.

"New Texas," Klüng helped me out.

Oh, God, no! I thought.

"It happens that we need somebody of your sort on that planet, Mr. Silk," Ghopal said. "Some of the trouble is in my department and some of it is in Mr. Klüng's; for that reason, perhaps it would be better if Coördinator Natalenko explained it to you."

"You know, I assume, our chief interest in New Texas?" Natalenko asked.

"I had some of it for breakfast, sir," I replied. "Supercow."

Natalenko tittered again. "Yes, New Texas is the butcher shop of the galaxy. In more ways than one, I'm afraid you'll find. They just butchered one of our people there a short while ago. Our Ambassador, in fact."

That would be Silas Cumshaw, and this was the first I'd heard about it.

I asked when it had happened.

"A couple of months ago. We just heard about it last evening, when the news came in on a freighter from there. Which serves to point up something you stressed in your article—the difficulties of trying to run a centralized democratic government on a galactic scale. But we have another interest, which may be even more urgent than our need for New Texan meat. You've heard, of course, of the z'Srauff."

That was a statement, not a question; Natalenko wasn't trying to insult me. I knew who the z'Srauff were; I'd run into them, here and there. One of the extra-solar intelligent humanoid races, who seemed to have been evolved from canine or canine-like ancestors, instead of primates. Most of them could speak Basic English, but I never saw one who would admit to understanding more of our language than the 850-word Basic vocabulary. They occupied a half-dozen planets in a small star-cluster about forty light-years beyond the Capella system. They had developed normal-space reaction-drive ships before we came into contact with them, and they had quickly picked up the hyperspace-drive from us back in those days when the Solar League was still playing Missionaries of Progress and trying to run a galaxy-wide Point-Four program.

In the past century, it had become almost impossible for anybody to get into their star-group, although z'Srauff ships were orbiting in on every planet that the League had settled or controlled. There were z'Srauff traders and small merchants all over the galaxy, and you almost never saw one of them without a camera. Their little meteor-mining boats were everywhere, and all of them carried more of the most modern radar and astrogational equipment than a meteor-miner's lifetime earnings would pay for.

I also knew that they were one of the chief causes of ulcers and premature gray hair at the League capital on Luna. I'd done a little reading on pre-spaceflight Terran history; I had been impressed by the parallel between the present situation and one which had culminated, two and a half centuries before, on the morning of 7 December, 1941.

"What," Natalenko inquired, "do you think Machiavelli, Junior would do about the z'Srauff?"

"We have a Department of Aggression," I replied. "Its mottoes are, 'Stop trouble before it starts,' and, 'If we have to fight, let's do it on the other fellow's real estate.' But this situation is just a little too delicate for literal application of those principles. An unprovoked attack on the z'Srauff would set every other non-human race in the

galaxy against us. . . . Would an attack by the
z'Srauff on New Texas constitute just provocation?"

"It might. New Texas is an independent planet.
Its people are descendants of emigrants from
Terra who wanted to get away from the rule of the
Solar League. We've been trying for half a century
to persuade the New Texan government to join
the League. We need their planet, for both strategic and commercial reasons. With the z'Srauff
for neighbors, they need us as much at least as we
need them. The problem is to make them understand that."

I nodded again. "And an attack by the z'Srauff
would do that, too, sir," I said.

Natalenko tittered again. "You see, gentlemen!
Our Mr. Silk picks things up very handily, doesn't
he?" He turned to Secretary of State Ghopal. "You
take it from there," he invited.

Ghopal Singh smiled benignly. "Well, that's it,
Stephen," he said. "We need a man on New Texas
who can get things done. Three things, to be
exact.

"First, find out why poor Mr. Cumshaw was
murdered, and what can be done about it to maintain our prestige without alienating the New Texans.

"Second, bring the government and people of
New Texas to a realization that they need the
Solar League as much as we need them.

"And, third, forestall or expose the plans for the
z'Srauff invasion of New Texas."

Is that all, now? I thought. *He doesn't want a
diplomat; he wants a magician.*

"And what," I asked, "will my official position be on New Texas, sir? Or will I have one, of any sort?"

"Oh, yes, indeed, Mr. Silk. Your official position will be that of Ambassador Plenipotentiary and Envoy Extraordinary. That, I believe, is the only vacancy which exists in the Diplomatic Service on that planet."

At Dumbarton Oaks Diplomatic Academy, they haze the freshmen by making them sit on a one-legged stool and balance a teacup and saucer on one knee while the upper classmen pelt them with ping-pong balls. Whoever invented that and the other similar forms of hazing was one of the great geniuses of the Service. So I sipped my coffee, set down the cup, took a puff from my cigarette, then said:

"I am indeed deeply honored, Mr. Secretary. I trust I needn't go into any assurances that I will do everything possible to justify your trust in me."

"I believe he will, Mr. Secretary," Natalenko piped, in a manner that chilled my blood.

"Yes, I believe so," Ghopal Singh said. "Now, Mr. Ambassador, there's a liner in orbit two thousand miles off Luna, which has been held from blasting off for the last eight hours, waiting for you. Don't bother packing more than a few things; you can get everything you'll need aboard, or at New Austin, the planetary capital. We have a man whom Coördinator Natalenko has secured for us, a native New Texan, Hoddy Ringo by name. He'll act as your personal secretary. He's aboard the ship now. You'll have to hurry, I'm afraid. . . . Well, bon voyage, Mr. Ambassador."

CHAPTER II

THE death-watch outside had grown to about fifteen or twenty. They were all waiting in happy anticipation as I came out of the Secretary's office.

"What did he do to you, Silk?" Courtlant Staynes asked, amusedly.

"Demoted me. Kicked me off the Hooligan Diplomats," I said glumly.

"Demoted you from the Consular Service?" Staynes asked scornfully. "Impossible!"

"Yes. He demoted me to the Cookie Pushers. Clear down to Ambassador."

They got a terrific laugh. I went out, wondering what sort of noises they'd make, the next morning, when the appointments sheet was posted.

I gathered a few things together, mostly small personal items, and all the microfilms that I could find on New Texas, then got aboard the Space Navy cutter that was waiting to take me to the ship. It was a four-hour trip and I put in the time going over my hastily-assembled microfilm library and using a stenophone to dictate a reading list for the spacetrip.

As I rolled up the stenophone-tape, I wondered what sort of secretary they had given me; and, in passing, why Natalenko's department had furnished him.

Hoddy Ringo . . .

Queer name, but in a galactic civilization, you find all sorts of names and all sorts of people bearing them, so I was prepared for anything.

And I found it.

I found him standing with the ship's captain, inside the airlock, when I boarded the big, spherical space-liner. A tubby little man, with shoulders and arms he had never developed doing secretarial work, and a good-natured, not particularly intelligent face.

See the happy moron, he doesn't give a damn, I thought.

Then I took a second look at him. He might be happy, but he wasn't a moron. He just looked like one. Natalenko's people often did, as one of their professional assets.

I also noticed that he had a bulge under his left armpit the size of an eleven-mm army automatic.

He was, I'd been told, a native of New Texas. I gathered, after talking with him for a while, that he had been away from his home planet for over five years, was glad to be going back, and especially glad that he was going back under the protection of Solar League diplomatic immunity.

In fact, I rather got the impression that, without such protection, he wouldn't have been going back at all.

I made another discovery. My personal secretary, it seemed, couldn't read stenotype. I found that out when I gave him the tape I'd dictated aboard the cutter, to transcribe for me.

"Gosh, boss. I can't make anything out of this

stuff," he confessed, looking at the combination shorthand-Braille that my voice had put onto the tape.

"Well, then, put it in a player and transcribe it by ear," I told him.

He didn't seem to realize that that could be done.

"How did you come to be sent as my secretary, if you can't do secretarial work?" I wanted to know.

He got out a bag of tobacco and a book of papers and began rolling a cigarette, with one hand.

"Why, shucks, boss, nobody seemed to think I'd have to do this kinda work," he said. "I was just sent along to show you the way around New Texas, and see you don't get inta no trouble."

He got his handmade cigarette drawing, and hitched the strap that went across his back and looped under his right arm. "A guy that don't know the way around can get inta a lotta trouble on New Texas. If you call gettin' killed trouble."

So he was a bodyguard . . . and I wondered what else he was. One thing, it would take him forty-two years to send a radio message back to Luna, and I could keep track of any other messages he sent, in letters or on tape, by ships. In the end, I transcribed my own tape, and settled down to laying out my three weeks' study-course on my new post.

I found, however, that the whole thing could be learned in a few hours. The rest of what I had was duplication, some of it contradictory, and it all boiled down to this:

Capella IV had been settled during the first wave of extrasolar colonization, after the Fourth

World—or First Interplanetary—War. Some time around 2100. The settlers had come from a place in North America called Texas, one of the old United States. They had a lengthy history— independent republic, admission to the United States, secession from the United States, recon- quest by the United States, and general intransi- gence under the United States, the United Nations and the Solar League. When the laws of non- Einsteinian physics were discovered and the hyperspace-drive was developed, practically the entire population of Texas had taken to space to find a new home and independence from every- body.

They had found Capella IV, a Terra-type planet, with a slightly higher mean temperature, a lower mass and lower gravitational field, about one- quarter water and three-quarters land-surface, at a stage of evolutionary development approxi- mately that of Terra during the late Pliocene. They also found supercow, a big mammal looking like the unsuccessful attempt of a hippopotamus to impersonate a dachshund and about the size of a nuclear-steam locomotive. On New Texas' plains, there were billions of them; their meat was fit for the gods of Olympus. So New Texas had become the meat-supplier to the galaxy.

There was very little in any of the microfilm- books about the politics of New Texas and such as it was, it was very scornful. There were such ex- pressions as 'anarchy tempered by assassination,' and 'grotesque parody of democracy.'

There would, I assumed, be more exact infor- mation in the material which had been shoved into my hand just before boarding the cutter from Luna, in a package labeled *TOP SECRET: TO BE*

OPENED ONLY IN SPACE, AFTER THE FIRST HYPERJUMP. There was also a big trunk that had been placed in my suite, sealed and bearing the same instructions.

I got Hoddy out of the suite as soon as the ship had passed out of the normal space-time continuum, locked the door of my cabin and opened the parcel.

It contained only two loose-leaf notebooks, both labeled with the Solar League and Department seals, both adorned with the customary bloodthirsty threats against the unauthorized and the indiscreet. They were numbered ONE and TWO.

ONE contained four pages. On the first, I read:

FINAL MESSAGE
OF THE FIRST SOLAR LEAGUE AMBASSADOR
TO
NEW TEXAS
ANDREW JACKSON HICKOCK

I agree with none of the so-called information about this planet on file with the State Department on Luna. The people of New Texas are certainly not uncouth barbarians. Their manners and customs, while lively and unconventional, are most charming. Their dress is graceful and practical, not grotesque; their soft speech is pleasing to the ear. Their flag is the original flag of the Republic of Texas; it is definitely not a barbaric travesty of our own emblem. And the underlying premises of their political system should, as far as possible, be incorporated into the organization of the Solar League. Here politics is an exciting and exacting game, in which only the true representative of all the people can survive.

DEPARTMENT ADDENDUM

After five years on New Texas, Andrew Jackson Hickock resigned, married a daughter of a local rancher and became a naturalized citizen of that planet. He is still active in politics there, often in opposition to Solar League policies.

That didn't sound like too bad an advertisement for the planet. I was even feeling cheerful when I turned to the next page, and:

FINAL MESSAGE
OF THE SECOND SOLAR LEAGUE
AMBASSADOR TO
NEW TEXAS
CYRIL GODWINSON

Yes and no; perhaps and perhaps not; pardon me; I agree with everything you say. Yes and no; perhaps and perhaps not; pardon me; I agree . . .

DEPARTMENT ADDENDUM

After seven years on New Texas, Ambassador Godwinson was recalled; adjudged hopelessly insane.

And then:

FINAL MESSAGE
OF THE THIRD SOLAR LEAGUE
AMBASSADOR TO NEW TEXAS
R. F. GULLIS

I find it very pleasant to inform you that when you are reading this, I will be dead.

DEPARTMENT ADDENDUM
Committed suicide after six months on New Texas.

I turned to the last page cautiously, found:

FINAL MESSAGE
OF THE FOURTH SOLAR LEAGUE
AMBASSADOR TO NEW TEXAS
SILAS CUMSHAW

I came to this planet ten years ago as a man of pronounced and outspoken convictions. I have managed to keep myself alive here by becoming an inoffensive nonentity. If I continue in this course, it will be only at the cost of my self-respect. Beginning tonight, I am going to state and maintain positive opinions on the relation between this planet and the Solar League.

DEPARTMENT ADDENDUM
Murdered at the home of Andrew J. Hickcock. (see p. 1.)

And that was the end of the first notebook. Nice, cheerful reading; complete, solid briefing.

I was, frankly, almost afraid to open the second notebook. I hefted it cautiously at first, saw that it contained only about as many pages as the first and that those pages were sealed with a band around them.

I took a quick peek, read the words on the band:

Before reading, open the sealed trunk which has been included with your luggage.

So I laid aside the book and dragged out the sealed trunk, hesitated, then opened it.

Nothing shocked me more than to find the trunk . . . full of clothes.

There were four pairs of trousers, light blue, dark blue, gray and black, with wide cuffs at the bottoms. There were six or eight shirts, their colors running the entire spectrum in the most violent shades. There were a couple of vests. There were two pairs of short boots with high heels and fancy leather-working, and a couple of hats with four-inch brims.

And there was a wide leather belt, practically a leather corset.

I stared at the belt, wondering if I was really seeing what was in front of me.

Attached to the belt were a pair of pistols in right- and left-hand holsters. The pistols were seven-mm Krupp-Tatta Ultraspeed automatics, and the holsters were the spring-ejection, quick-draw holsters which were the secret of the State Department Special Services.

This must be a mistake, I thought. *I'm an Ambassador now and Ambassadors never carry weapons.*

The sanctity of an Ambassador's person not only made the carrying of weapons unnecessary, so that an armed Ambassador was a contradiction of diplomatic terms, but it would be an outrageous insult to the nation to which he had been accredited.

Like taking a poison-taster to a friendly dinner.

Maybe I was supposed to give the belt and the holsters to Hoddy Ringo. . . .

So I tore the sealed band off the second notebook and read through it.

I was to wear the local costume on New Texas.

That was something unusual; even in the Hooligan Diplomats, we leaned over backward in wearing Terran costume to distinguish ourselves from the people among whom we worked.

I was further advised to start wearing the high boots immediately, on shipboard, to accustom myself to the heels. These, I was informed, were traditional. They had served a useful purpose, in the early days on Terran Texas, when all travel had been on horseback. On horseless and mechanized New Texas, they were a useless but venerated part of the cultural heritage.

There were bits of advice about the hat, and the trousers, which for some obscure reason were known as Levis. And I was informed, as an order, that I was to wear the belt and the pistols at all times outside the Embassy itself.

That was all of the second notebook.

The two notebooks, plus my conversation with Ghopal, Klüng and Natalenko, completed my briefing for my new post.

I slid off my shoes and pulled on a pair of boots. They fitted perfectly. Evidently I had been tapped for this job as soon as word of Silas Cumshaw's death had reached Luna and there must have been some fantastic hurrying to get my outfit ready.

I didn't like that any too well, and I liked the order to carry the pistols even less. Not that I had any objection to carrying weapons, *per se*: I had been born and raised on Theta Virgo IV, where the children aren't allowed outside the house unattended until they've learned to shoot.

But I did have strenuous objections to being sent, virtually ignorant of local customs, on a mission where I was ordered to commit deliberate provocation of the local government, immediately on the heels of my predecessor's violent death.

The author of *Probable Future Courses of Solar League Diplomacy* had recommended the use of provocation to justify conquest. If the New Texans murdered two Solar League Ambassadors in a row, nobody would blame the League for moving in with a space-fleet and an army. . . .

I was beginning to understand how Doctor Guillotin must have felt while his neck was being shoved into his own invention.

I looked again at the notebooks, each marked in red: *Familiarize yourself with contents and burn or disintegrate.*

I'd have to do that, of course. There were a few non-humans and a lot of non-League people aboard this ship. I couldn't let any of them find out what we considered a full briefing for a new Ambassador.

So I wrapped them in the original package and went down to the lower passenger zone, where I found the ship's third officer. I told him that I had some secret diplomatic matter to be destroyed and he took me to the engine room. I shoved the package into one of the mass-energy convertors and watched it resolve itself into its constitutent protons, neutrons and electrons.

On the way back, I stopped in at the ship's bar.

Hoddy Ringo was there, wrapped up in—and I use the words literally—a young lady from the Alderbaran system. She was on her way home from one of the quickie divorce courts on Terra and was celebrating her marital emancipation. They were so entangled with each other that they didn't notice me. When they left the bar, I slipped after them until I saw them enter the lady's stateroom. That, of course, would have Hoddy immobilized—better word, *located*—for a while. So I went back to our suite, picked the lock of Hoddy's room, and allowed myself half an hour to search his luggage.

All of his clothes were new, but there were not a great many of them. Evidently he was planning to re-outfit himself on New Texas. There were a few odds and ends, the kind any man with a real home planet will hold on to, in the luggage.

He had another eleven-mm pistol, made by Consolidated-Martian Metalworks, mate to the one he was carrying in a shoulder-holster, and a wide two-holster belt like the one furnished me, but quite old.

I greeted the sight and the meaning of the old holsters with joy: they weren't the State Department Special Services type. That meant that Hoddy was just one of Natalenko's run-of-the-gallows cutthroats, not important enough to be issued the secret equipment.

But I was a little worried over what I found hidden in the lining of one of his bags, a letter addressed to Space-Commander Lucius C. Stonehenge, Agression Department Attaché, New Austin Embassy. I didn't have either the time or the equipment to open it. But, knowing our various Departments, I tried to reassure myself with the thought that it was only a letter-of-credence, with the real message to be delivered orally.

About the real message I had no doubts: *arrange the murder of Ambassador Stephen Silk in such a way that it looks like another New Texan job. . . .*

Starting that evening—or what passed for evening aboard a ship in hyperspace—Hoddy and I began a positively epochal binge together.

I had it figured this way: as long as we were on board ship, I was perfectly safe. On the ship, in fact, Hoddy would definitely have given his life to save mine. I'd have to be killed on New Texas to give Klüng's boys their excuse for moving in.

And there was always the chance, with no chance too slender for me to ignore, that I might be able to get Hoddy drunk enough to talk, yet still be sober enough myself to remember what he said.

Exact times, details, faces, names, came to me through a sort of hazy blur as Hoddy and I drank something he called superbourbon—a New Texan drink that Bourbon County, Kentucky, would never have recognized. They had no corn on New Texas. This stuff was made out of something called superyams.

There were at least two things I got out of the binge. First, I learned to slug down the national drink without batting an eye. Second, I learned to control my expression as I uncovered the fact that everything on New Texas was supersomething.

I was also cautious enough, before we really got started, to leave my belt and guns with the purser. I didn't want Hoddy poking around those secret holsters. And I remember telling the captain to radio New Austin as soon as we came out of our last hyperspace-jump, then to send the ship's doctor around to give me my hangover treatments.

But the one thing I wanted to remember, as the hangover shots brought me back to normal life, I found was the one thing I couldn't remember. What was the name of that girl—a big, beautiful blond—who joined the party along with Hoddy's grass widow from Alderbaran and stayed with it to the end?

Damn, I wished I could remember her name!

When we were fifteen thousand miles off-planet and the lighters from New Austin spaceport were reported on the way, I got into the skin-tight Levis, the cataclysmic-colored shirt, and the loose vest, tucked my big hat under my arm, and went to the purser's office for my guns, buckling them on. When I got back to the suite, Hoddy had put on his pistols and was practicing quick draws in front of the mirror. He took one look at my armament and groaned.

"You're gonna get yourself killed for sure, with that rig, an' them popguns," he told me.

"These popguns'll shoot harder and make bigger holes than that pair of museum-pieces you're carrying," I replied.

"An' them holsters!" Hoddy continued. "Why, it'd take all day to get your guns outa them! You better let me find you a real rig, when we get to New Austin. . . ."

There was a chance, of course, that he knew what I was using and wanted to hide his knowledge. I doubted that.

"Sure, you State Department guys always know everything," he went on. "Like them microfilm-books you was readin'. I try to tell you what things is really like on New Texas, an' you let it go in one ear an' out the other."

Then he wandered off to say good-bye to the grass widow from Alderbaran, leaving me to make the last-minute check on the luggage. I was hoping I'd be able to see that blond . . . what *was* her name; Gail something-or-other. Let's see, she'd been at some Terran university, and she was on her way home to . . . to New Texas! Of course!

I saw her, half an hour later, in the crowd around the airlock when the lighters came alongside, and I tried to push my way toward her. As I did, the airlock opened, the crowd surged toward it, and she was carried along. Then the airlock closed, after she had passed through and before I could get to it. That meant I'd have to wait for the second lighter.

So I made the best of it, and spent the next half-hour watching the disc of the planet grow into a huge ball that filled the lower half of the viewscreen and then lose its curvature, and instead of moving in toward the planet, we were going down toward it.

CHAPTER III

NEW AUSTIN spaceport was a huge place, a good fifty miles outside the city. As we descended, I could see that it was laid out like a wheel, with the landings and the blast-off stands around the hub, and high buildings—packing houses and refrigeration plants—along the many spokes. It showed a technological level quite out of keeping with the accounts I had read, or the stories Hoddy had told, about the simple ranch life of the planet. Might be foreign capital invested there, and I made a mental note to find out whose.

On the other hand, Old Texas, on Terra, had been heavily industrialized; so much so that the state itself could handle the gigantic project of building enough spaceships to move almost the whole population into space.

Then the landing-field was rushing up at us, with the nearer ends of the roadways and streets drawing close and the far ends lengthening out away from us. The other lighter was already down, and I could see a crowd around it.

There was a crowd waiting for us when we got out and went down the escalators to the ground, and as I had expected, a special group of men waiting for me. They were headed by a tall, slender individual in the short black Eisenhower jacket, gray-striped trousers and black homburg that was the uniform of the Diplomatic Service, alias the Cookie Pushers.

Over their heads at the other rocket-boat, I could see the gold-gleaming head of the girl I'd met on the ship.

I tried to push through the crowd and get to her. As I did, the Cookie Pusher got in my way.

"Mr. Silk! Mr. Ambassador! Here we are!" he was clamoring. "The car for the Embassy is right over here!" He clutched my elbow. "You have no idea how glad we all are to see you, Mr. Ambassador!"

"Yes, yes; of course. Now, there's sombody over there I have to see, at once." I tried to pull myself loose from his grasp.

Across the concrete between the two lighters, I could see the girl push out of the crowd around her and wave a hand to me. I tried to yell to her; but just then another lighter, loaded with freight, started to lift out at another nearby stand, with the roar of half a dozen Niagaras. The thin man in the striped trousers added to the uproar by shouting into my ear and pulling at me.

"We haven't time!" he finally managed to make himself heard. "We're dreadfully late now, sir! You must come with us."

Hoddy, too, had caught hold of me by the other arm.

"Come on, boss. There's gotta be some reason why he's got himself in an uproar about whatever it is. You'll see her again."

Then, the whole gang—Hoddy, the thin man with the black homburg, his younger accomplice in identical garb, and the chauffeur—all closed in on me and pushed me, pulled me, half-carried me, fifty yards across the concrete to where their air-car was parked. By this time, the tall blond had gotten clear of the mob around her and was waving frantically at me. I tried to wave back, but I was literally crammed into the car and flung down on the seat. At the same time, the chauffeur was jumping in, extending the car's wings, jetting up.

"Great God!" I bellowed. "This is the damnedest piece of impudence I've ever had to suffer from any subordinates in my whole State Department experience! I want an explanation out of you, and it'd better be a good one!"

There was a deafening silence in the car for a moment. The thin man moved himself off my lap, then sat there looking at me with the heartbroken eyes of a friendly dog that had just been kicked for something which wasn't really its fault.

"Mr. Ambassador, you can't imagine how sorry we all are, but if we hadn't gotten you away from the spaceport and to the Embassy at once, we would all have been much sorrier."

"Somebody here gunnin' for the Ambassador?" Hoddy demanded sharply.

"Oh, no! I hadn't even thought of that," the thin man almost gibbered. "But your presence at the Embassy is of immediate and urgent necessity. You have no idea of the state into which things have gotten. . . . Oh, pardon me, Mr. Ambassador. I am Gilbert W. Thrombley, your chargé d'affaires." I shook hands with him. "And Mr. Benito Gomez, the Secretary of the Embassy." I shook hands with him, too, and started to introduce Mr. Hoddy Ringo.

Hoddy, however, had turned to look out the rear window; immediately, he gave a yelp.

"We got a tail, boss! Two of them! Look back there!"

There were two black eight-passenger aircars, of the same model, whizzing after us, making an obvious effort to overtake us. The chauffeur cursed and fired his auxilliary jets, then his rocket-booster.

Immediately, black rocket-fuel puffs shot away from the pursuing aircars.

Hoddy turned in his seat, cranked open a porthole-slit in the window, and poked one of his eleven-mm's out, letting the whole clip go. Thrombley and Gomez slid down onto the floor, and both began trying to drag me down with them, imploring me not to expose myself.

As far as I could see, there was nothing to expose myself to. The other cars kept coming, but neither of them were firing at us. There was also no indication that Hoddy's salvo had had any effect on them. Our chauffeur went into a perfect frenzy of twisting and dodging, at the same time using his radiophone to tell sombody to get the goddamn gate open in a hurry. I saw the blue skies and green plains of New Texas replacing one another above, under, in front of and behind us. Then the car set down on a broad stretch of concrete, the wings were retracted, and we went whizzing down a city street.

We whizzed down a number of streets. We cut corners on two wheels, and on one wheel, and, I was prepared to swear, on no wheels. A couple of times, with the wings retracted, we actually jetted into the air and jumped over vehicles in front of us, landing again with bone-shaking jolts. Then we made an abrupt turn and shot in under a concrete arch, and a big door banged shut behind us, and we stopped, in the middle of a wide patio, the front of the car a few inches short of a fountain. Four or five people, in diplomatic striped trousers, local dress and the uniform of the Space Marines, came running over.

Thrombley pulled himself erect and half-climbed, half-fell, out of the car. Gomez got out on the other side with Hoddy; I climbed out after Thrombley.

A tall, sandy-haired man in the uniform of the Space Navy came over.

"What the devil's the matter, Thrombley?" he demanded. Then, seeing me, he gave me as much of a salute as a naval officer will ever bestow on anybody in civilian clothes.

"Mr. Silk?" He looked at my costume and the pistols on my belt in well-bred concealment of surprise. "I'm your military attaché, Stonehenge; Space-Commander, Space Navy."

I noticed that Hoddy's ears had pricked up, but he wasn't making any effort to attract Stonehenge's attention. I shook hands with him, introduced Hoddy, and offered my cigarette case around.

"You seem to have had a hectic trip from the spaceport, Mr. Ambassador. What happened?"

Thrombley began accusing our driver of trying to murder the lot of us. Hoddy brushed him aside and explained:

"Just after we'd took off, two other cars took off after us. We speeded up, and they speeded up, too. Then your fly-boy, here, got fancy. That shook 'em off. Time we got into the city, we'd dropped them. Nice job of driving. Probably saved our lives."

"Shucks, that wasn't nothin'," the driver disclaimed. "When you drive for politicians, you're either good or you're good and dead."

"I'm surprised they started so soon," Stonehenge said. Then he looked around at my fellow-passengers, who seemed to have realized, by now, that they were no longer dangling by their fingernails over the brink of the grave. "But gentlemen, let's not keep the Ambassador standing out here in the hot sun."

So we went over the arches at the side of the patio, and were about to sit down when one of the Embassy servants came up, followed by a man in a loose vest and blue Levis and a big hat. He had a pair of automatics in his belt, too.

"I'm Captain Nelson; New Texas Rangers," he introduced himself. "Which one of you-all is Mr. Stephen Silk?"

I admitted it.

The Ranger pushed back his wide hat and grinned at me.

"I just can't figure this out," he said. "You're in the right place and the right company, but we got a report, from a mighty good source, that you'd been kidnaped at the spaceport by a gang of thugs!"

"A blond source?" I made curving motions with my hands. "I don't blame her. My efficient and conscientious chargé d'affaires, Mr. Thrombley, felt that I should reach the Embassy, here, as soon as possible, and from where she was standing, it must have looked like a kidnaping.

Fact is, it looked like one from where I was standing, too. Was that you and your people who were chasing us? Then I must apologize for opening fire on you . . . I hope nobody was hurt."

"No, our cars are pretty well armored. You scored a couple of times on one of them, but no harm done. I reckon after what happened to Silas Cumshaw, you had a right to be suspicious."

I noticed that refreshments, including several bottles, had been placed on a big wicker table under the arched veranda.

"Can I offer you a drink, Captain, in token of mutual amity?" I asked.

"Well, now, I'd like to, Mr. Ambassador, but I'm on duty . . ." he began.

"You can't be. You're an officer of the Planetary Government of New Texas, and in this Embassy, you're in the territory of the Solar League."

"That's right, now, Mr. Ambassador," he grinned. "Extraterritoriality. Wonderful thing, extraterritoriality." He looked at Hoddy, who, for the first time since I had met him, was trying to shrink into the background. "And diplomatic immunity, too. Ain't it, Hoddy?"

After he had had his drink and departed, we all sat down. Thrombley began speaking almost at once.

"Mr. Ambassador, you must, you simply must, issue a public statement, immediately, sir. Only a public statement, issued promptly, will relieve the crisis into which we have all been thrust."

"Oh, come, Mr. Thrombley," I objected. "Captain Nelson'll take care of all that in his report to his superiors."

Thrombley looked at me for a moment as

though I had been speaking to him in Hottentot, then waved his hands in polite exasperation.

"Oh, no, no! I don't mean that, sir. I mean a public statement to the effect that you have assumed full responsibility for the Embassy. Where is that thing? Mr. Gomez!"

Gomez gave him four or five sheets, stapled together. He laid them on the table, turned to the last sheet, and whipped out a pen.

"Here, sir; just sign here."

"Are you crazy?" I demanded. "I'll be damned if I'll sign that. Not till I've taken an inventory of the physical property of the Embassy, and familiarized myself with all its commitments, and had the books audited by some firm of certified public accountants."

Thrombley and Gomez looked at one another. They both groaned.

"But we must have a statement of assumption of responsibility . . ." Gomez dithered.

". . . or the business of the Embassy will be at a dead stop, and we can't do anything," Thrombley finished.

"Wait a moment, Thrombley," Stonehenge cut in. "I understand Mr. Silk's attitude. I've taken command of a good many ships and installations, at one time or another, and I've never signed for anything I couldn't see and feel and count. I know men who retired as brigadier generals or vice-admirals, but they retired loaded with debts incurred because as second lieutenants or ensigns they forgot that simple rule."

He turned to me. "Without any disrespect to the chargé d'affaires, Mr. Silk, this Embassy has been pretty badly disorganized since Mr. Cumshaw's death. No one felt authorized, or, to put it more accurately, no one dared, to declare himself acting head of the Embassy—"

"Because that would make him the next target?" I interrupted. "Well, that's what I was sent here for. Mr. Gomez, as Secretary of the Embassy, will you please, at once, prepare a statement for the press and telecast release to the effect that I am now the authorized head of this Embassy, responsible from this hour for all its future policies and all its present commitments insofar as they obligate the government of the Solar League. Get that out at once. Tomorrow, I will present my credentials to the Secretary of State here. Thereafter, Mr. Thrombley, you can rest in the assurance that I'll be the one they'll be shooting at."

"But you can't wait that long, Mr. Ambassador," Thrombley almost wailed. "We must go immediately to the Statehouse. The reception for you is already going on."

I looked at my watch, which had been regulated aboard ship for Capella IV time. It was just 1315.

"What time do they hold diplomatic receptions on this planet, Mr. Thrombley?" I asked.

"Oh, any time at all, sir. This one started about 0900 when the news that the ship was in orbit off-planet got in. It'll be a barbecue, of course, and—"

"Barbecued supercow! Yipeee!" Hoddy yelled. "What I been waitin' for for five years!"

It would be the vilest cruelty not to take him along, I thought. And it would also keep him and Stonehenge apart for a while.

"But we must hurry, Mr. Ambassador,"

Thrombley was saying. "If you will change, now, to formal dress . . ."

And he was looking at me, gasping. I think it was the first time he had actually seen what I was wearing.

"In native dress, Mr. Ambassador!"

Thrombley's eyes and tone were again those of an innocent spaniel caught in the middle of a marital argument.

Then his gaze fell to my belt and his eyes became saucers. "Oh, dear! And armed!"

My chargé d'affaires was shuddering and he could not look directly at me.

"Mr. Ambassador, I understand that you were recently appointed from the Consular Service. I sincerely hope that you will not take it amiss if I point out, here in private, that—"

"Mr. Thrombley, I am wearing this costume and these pistols on the direct order of Secretary of State Ghopal Singh."

That set him back on his heels.

"I . . . I can't believe it!" he exclaimed. "An ambassador is never armed."

"Not when he's dealing with a government which respects the comity of nations and the usages of diplomatic practice, no," I replied. "But the fate of Mr. Cumshaw clearly indicates that the government of New Texas is not such a government. These pistols are in the nature of a not-too-subtle hint of the manner in which this government, here, is being regarded by the government of the Solar League." I turned to Stonehenge. "Commander, what sort of an Embassy guard have we?" I asked.

"Space Marines, sergeant and five men. I double as guard officer, sir."

"Very well. Mr. Thrombley insists that it is necessary for me to go to this fish-fry or whatever it is immediately. I want two men, a driver and an auto-rifleman, for my car. And from now on, I would suggest, Commander, that you wear your sidearm at all times outside the Embassy."

"Yes, sir!" and this time, Stonehenge gave me a real salute.

"Well, I must phone the Statehouse, then," Thrombley said. "We will have to call on Secretary of State Palme, and then on President Hutchinson."

With that, he got up, excused himself, motioned Gomez to follow, and hurried away.

I got up, too, and motioned Stonehenge aside.

"Aboard ship, coming in, I was told that there's a task force of the Space Navy on maneuvers about five light-years from here," I said.

"Yes, sir. Task Force Red-Blue-Green, Fifth Space Fleet. Fleet Admiral Sir Rodney Tregaskis."

"Can we get hold of a fast space-boat, with hyperdrive engines, in a hurry?"

"Eight or ten of them always around New Austin spaceport, available for charter."

"All right; charter one and get out to that fleet. Tell Admiral Tregaskis that the Ambassador at New Austin feels in need of protection; possibility of z'Srauff invasion. I'll give you written orders. I want the Fleet within radio call. How far out would that be, with our facilities?"

"The Embassy radio isn't reliable beyond about sixty light-minutes, sir."

"Then tell Sir Rodney to bring his fleet in that close. The invasion, if it comes, will probably not come from the direction of the z'Srauff star-cluster; they'll probably jump past us and move in from the other side. I hope you don't think I'm having nightmares, Commander. Danger of a z'Srauff invasion was pointed out to me by persons on the very highest level, on Luna."

Stonehenge nodded. "I'm always having the same kind of nightmares, sir. Especially since this special envoy arrived here, ostensibly to negotiate a meteor-mining treaty." He hesitated for a moment. "We don't want the New Texans to know, of course, that you've sent for the fleet?"

"Naturally not."

"Well, if I can wait till about midnight before I leave, I can get a boat owned, manned and operated by Solar League people. The boat's a dreadful-looking old tub, but she's sound and fast. The gang who own her are pretty notorious characters—suspected of smuggling, piracy, and what not—but they'll keep their mouths shut if well paid."

"Then pay them well," I said. "And it's just as well you're not leaving at once. When I get back from this clambake, I'll want to have a general informal council, and I certainly want you in on it."

On the way to the Statehouse in the aircar, I kept wondering just how smart I had been.

I was pretty sure that the z'Srauff was getting ready for a sneak attack on New Texas, and, as Solar League Ambassador, I of course had the right to call on the Space Navy for any amount of armed protection.

Sending Stonehenge off on what couldn't be less than an eighteen-hour trip would delay anything he and Hoddy might be cooking up, too.

On the other hand, with the fleet so near, they might decide to have me rubbed out in a hurry, to justify seizing the planet ahead of the z'Srauff.

I was in that pleasant spot called, "Damned if you do and damned if you don't. . . ."

CHAPTER IV

THE Statehouse appeared to cover about a square mile of ground and it was an insane jumble of buildings piled beside and on top of one another, as though it had been in continuous construction ever since the planet was colonized, eighty-odd years before.

At what looked like one of the main entrances, the car stopped. I told our Marine driver and auto-rifleman to park the car and take in the barbecue, but to leave word with the doorman where they could be found. Hoddy, Thrombley and I then went in, to be met by a couple of New Texas Rangers, one of them the officer who had called at the Embassy. They guided us to the office of the Secretary of State.

"We're dreadfully late," Thrombley was fretting. "I do hope we haven't kept the Secretary waiting too long."

From the looks of him, I was afraid we had. He jumped up from his desk and hurried across the room as soon as the receptionist opened the door for us, his hand extended.

"Good afternoon, Mr. Thrombley," he burbled nervously. "And this is the new Ambassador, I suppose. And this—" He caught sight of Hoddy

Ringo, bringing up the rear and stopped short, hand flying to open mouth. "Oh, dear me!"

So far, I had been building myself a New Texas stereotype from Hoddy Ringo and the Ranger officer who had chased us to the Embassy. But this frightened little rabbit of a fellow simply didn't fit it. An alien would be justified in assigning him to an entirely different species.

Thrombley introduced me. I introduced Hoddy as my confidential secretary and advisor. We all shook hands, and Thrombley dug my credentials out of his briefcase and handed them to me, and I handed them to the Secretary of State, Mr. William A. Palme. He barely glanced at them, then shook my hand again fervently and mumbled something about "inexpressible pleasure" and "entirely acceptable to my government."

That made me the accredited and accepted Ambassador to New Texas.

Mr. Palme hoped, or said he hoped, that my stay in New Texas would be long and pleasant. He seemed rather less than convinced that it would be. His eyes kept returning in horrified fascination to my belt. Each time they would focus on the butts of my Krupp-Tattas, he would pull them resolutely away again.

"And now, we must take you to President Hutchinson; he is most anxious to meet you, Mr. Silk. If you will please come with me . . ."

Four or five Rangers who had been loitering the hall outside moved to follow us as we went toward the elevator. Although we had come into the building onto a floor only a few feet above street-level, we went down three floors from the hallway outside the Secretary of State's office, into a huge room, the concrete floor of which was oil-stained, as though vehicles were continually being driven in and out. It was about a hundred feet wide, and two or three hundred in length. Daylight was visible through open doors at the end. As we approached them, the Rangers fanning out on either side and in front of us, I could hear a perfect bedlam of noise outside—shouting, singing, dance-band music, interspersed with the banging of shots.

When we reached the doors at the end, we emerged into one end of a big rectangular plaza, at least five hundred yards in length. Most of the uproar was centered at the opposite end, where several thousand people, in costumes colored through the whole spectrum, were milling about. There seemed to be at least two square-dances going on, to the music of competing bands. At the distant end of the plaza, over the heads of the crowd, I could see the piles and tracks of an overhead crane, towering above what looked like an open-hearth furnace. Between us and the bulk of the crowd, in a cleared space, two medium tanks, heavily padded with mats, were ramming and trying to overturn each other, the mob of spectators crowding as close to them as they dared. The din was positively deafening, though we were at least two hundred yards from the center of the crowd.

"Oh, dear, I always dread these things!" Palme was saying.

"Yes, absolutely *anything* could happen," Thrombley twittered.

"Man, this is a real barbecue!" Hoddy gloated. "Now I really feel at home!"

"Over this way, Mr. Silk," Palme said, guiding me toward the short end of the plaza, on our left. "We will see the President and then . . ."

He gulped.

". . . then we will all go to the barbecue."

In the center of the short end of the plaza, dwarfed by the monster bulks of steel and concrete and glass around it, stood a little old building of warm-tinted adobe. I had never seen it before, but somehow it was familiar-looking. And then I remembered. Although I had never seen it before, I had seen it pictured many times; pictured under attack, with gunsmoke spouting from windows and parapets.

I plucked Thrombley's sleeve.

"Isn't that a replica of the Alamo?"

He was shocked. "Oh, dear, Mr. Ambassador, don't let anybody hear you ask that. That's no replica. It *is* the Alamo. *The* Alamo."

I stood there a moment, looking at it. I was remembering, and finally understanding, what my psycho-history lessons about the "Romantic Freeze" had meant.

They had taken this little mission-fort down, brick by adobe brick, loaded it carefully into a spaceship, brought it here, forty two light-years away from Terra, and reverently set it up again. Then they had built a whole world and a whole social philosophy around it.

It had been the dissatisfied, of course, the discontented, the dreamers, who had led the vanguard of man's explosion into space following the discovery of the hyperspace drive. They had gone from Terra cherishing dreams of things that had been dumped into the dust bin of history, carry-

ing with them pictures of ways of life that had
passed away, or that had never really been. Then,
in their new life, on new planets, they had set to
work making those dreams and those pictures
live.

And, many times, they had come close to suc-
ceeding.

These Texans, now: they had left behind the
cold fact that it had been their state's great industrial complex that had made their migration possible. They ignored the fact that their life here on
Capella IV was possible only by application of
modern industrial technology. That rodeo down
the plaza—tank-tilting instead of bronco-busting.
Here they were, living frozen in a romantic dream,
a world of roving cowboys and ranch kingdoms.

No wonder Hoddy hadn't liked the books I had
been reading on the ship. They shook the fabric of
that dream.

There were people moving about, at this relatively quiet end of the plaza, mostly in the direction of the barbecue. Ten or twelve Rangers loi-
tered at the front of the Alamo, and with them I
saw the dress blues of my two Marines. There was
a little three-wheeled motorcart among them,
from which they were helping themselves to food
and drink. When they saw us coming, the two
Marines shoved their sandwiches into the hands
of a couple of Rangers and tried to come to attention.

"At ease, at ease," I told them. "Have a good
time, boys. Hoddy, you better get in on some of
this grub; I may be inside for quite a while."

As soon as the Rangers saw Hoddy, they hastily

got things out of their right hands. Hoddy grinned at them.

"Take it easy, boys," he said. "I'm protected by the game laws. I'm a diplomat, I am."

There were a couple of Rangers lounging outside the door of the President's office and both of them carried autorifles, implying things I didn't like.

I had seen the President of the Solar League wandering around the dome-city of Artemis unattended, looking for all the world like a professor in his academic halls. Since then, maybe before then, I had always had a healthy suspicion of governments whose chiefs had to surround themselves with bodyguards.

But the President of New Texas, John Hutchinson, was alone in his office when we were shown in. He got up and came around his desk to greet us, a slender, stoop-shouldered man in a black-and-gold laced jacket. He had a narrow compressed mouth and eyes that seemed to be watching every corner of the room at once. He wore a pair of small pistols in cross-body holsters under his coat, and he always kept one hand or the other close to his abdomen.

He was like, and yet unlike, the Secretary of State. Both had the look of hunted animals; but where Palme was a rabbit, twitching to take flight at the first whiff of danger, Hutchinson was a cat who hears hounds baying—ready to run if he could, or claw if he must.

"Good day, Mr. Silk," he said, shaking hands with me after the introductions. "I see you're heeled; you're smart. You wouldn't be here today if poor Silas Cumshaw'd been as smart as you are. Great man, though; a wise and farseeing states- man. He and I were real friends."

"You know who Mr. Silk brought with him as bodyguard?" Palme asked. "Hoddy Ringo!"

"Oh, my God! I thought this planet was rid of him!" The President turned to me. "You got a good trigger-man, though, Mr. Ambassador. Good man to watch your back for you. But lot of folks here won't thank you for bringing him back to New Texas."

He looked at his watch. "We have time for a little drink, before we go outside, Mr. Silk," he said. "Care to join me?"

I assented and he got a bottle of superbourbon out of his desk, with four glasses. Palme got some water tumblers and brought the pitcher of ice- water from the cooler.

I noticed that the New Texas Secretary of State filled his three-ounce liquor glass to the top and gulped it down at once. He might act as though he were descended from a long line of maiden aunts, but he took his liquor in blasts that would have floored a spaceport labor-boss.

We had another drink, a little slower, and chat- ted for a while, and then Hutchinson said, regret- fully that we'd have to go outside and meet the folks. Outside, our guards—Hoddy, the two Marines, the Rangers who had escorted us from Palme's office, and Hutchinson's retinue— surrounded us, and we made our way down the plaza, through the crowd. The din—ear-piercing yells, whistles, cowbells, pistol shots, the cacophony of the two dance-bands, and the chorus-singing, of which I caught only the words:

The skies of freedom are above you!—was as bad as New Year's Eve in Manhattan or Nairobi or New Moscow, on Terra.

"Don't take all this as a personal tribute, Mr. Silk!" Hutchinson screamed into my ear. "On this planet, to paraphrase Nietzsche, a good barbecue halloweth any cause!"

That surprised me, at the moment. Later I found out that John Hutchinson was one of the leading scholars on New Texas and had once been president of one of their universities. New Texas Christian, I believe.

As we got up onto the platform, close enough to the barbecue pits to feel the heat from them, somebody let off what sounded like a fifty-mm anti-tank gun five or six times. Hutchinson grabbed a microphone and bellowed into it: "Ladies and gentlemen! Your attention, please!"

The noise began to diminish, slowly, until I could hear one voice, in the crowd below:

"Shut up, you damn fools! We can't eat till this is over!"

Hutchinson introduced me, in very few words. I gathered that lengthy speeches at barbecues were not popular on New Texas.

"Ladies and gentlemen!" I yelled into the microphone. "Appreciative as I am of this honor, there is one here who is more deserving of your notice than I; one to whom I, also, pay homage. He's over there on the fire, and I want a slice of him as soon as possible!"

That got a big ovation. There was, beside the water pitcher, a bottle of superbourbon. I ostentatiously threw the water out of the glass, poured a big shot of the corrosive stuff, and downed it.

"For God's sake, let's eat!" I finished. Then I turned to Thrombley, who was looking like a priest who has just seen the bishop spit in the holy-water font. "Stick close to me," I whispered. "Cue me in on the local notables, and the other members of the Diplomatic Corps." Then we all got down off the platform, and a band climbed up and began playing one of those raucous "cowboy ballads" which had originated in Manhattan about the middle of the Twentieth Century.

"The sandwiches'll be here in a moment, Mr. Ambassador," Hutchinson screamed—in effect, whispered—in my ear. "Don't feel any reluctance about shaking hands with a sandwich in your other hand; that's standard practice, here. You struck just the right note, up there. That business with the liquor was positively inspired!"

The sandwiches—huge masses of meat and hot relish, wrapped in tortillas of some sort—arrived and I bit into one.

I'd been eating supercow all my life, frozen or electronbeamed for transportation, and now I was discovering that I had never really eaten supercow before. I finished the first sandwich in surprisingly short order and was starting on my second when the crowd began coming.

First, the Diplomatic Corps, the usual collection of weirdies, human and otherwise. . . .

There was the Ambassador from Tara, in a suit of what his planet produced as a substitute for Irish homespuns. His Embassy, if it was like the others I had seen elsewhere, would be an outsize cottage with whitewashed walls and a thatched roof, with a bowl of milk outside the door for the Little People . . .

The Ambassador from Alpheratz II, the South African Nationalist planet, with a full beard, and old fashioned plug hat and tail-coat. They were a frustrated lot. They had gone into space to practice *apartheid* and had settled on a planet where there was no other intelligent race to be superior to . . .

The Mormon Ambassador from Deseret—Delta Camelopardalis V . . .

The Ambassador from Spica VII, a short jolly-looking little fellow, with a head like a seal's, long arms, short legs and a tail like a kangaroo's . . .

The Ambassador from Beta Cephus VI, who could have passed for human if he hadn't had blood with a copper base instead of iron. His skin was a dark green and his hair was a bright blue . . .

I was beginning to correct my first impression that Thrombley was a complete dithering fool. He stood at my left elbow, whispering the names, and governments and home planets of the Ambassadors as they came up, handing me little slips of paper on which he had written phonetically correct renditions of the greetings I would give them in their own language. I was still twittering a reply to the greeting of Nanadabadian, from Beta Cephus VI, when he whispered to me:

"Here it comes, sir. The z'Srauff!"

The z'Srauff were reasonably close to human stature and appearance, allowing for the fact that their ancestry had been canine instead of simian. They had, of course, longer and narrower jaws than we have, and definitely carnivorous teeth.

There were stories floating around that they

enjoyed barbecued Terran even better than they did supercow and hot relish.

This one advanced, extending his three-fingered hand.

"I am most happy to make connection with Solar League representative," he said. "I am named Gglafrr Ddespttann Vuvuvu."

No wonder Thrombley let him introduce himself. I answered in the Basic English that was all he'd admit to understanding:

"The name of your great nation has gone before you to me. The stories we tell to our young of you are at the top of our books. I have hope to make great pleasure in you and me to be friends."

Gglafrr Vuvuvu's smile wavered a little at the oblique reference to the couple of trouncings our Space Navy had administered to z'Srauff ships in the past. "We will be in the same place again times with no number," the alien replied. "I have hope for you that time you are in this place will be long and will put pleasure in your heart."

Then the pressure of the line behind him pushed him on. Cabinet Members; Senators and Representatives; prominent citizens, mostly Judge so-and-so, or Colonel this-or-that. It was all a blur, so much so that it was an instant before I recognized the gleaming golden hair and the statuesque figure.

"Thank you! I have met the Ambassador." The lovely voice was shaking with restrained anger.

"Gail!" I exclaimed.

"Your father coming to the barbecue, Gail?" President Hutchinson was asking.

"He ought to be here any minute. He sent me on

ahead from the hotel. He wants to meet the Ambassador. That's why I joined the line."

"Well, suppose I leave Mr. Silk in your hands for a while," Hutchinson said. "I ought to circulate around a little."

"Yes. Just leave him in my hands!" she said vindictively.

"What's wrong, Gail?" I wanted to know. "I know, I was supposed to meet you at the spaceport, but—"

"You made a beautiful fool of me at the spaceport!"

"Look, I can explain everything. My Embassy staff insisted on hurrying me off—"

Somebody gave a high-pitched whoop directly behind me and emptied the clip of a pistol. I couldn't even hear what else I said. I couldn't hear what she said, either, but it was something angry.

"You have to listen to me!" I roared in her ear. "I can explain everything!"

"Any diplomat can explain anything!" she shouted back.

"Look, Gail, you're hanging an innocent man!" I yelled back at her. "I'm entitled to a fair trial!"

Somebody on the platform began firing his pistol within inches of the loud-speakers and it sounded like an H-bomb going off. She grabbed my wrist and dragged me toward a door under the platform.

"Down here!" she yelled. "And this better be good, Mr. Silk!"

We went down a spiral ramp, lighted by widely-scattered overhead lights.

"Space-attack shelter," she explained. "And

look: what goes on in space-ships is one thing, but it's as much as a girl's reputation is worth to come down here during a barbecue."

There seemed to be quite few girls at that barbecue who didn't care what happened to their reputations. We discovered that after looking into a couple of passageways that branched off the entrance.

"Over this way," Gail said, "Confederate Courts Building. There won't be anything going on over here, now."

I told her, with as much humorous detail as possible, about how Thrombley had shanghaied me to the Embassy, and about the chase by the Rangers. Before I was half through, she was laughing heartily, all traces of her anger gone. Finally, we came to a stairway, and at the head of it to a small door.

"It's been four years that I've been away from here," she said. "I think there's a reading room of the Law Library up here. Let's go in and enjoy the quiet for a while."

But when we opened the door, there was a Ranger standing inside.

"Come to see a trial, Mr. Silk? Oh, hello, Gail. Just in time; they're going to prepare for the next trial."

As he spoke, something clicked at the door. Gail looked at me in consternation.

"Now we're locked in," she said. We can't get out till the trial's over."

CHAPTER V

I LOOKED AROUND.

We were on a high balcony, at the end of a long, narrow room. In front of us, windows rose to the ceiling, and it was evident that the floor of the room was about twenty feet below ground level. Outside, I could see the barbecue still going on, but not a murmur of noise penetrated to us. What seemed to be the judge's bench was against the outside wall, under the tall windows. To the right of it was a railed stand with a chair in it, and in front, arranged in U-shape, were three tables at which a number of men were hastily conferring. There were nine judges in a row on the bench, all in black gowns. The spectators' seats below were filled with people, and there were quite a few up here on the balcony.

"What is this? Supreme Court?" I asked as Gail piloted me to a couple of seats where we could be alone.

"No, Court of Political Justice," she told me. "This is the court that's going to try those three Bonney brothers, who killed Mr. Cumshaw."

It suddenly occurred to me that this was the first time I had heard anything specific about the death of my predecessor.

"That isn't the trial that's going on now, I hope?"

"Oh, no; that won't be for a couple of days. Not till after you can arrange to attend. I don't know what this trial is. I only got home today, myself."

"What's the procedure here?" I wanted to know.

"Well, those nine men are judges," she began. "The one in the middle is President Judge Nelson. You've met his son—the Ranger officer who chased you from the spaceport. He's a regular jurist. The other eight are prominent citizens who are drawn from a panel, like a jury. The men at the table on the left are the prosecution: friends of the politician who was killed. And the ones on the right are the defense: they'll try to prove that the dead man got what was coming to him. The ones in the middle are friends of the court: they're just anybody who has any interest in the case—people who want to get some point of law cleared up, or see some precedent established, or something like that."

"You seem to assume that this is a homicide case," I mentioned.

"They generally are. Sometimes mayhem, or wounding, or simple assault, but—"

There had been some sort of conference going on in the open space of floor between the judges' bench and the three tables. It broke up, now, and the judge in the middle rapped with his gavel.

"Are you gentlemen ready?" he asked. "All right, then. Court of Political Justice of the Confederate Continents of New Texas is now in session. Case of the friends of S. Austin Maverick, deceased, late of James Bowie Continent, versus Wilbur Whately."

"My God, did somebody finally kill Aus Maverick?" Gail whispered.

On the center table, in front of the friends of the court, both sides seemed to have piled their exhibits; among the litter I saw some torn clothing, a big white sombrero covered with blood, and a long machete.

"The general nature of the case," the judge was saying, "is that the defendant, Wilbur Whately, of Sam Houston Continent, is here charged with divers offenses arising from the death of the Honorable S. Austin Maverick, whom he killed on the front steps of the Legislative Assembly Building, here in New Austin . . ."

What goes on here? I thought angrily. This is the rankest instance of a pre-judged case I've ever seen. I started to say as much to Gail, but she hushed me.

"I want to hear the specifications," she said.

A man at the prosecution table had risen.

"Please the court," he began, "the defendant, Wilbur Whately, is here charged with political irresponsibility and excessive atrocity in exercising his constitutional right of criticism of a practicing politician.

"The specifications are, as follows: That, on the afternoon of May Seventh, Anno Domini 2193, the defendant here present did arm himself with a machete, said machete not being one of his normal and accustomed weapons, and did loiter in wait on the front steps of the Legislative Assembly Building in the city of New Austin, Continent of

Sam Houston, and did approach the decedent, addressing him in abusive, obscene, and indecent language, and did set upon and attack him with the machete aforesaid, causing the said decedent, S. Austin Maverick, to die."

The court wanted to know how the defendant would plead. Somebody, without bothering to rise, said, "Not guilty, Your Honor," from the defense table.

There was a brief scraping of chairs; four of five men from the defense and the prosecution tables got up and advanced to confer in front of the bench, comparing sheets of paper. The man who had read the charges, obviously the chief prosecutor, made himself the spokesman.

"Your Honor, defense and prosecution wish to enter the following stipulations: That the decedent was a practicing politician within the meaning of the Constitution, that he met his death in the manner stated in the coroner's report, and that he was killed by the defendant, Wilbur Whately."

"Is that agreeable to you, Mr. Vincent?" the judge wanted to know.

The defense answered affirmatively. I sat back, gaping like a fool. Why, that was practically—no, it *was*—a confession.

"All right, gentlemen," the judge said. "Now we have all that out of the way, let's get on with the case."

As though there were any case to get on with! I fully expected them to take it on from there in song, words by Gilbert and music by Sullivan.

"Well, Your Honor, we have a number of character witnesses," the prosecution—prosecution, for God's sake!—announced.

"Skip them," the defense said. "We stipulate."

"But you can't stipulate character testimony," the prosecution argued. "You don't know what our witnesses are going to testify to."

"Sure we do: they're going to give us a big long shaggy-dog story about the Life and Miracles of Saint Austin Maverick. We'll agree in advance to all that; this case is concerned only with his record as a politician. And as he spent the last fifteen years in the Senate, that's all a matter of public record. I assume that the prosecution is going to introduce all that, too?"

"Well, naturally . . ." the prosecutor began.

"Including his public acts on the last day of his life?" the counsel for the defense demanded. "His actions on the morning of May seventh as chairman of the Finance and Revenue Committee? You going to introduce that as evidence for the prosecution?"

"Well, now . . ." the prosecutor began.

"Your Honor, we ask to have a certified copy of the proceedings of the Senate Finance and Revenue Committee for the morning of May Seventh, 2193, read into the record of this court," the counsel for the defense said. "And thereafter, we rest our case."

"Has the prosecution anything to say before we close the court?" Judge Nelson inquired.

"Well, Your Honor, this seems . . . that is, we ought to hear both sides of it. My old friend, Aus Maverick, was really a fine man; he did a lot of good for the people of his continent . . ."

"Yeah, we'd of lynched him, when he got back, if somebody hadn't chopped him up here in New Austin!" a voice from the rear of the courtroom broke in.

The prosecution hemmed and hawed for a moment, and then announced, in a hasty mumble, that it rested.

"I will now close the court," Judge Nelson said. "I advise everybody to keep your seats. I don't think it's going to be closed very long."

And then, he actually closed the court; pressing a button on the bench, he raised a high black screen in front of him and his colleagues. It stayed up for some sixty seconds, and then dropped again.

"The Court of Political Justice has reached a verdict," he announced. "Wilbur Whately, and your attorney, approach and hear the verdict."

The defense lawyer motioned a young man who had been sitting beside him to rise. In the silence that had fallen, I could hear the defendant's boots squeaking as he went forward to hear his fate. The judge picked up a belt and a pair of pistols that had been lying in front of him.

"Wilbur Whately," he began, "this court is proud to announce that you have been unanimously acquitted of the charge of political irresponsibility, and of unjustified and excessive atrocity.

"There was one dissenting vote on acquitting you of the charge of political irresponsibility; one of the associate judges felt that the late unmitigated scoundrel, Austin Maverick, ought to have been skinned alive, an inch at a time. You are, however, acquitted of that charge, too.

"You all know," he continued, addressing the entire assemblage, "the reason for which this young hero cut down that monster of political iniquity, S. Austin Maverick. On the very morning of his justly-merited death, Austin Maverick, using the powers of his political influence, rammed through the Finance and Revenue Committee a bill entitled 'An Act for the Taxing of Personal Incomes, and for the Levying of a Withholding Tax.' Fellow citizens, words fail me to express my horror of this diabolic proposition, this proposed instrument of tyrannical extortion, borrowed from the Dark Ages of the Twentieth Century! Why, if this young nobleman had not taken his blade in hand, I'd have killed the sonofabitch, myself!''

He leaned forward, extending the belt and holsters to the defendant.

''I therefore restore to you your weapons, taken from you when, in compliance with the law, you were formally arrested. Buckle them on, and, assuming your weapons again, go forth from this court a free man, Wilbur Whately. And take with you that machete with which you vindicated the liberties and rights of all New Texans. Bear it reverently to your home, hang it among your lares and penates, cherish it, and dying, mention it within your will, bequeathing it as a rich legacy unto your issue! Court adjourned; next session 0900 tomorrow. For Chrissake, let's get out of here before the barbecue's over!''

Some of the spectators, drooling for barbecued supercow, began crowding and jostling toward the exits; more of them were pushing to the front of the courtroom, cheering and waving their hipflasks. The prosecution and about half of the friends of the court hastily left by a side door, probably to issue statements disassociating themselves from the deceased Maverick.

''So that's the court that's going to try the men

who killed Ambassador Cumshaw," I commented, as Gail and I went out. "Why, the purpose
of that court seems to be to acquit murderers."

"Murderers?" She was indignant. "That wasn't
murder. He just killed a politician. All the court
could do was determine whether or not the politician needed it, and while I never heard about
Maverick's income-tax proposition, I can't see
how they could have brought in any other kind of
a verdict. Of all the outrageous things!"

I was thoughtfully silent as we went out into the
plaza, which was still a riot of noise and poly-
chromatic costumes. And my thoughts were as
weltered as the scene before me.

Apparently, on New Texas, killing a politician
wasn't regarded as *mallum in se*, and was *mallum
prohibitorum* only to the extent that what happened to the politician was in excess of what he
deserved. I began to understand why Palme was
such a scared rabbit, why Hutchinson had that
hunted look and kept his hands always within
inches of his pistols.

I began to feel more pity than contempt for
Thrombley, too. *He's been on this planet too long
and he should never have been sent here in the
first place. I'll rotate him home as soon as possible. . . .*

Then the full meaning of what I had seen finally
got through to me: if they were going to try the
killers of Cumshaw in that court, that meant that
on New Texas, foreign diplomats were regarded
as practicing politicians . . .

That made me a practicing politician too!

And that's why, when we got back to the vicin-

ity of the bandstand, I had my right hand close to
my pistol, with my thumb on the inconspicuous
little spot of silver inlay that operated the secret
holster mechanism.

I saw Hutchinson and Palme and Thrombley
ahead. With them was a newcomer, a portly,
ruddy-faced gentleman with a white mustache
and goatee, dressed in a white suit. Gail broke
away from me and ran toward him. This, I
thought, would be her father; now I would be
introduced and find out just what her last name
was. I followed, more slowly, and saw a waiter,
with a wheeled serving-table, move in behind the
group which she had joined.

So I saw what none of them did—the waiter
suddenly reversed his long carving-knife and
poised himself for a blow at President Hutchinson's back. I simply pressed the little silver stud
on my belt, the Krupp-Tatta popped obediently
out of the holster into my open hand. I thumbed
off the safety and swung up; when my sights
closed on the rising hand that held the knife, I
fired.

Hoddy Ringo, who had been holding a
sandwich, with one hand and a drink with the
other, dropped both and jumped on the man
whose hand I had smashed. A couple of Rangers
closed in and grabbed him, also. The group
around President Hutchinson had all turned and
were staring from me to the man I had shot, and
from him to the knife with the broken handle,
lying on the ground.

Hutchinson spoke first. "Well, Mr. Ambassador! My Government thanks your Government!
That was nice shooting!"

"Hey, you been holdin' out on me!" Hoddy accused. "I never knew you was that kinda gun-fighter!"

"There's a new wrinkle," the man with the white goatee said. "We'll have to screen the help at these affairs a little more closely." He turned to me. "Mr. Ambassador, New Texas owes you a great deal for saving the President's life. If you'll get that pistol out of your hand, I'd be proud to shake it, sir."

I holstered my automatic, and took his hand. Gail was saying, "Stephen, this is my father," and at the same time, Palme, the Secretary of State, was doing it more formally:

"Ambassador Silk, may I present one of our leading citizens and large ranchers, Colonel Andrew Jackson Hickock."

Dumbarton Oaks had taught me how to maintain the proper diplomat's unchanging expression; drinking superbourbon had been a post-graduate course. I needed that training as I finally learned Gail's last name.

CHAPTER VI

IT WAS early evening before we finally managed to get away from the barbecue. Thrombley had called the Embassy and told them not to wait dinner for us, so the staff had finished eating and were relaxing in the patio when our car came in through the street gate. Stonehenge and another man came over to meet us as we got out—a man I hadn't met before.

He was a little fellow, half-Latin, half-Oriental; in New Texas costume and wearing a pair of pistols like mine, in State Department Special Services holsters. He didn't look like a Dumbarton Oaks product: I thought he was more likely an alumnus of some private detective agency.

"Mr. Francisco Parros, our Intelligence man," Stonehenge introduced him.

"Sorry I wasn't here when you arrived, Mr. Silk," Parros said. "Out checking on some things. But I saw that bit of shooting, on the telecast screen in a bar over town. You know, there was a camera right over the bandstand that caught the whole thing—you and Miss Hickock coming toward the President and his party, Miss Hickock running forward to her father, the waiter going up behind Hutchinson with the knife, and then that beautiful draw and snap shot. They ran it again a couple of times on the half-hourly newscast. Everybody in New Austin, maybe on New Texas, is talking about it, now.''

"Yes, indeed, sir," Gomez, the Embassy Secretary, said, joining us. "You've made yourself more popular in the eight hours since you landed than poor Mr. Cumshaw had been able to do in the ten years he spent here. But, I'm afraid, sir, you've given me a good deal of work, answering your fan-mail.''

We went over and sat down at one of the big tables under the arches at the side of the patio.

"Well, that's all to the good," I said. "I'm going to need a lot of local good will, in the next few weeks. No thanks, Mr. Parros," I added, as the Intelligence man picked up a bottle and made to pour for me. "I've been practically swimming in superbourbon all afternoon. A little black coffee, if you don't mind. And now, gentlemen, if you'll all be seated, we'll see what has to be done.''

"A council of war, in effect, Mr. Ambassador?" Stonehenge inquired.

"Let's call it a council to estimate the situation. But I'll have to find out from you first exactly what the situation here is.''

Thrombley stirred uneasily. "But sir, I confess that I don't understand. Your briefing on Luna . . .''

"Was practically nonexistent. I had a total of six hours to get aboard ship, from the moment I was notified that I had been appointed to this Embassy.''

"Incredible!" Thrombley murmured.

I wondered what he'd say if I told him that I thought it was deliberate.

"Naturally, I spent some time on the ship reading up on this planet, but I know practically nothing about what's been going on here in, say, the last year. And all I know about the death of Mr. Cumshaw is that he is said to have been killed by three brothers named Bonney."

"So you'll want just about everything, Mr. Silk," Thrombley said. "Really, I don't know where to begin."

"Start with why and how Mr. Cumshaw was killed. The rest, I believe, will key into that."

So they began; Thrombley, Stonehenge and Parros doing the talking. It came to this:

Ever since we had first established an Embassy on New Texas, the goal of our diplomacy on this planet had been to secure it into the Solar League. And it was a goal which seemed very little closer to realization now than it had been twenty-three years before.

"You must know, by now, what politics on this planet are like, Mr. Silk," Thrombley said.

"I have an idea. One Ambassador gone native, another gone crazy, the third killed himself, the fourth murdered."

"Yes, indeed. I've been here fifteen years, myself . . ."

"That's entirely too long for anybody to be stationed in this place," I told him. "If I'm not murdered, myself, in the next couple of weeks, I'm going to see that you and any other member of this staff who's been here over ten years are rotated home for a tour of duty at Department Headquarters."

"Oh, would you, Mr. Silk? I would be so happy . . ."

Thrombley wasn't much in the way of an ally,

but at least he had a sound, selfish motive for helping me stay alive. I assured him I would get him sent back to Luna, and then went on with the discussion.

Up until six months ago, Silas Cumshaw had modeled himself after the typical New Texas politician. He had always worn at least two faces, and had always managed to place himself on every side of every issue at once. Nothing he ever said could possibly be construed as controversial. Naturally, the cause of New Texan annexation to the Solar League had made no progress whatever.

Then, one evening, at a banquet, he had executed a complete 180-degree turn, delivering a speech in which he proclaimed that union with the Solar League was the only possible way in which New Texans could retain even a vestige of local sovereignty. He had talked about an invasion as though the enemy's ships were already coming out of hyperspace, and had named the invader, calling the z'Srauff "our common enemy." The z'Srauff Ambassador, also present, had immediately gotten up and stalked out, amid a derisive chorus of barking and baying from the New Texans. The New Texans were first shocked and then wildly delighted; they had been so used to hearing nothing but inanities and high-order abstractions from their public figures that the Solar League Ambassador had become a hero overnight.

"Sounds as though there is a really strong sentiment at what used to be called the grass-roots level in favor of annexation," I commented.

"There is," Parros told me. "Of course, there is a very strong isolationist, anti-annexation, sentiment, too. The sentiment in favor of annexation is based on the point Mr. Cumshaw made—the danger of conquest by the z'Srauff. Against that, of course, there is fear of higher taxes, fear of loss of local sovereignty, fear of abrogation of local customs and institutions, and chauvinistic pride."

"We can deal with some of that by furnishing guarantees of local self-government; the emotional objections can be met by convincing them that we need the great planet of New Texas to add glory and luster to the Solar League," I said. "You think, then, that Mr. Cumshaw was assassinated by opponents of annexation?"

"Of course, sir," Thrombley replied. "These Bonneys were only hirelings. Here's what happened, on the day of the murder:

"It was the day after a holiday, a big one here on New Texas, celebrating some military victory by the Texans on Terra, a battle called San Jacinto. We didn't have any business to handle, because all the local officials were home nursing hangovers, so when Colonel Hickock called—"

"Who?" I asked sharply.

"Colonel Hickock. The father of the young lady you were so attentive to at the barbecue. He and Mr. Cumshaw had become great friends, beginning shortly before the speech the Ambassador made at that banquet. He called about 0900, inviting Mr. Cumshaw out to his ranch for the day, and as there was nothing in the way of official business, Mr. Cumshaw said he'd be out by 1030.

"When he got there, there was an aircar circling about, near the ranchhouse. As Mr. Cumshaw got out of his car and started up the front steps, somebody in this car landed it on the driveway and began shooting with a twenty-mm auto-rifle. Mr. Cumshaw was hit several times, and killed instantly."

"The fellows who did the shooting were damned lucky," Stonhenge took over. "Hickock's a big rancher. I don't know how much you know about supercow-ranching, sir, but those things have to be herded with tanks and light aircraft, so that every rancher has at his disposal a fairly good small air-armor combat team. Naturally, all the big ranchers are colonels in the Armed Reserve. Hickock has about fifteen fast fighters, and thirty medium tanks armed with fifty-mm guns. He also has some AA-guns around his ranch house—every once in a while, these ranchers get to squabbling among themselves.

"Well, these three Bonney brothers were just turning away when a burst from the ranch house caught their jet assembly, and they could only get as far as Bonneyville, thirty miles away, before they had to land. They landed right in front of the town jail.

"This Bonneyville's an awful shantytown; everybody in it is related to everybody else. The mayor, for instance, Kettle-Belly Sam Bonney, is an uncle of theirs.

"These three boys—Switchblade Joe Bonney, Jack-High Abe Bonney and Turkey-Buzzard Tom Bonney—immediately claimed sanctuary in the jail, on the grounds that they had been near to—get that; I think that indicates the line they're going to take at the trial—*near* to a political assassination. They were immediately given the protection of the jail, which is about the only well-constructed building in the place, practically a fort."

"You think that was planned in advance?" I asked.

Parros nodded emphatically. "I do. There was a hell of a big gang of these Bonneys at the jail, almost the entire able-bodied population of the place. As soon as Switchblade and Jack-High and Turkey-Buzzard landed, they were rushed inside and all the doors barred. About three minutes later, the Hickock outfit started coming in, first aircraft and then armor. They gave that town a regular Georgie Patton style blitzing."

"Yes. I'm only sorry I wasn't there to see it," Stonehenge put in. "They knocked down or burned most of the shanties, and then they went to work on the jail. The aircraft began dumping these firebombs and stun-bombs that they use to stop supercow stampedes, and the tank-guns began to punch holes in the walls. As soon as Kettle-Belly saw what he had on his hands, he radioed a call for Ranger protection. Our friend Captain Nelson went out to see what the trouble was."

"Yes. I got the story of that from Nelson," Parros put in. "Much as he hated to do it, he had to protect the Bonneys. And as soon as he'd taken a hand, Hickock had to call off his gang. But he was smart. He grabbed everything relating to the killing—the aircar and the twenty-mm auto-rifle in particular—and he's keeping them under cover. Very few people know about that, or about the fact that on physical evidence alone, he has the killing pinned on the Bonneys so well that they'll never get away with this story of being merely innocent witnesses."

"The rest, Mr. Silk, is up to us," Thrombley said. "I have Colonel Hickock's assurance that he will give us every assistance, but we simply must see to it that those creatures with the outlandish names are convicted."

I didn't have a chance to say anything to that: at that moment, one of the servants ushered Captain Nelson toward us.

"Good evening, Captain," I greeted the Ranger. "Join us, seeing that you're on foreign soil and consequently not on duty."

He sat down with us and poured a drink.

"I thought you might be interested," he said. "We gave that waiter a going-over. We wanted to know who put him up to it. He tried to sell us the line that he was a New Texan patriot, trying to kill a tyrant, but we finally got the truth out of him. He was paid a thousand pesos to do the job, by a character they call Snake-Eyes Sam Bonney. A cousin of the three who killed Mr. Cumshaw."

"Nephew of Kettle-Belly Sam," Parros interjected. "You pick him up?"

Nelson shook his head disgustedly. "He's out in the high grass somewhere. We're still looking for him. Oh, yes, and I just heard that the trial of Switchblade, and Jack-High and Turkey-Buzzard is scheduled for three days from now. You'll be notified in due form tomorrow, but I thought you might like to know in advance."

"I certainly do, and thank you, Captain. . . . We were just talking about you when you arrived," I mentioned. "About the arrest, or rescue, or whatever you call it, of that trio."

"Yeah. One of the jobs I'm not particularly proud of. Pity Hickock's boys didn't get hold of them before I got there. It'd of saved everybody a lot of trouble."

"Just what impression did you get at the time, Captain?" I asked. "You think Kettle-Belly knew in advance what they were going to do?"

"Sure he did. They had the whole jail fortified. Not like a jail usually is, to keep people from getting out; but like a fort, to keep people from getting in. There were no prisoners inside. I found out that they had all been released that morning."

He stopped, seemed to be weighing his words, then continued, speaking very slowly.

"Let me tell you first some things I can't testify to, couple of things that I figure went wrong with their plans.

"One of Colonel Hickock's men was on the porch to greet Mr. Cumshaw and he recognized the Bonneys. That was lucky; otherwise we might still be lookin' and wonderin' who did the shootin', which might not have been good for New Texas."

He cocked an eyebrow and I nodded. The Solar League, in similar cases, had regarded such planetary governments as due for change without notice and had promptly made the change.

"Number two," Captain Nelson continued, "that AA-shot which hit their aircar. I don't think they intended to land at the jail—it was just sort of a reserve hiding-hole. But because they'd been hit, they had to land. And they'd been slowed down so much that they couldn't dispose of the evidence before the Colonel's boys were tappin' on the door 'n' askin', couldn't they come in."

"I gather the Colonel's task-force was becoming insistent," I prompted him.

The big Ranger grinned. "Now we're on things I can testify to.

"When I got there, what had been the cell-block was on fire, and they were trying to defend the mayor's office and the warden's office. These Bonneys gave me the line that they'd been witnesses to the killing of Mr. Cumshaw by Colonel Hickock and that the Hickock outfit was trying to rub them out to keep them from testifying. I just laughed and started to walk out. Finally, they confessed that they'd shot Mr. Cumshaw, but they claimed it was right of action against political malfeasance. When they did that, I had to take them in."

"They confessed to you, before you arrested them?" I wanted to be sure of that point.

"That's right. I'm going to testify to that, Monday, when the trial is held. And that ain't all: we got their fingerprints off the car, off the gun, off some shells still in the clip, and we have the gun identified to the shells that killed Mr. Cumshaw. We got their confession fully corroborated."

I asked him if he'd give Mr. Parros a complete statement of what he'd seen and heard at Bonneyville. He was more than willing and I suggested that they go into Parros' office, where they'd be undisturbed. The Ranger and my Intelligence man got up and took a bottle of super-bourbon with them. As they were leaving, Nelson turned to Hoddy, who was still with us.

"You'll have to look to your laurels, Hoddy," Nelson said. "Your Ambassador seems to be making quite a reputation for himself as a gunfighter."

"Look," Hoddy said, and though he was facing Nelson, I felt he was really talking to Stonehenge, "before I'd go up against this guy, I'd shoot myself. That way, I could be sure I'd get a nice painless job."

After they were gone, I turned to Stonehenge and Thrombley. "This seems to be a carefully prearranged killing."

They agreed.

"Then they knew *in advance* that Mr. Cumshaw would be on Colonel Hickock's front steps at about 1030. *How did they find that out?*"

"Why . . . why, I'm sure I don't know," Thrombley said. It was most obvious that the idea had never occurred to him before and a side glance told me that the thought was new to Stonhenge also. "Colonel Hickock called at 0900. Mr. Cumshaw left the Embassy in an aircar a few minutes later. It took an hour and a half to fly out to the Hickock ranch. . . ."

"I don't like the implications, Mr. Silk," Stonehenge said. "I can't believe that was how it happened. In the first place, Colonel Hickock isn't that sort of man: he doesn't use his hospitality to trap people to their death. In the second place, he wouldn't have needed to use people like these Bonneys. His own men would do anything for him. In the third place, he is one of the leaders of the annexation movement here and this was obviously an anti-annexation job. And in the fourth place—"

"Hold it!" I checked him. "Are you sure he's really on the annexation side?"

He opened his mouth to answer me quickly, then closed it, waited a moment, answered me slowly. "I can guess what you are thinking, Mr. Silk. But, remember, when Colonel Hickock came here as our first Ambassador, he came here as a man with a mission. He had studied the problem and he believed in what he came for. He has never changed.

"Let me emphasize this, sir: *we* know he has never changed. For our own protection, we've had to check on every real leader of the annexation movement, screening them for crackpots who might do us more harm than good. The Colonel is with us all the way.

"And now, in the fourth place, underlined by what I've just said, the Colonel and Mr. Cumshaw were really friends."

"Now you're talking!" Hoddy burst in. "I've knowed A. J. ever since I was a kid. Ever since he married old Colonel MacTodd's daughter. That just ain't the way A. J. works!"

"On the other hand, Mr. Ambassador," Thrombley said, keeping his gaze fixed on Hoddy's hands and apparently ready to both duck and shut up if Hoddy moved a finger, "you will recall, I think, that Colonel Hickock did do everything in his power to see that these Bonney brothers did not reach court alive. And, let me add," he was getting bolder, tilting his chin up a little, "it's a choice as simple as this: either Colonel Hickock told them, or we have—and this is unbelievable—a traitor in the Embassy itself."

That statement rocked even Hoddy. Even

though he was probably no more than one of Natalenko's little men, he still couldn't help knowing how thoroughly we were screened, indoctrinated, and—let's face it—mind-conditioned. A traitor among us was unthinkable because we just couldn't think that way.

The silence, the sorrow, were palpable. Then I remembered, told them, Hickock himself had been a Department man.

Stonehenge gripped his head between his hands and squeezed as if trying to bring out an idea. "All right, Mr. Ambassador, where are we now? Nobody who knew could have told the Bonney boys where Mr. Cumshaw would be at 1030, yet the three men were there waiting for him. You take it from there. I'm just a simple military man and I'm ready to go back to the simple military life as soon as possible."

I turned to Gomez. "There could be an obvious explanation. Bring us the official telescreen log. Let's see what calls were made. Maybe Mr. Cumshaw himself said something to someone that gave his destination away."

"That won't be necessary," Thrombley told me. "None of the junior clerks were on duty, and I took the only three calls that came in, myself. First, there was the call from Colonel Hickock. Then, the call about the wrist watch. And then, a couple of hours later, the call from the Hickock ranch, about Mr. Cumshaw's death."

"What was the call about the wrist watch?" I asked.

"Oh, that was from the z'Srauff Embassy," Thrombley said. "For some time, Mr. Cumshaw had been trying to get one of the very precise watches which the z'Srauff manufacture on their home planet. The z'Srauff Ambassador called, that day, to tell him that they had one for him and wanted to know when it was to be delivered. I told them the Ambassador was out, and they wanted to know where they could call him and I—"

I had never seen a man look more horror-stricken.

"Oh, my God! I'm the one who told them!"

What could I say? Not much, but I tried. "How could you know, Mr. Thrombley? You did the natural, the normal, the proper thing, on a call from one Ambassador to another."

I turned to the others, who, like me, preferred not to look at Thrombley. "They must have had a spy outside who told them the Ambassador had left the Embassy. Alone, right? And that was just what they'd been waiting for.

"But what's this about the watch, though. There's more to this than a simple favor from one Ambassador to another."

"My turn, Mr. Ambassador," Stonehenge interrupted. "Mr. Cumshaw had been trying to get one of the things at my insistence. Naval Intelligence is very much interested in them and we want a sample. The z'Srauff watches are very peculiar—they're operated by radium decay, which, of course is a universal constant. They're uniform to a tenth second and they're all synchronized with the official time at the capital city of the principal z'Srauff planet. The time used by the z'Srauff Navy."

Stonehenge deliberately paused, let that last phrase hang heavily in the air for a moment, then he continued.

"They're supposed to be used in religious observances—timing hours of prayer, I believe. They can, of course, have other uses.

"For example, I can imagine all those watches giving the wearer a light electric shock, or ringing a little bell, all over New Texas, at exactly the same moment. And then I can imagine all the z'Srauff running down into nice deep holes in the ground."

He looked at his own watch. "And that reminds me: my gang of pirates are at the spaceport by now, ready to blast off. I wonder if someone could drive me there."

"I'll drive him, boss," Hoddy volunteered. "I ain't doin' nothin' else."

I was wondering how I could break that up, plausibly and without betraying my suspicions, when Parros and Captain Nelson came out and joined us.

"I have a lot of stuff here," Parros said. "Stuff we never seemed to have noticed. For instance—"

I interrupted. "Commander Stonehenge's going to the spaceport, now," I said. "Suppose you ride with him, and brief him on what you learned, on the way. Then, when he's aboard, come back and tell us."

Hoddy looked at me for a long ten seconds. His expression started by being exasperated and ended by betraying grudging admiration.

CHAPTER VII

THE next morning, which was Saturday, I put Thrombley in charge of the routine work of the Embassy, but first instructed him to answer all inquiries about me with the statement, literally true, that I was too immersed in work of clearing up matters left unfinished after the death of the former Ambassador for any social activities. Then I called the Hickock ranch in the west end of Sam Houston Continent, mentioning an invitation the Colonel and his daughter had extended me, and told them I would be out to see them before noon that same day. With Hoddy Ringo driving the car, I arrived about 1000, and was welcomed by Gail and her father, who had flown out the evening before, after the barbecue.

Hoddy, accompanied by a Ranger and one of Hickock's ranch hands, all three disguised in shabby and grease-stained cast-offs borrowed at the ranch, and driving a dilapidated aircar from the ranch junkyard, were sent to visit the slum village of Bonneyville. They spent all day there, posing as a trio of range tramps out of favor with the law.

I spent the day with Gail, flying over the range, visiting Hickock's herd camps and slaughtering crews. It was a pleasant day and I managed to make it constructive as well.

Because of their huge size—they ran to a live weight of around fifteen tons—and their uncertain disposition, supercows are not really domesticated. Each rancher owned the herds on his own land, chiefly by virtue of constant watchfulness over them. There were always a couple of helicopters hovering over each herd, with fast fighter planes waiting on call to come in and drop firebombs or stun-bombs in front of them if they showed a disposition to wander too far. Naturally, things of this size could not be shipped live to the market; they were butchered on the range, and the meat hauled out in big 'copter-trucks.

Slaughtering was dangerous and exciting work. It was done with medium tanks mounting fifty-mm guns, usually working at the rear of the herd, although a supercow herd could change directions almost in a second and the killing-tanks would then find themselves in front of a stampede. I saw several such incidents. Once Gail and I had to dive in with our car and help turn such a stampede.

We got back to the ranch house shortly before dinner. Gail went at once to change clothes; Colonel Hickock and I sat down together for a drink in his library, a beautiful room. I especially admired the walls, panelled in plastic-hardened supercow-leather.

"What do you think of our planet now, Mr. Silk?" Colonel Hickock asked.

"Well, Colonel, your final message to the State was part of the briefing I received," I replied. "I must say that I agree with your opinions. Espe-

cially with your opinion of local political practices. Politics is nothing, here, if not exciting and
exacting."

"You don't understand it though." That was
about half-question and half-statement. "Particularly our custom of using politicians as clay pi-
geons."

"Well, it is rather unusual. . . ."

"Yes." The dryness in his tone was a paragraph
of comment on my understatement. "And it's
fundamental to our system of government.

"You were out all afternoon with Gail; you saw
how we have to handle the supercow herds. Well,
it is upon the fact that every rancher must have at
his disposal a powerful force of aircraft and armor, easily convertible to military uses, that our
political freedom rests. You see, our government
is, in effect, an oligarchy of the big landowners
and ranchers, who, in combination, have enough
military power to overturn any Planetary government overnight. And, on the local level, it is a
paternalistic feudalism.

"That's something that would have stood the
hair of any Twentieth Century 'Liberal' on end.
And it gives us the freest government anywhere in
the galaxy.

"There were a number of occasions, much less
frequent now than formerly, when coalitions of
big ranches combined their strength and marched
on the Planetary government to protect their
rights from government encroachment. This sort
of thing could only be resorted to in defense of
some inherent right, and never to infringe on the
rights of others. Because, in the latter case, other
armed coalitions would have arisen, as they did

once or twice during the first three decades of New Texan history, to resist.

"So the right of armed intervention by the people when the government invaded or threatened their rights became an acknowledged part of our political system.

"And—this arises as a natural consequence— you can't give a man with five hundred employees and a force ot tanks and aircraft the right to resist the government, then at the same time deny that right to a man who has only his own pistol or machete."

"I notice the President and the other officials have themselves surrounded by guards to protect them from individual attack," I said. "Why doesn't the government, as such, protect itself with an army and air force large enough to resist any possible coalition of the big ranchers?"

"Because we won't let the government get that strong!" the Colonel said forcefully. "That's one of the basic premises. We have no standing army, only the New Texas Rangers. And the legislature won't authorize any standing army, or appropriate funds to support one. Any member of the legislature who tried it would get what Austin Maverick got, a couple of weeks ago, or what Sam Saltkin got, eight years ago, when he proposed a law for the compulsory registration and licensing of firearms. The opposition to that tax scheme of Maverick's wasn't because of what it would cost the public in taxes, but from fear of what the government could do with the money after they got it.

"Keep a government poor and weak and it's your servant; let it get rich and powerful and it's

your master. We don't want any masters here on
New Texas."

"But the President has a bodyguard," I noted.

"Casualty rate was too high," Hickock explained. "Remember, the President's job is in-
herently impossible: he has to represent *all* the
people."

I thought that over, could see the illogical logic,
but . . . "How about your rancher oligarchy?"

He laughed. "Son, if I started acting like a master around this ranch in the morning, they'd find
my body in an irrigation ditch before sunset.

"Sure, if you have a real army, you can keep the
men under your thumb—use one regiment or one
division to put down mutiny in another. But
when you have only five hundred men, all of
whom know everybody else and all of them
armed, you just act real considerate of them if you
want to keep on living."

"Then would you say that the opposition to
annexation comes from the people who are afraid
that if New Texas enters the Solar League, there
will be League troops sent here and this . . . this
interesting system of insuring government responsibility to the public would be brought to an
end?"

"Yes. If you can show the people of this planet
that the League won't interfere with local political
practices, you'll have a 99.95 percent majority in
favor of annexation. We're too close to the z'Srauff
star-cluster, out here, not to see the benefits of
joining the Solar League."

We left the Hickock ranch on Sunday afternoon
and while Hoddy guided our air-car back to New
Austin, I had a little time to revise some of my

ideas about New Texas. That is, I had time to think during those few moments when Hoddy wasn't taking advantage of our diplomatic immunity to invent new air-ground traffic laws.

My thoughts alternated between the pleasure of remembering Gail's gay company and the gloom of understanding the complete implications of the Colonel's clarifying lectures. Against the background of his remarks, I could find myself appreciating the Ghopal-Klüng-Natalenko reasoning: the only way to cut the Gordian knot was to have another Solar League Ambassador killed.

And, whenever I could escape thinking about the fact that the next Ambassador to be the clay pigeon was me, I found myself wondering if I wanted the League to take over. Annexation, yes; New Texas customs would be protected under a treaty of annexation. But the "justified conquest" urged by Machiavelli, Jr.? No.

I was still struggling with the problem when we reached the Embassy about 1700. Everyone was there, including Stonehenge, who had returned two hours earlier with the good news that the fleet had moved into position only sixty light-minutes off Capella IV. I had reached the point in my thinking where I had decided it was useless to keep Hoddy and Stonehenge apart except as an exercise in mental agility. Inasmuch as my brain was already weight-lifting, swinging from a flying trapeze to elusive flying rings while doing triple somersaults and at the same time juggling seven Indian clubs, I skipped the whole matter.

But I'm fairly certain that it wasn't till then that Hoddy had a chance to deliver his letter-of-credence to Stonehenge.

After dinner, we gathered in my office for our coffee and a final conference before the opening of the trial the next morning.

Stonehenge spoke first, looking around the table at everyone except me.

"No matter what happens, we have the fleet within call. Sir Rodney's been active picking up those z'Srauff meteor-mining boats. They no longer have a tight screen around the system. We do. I don't think that anyone, except us, knows that the fleet's where it is."

No matter what happens, I thought glumly, and the phrase explained why he hadn't been able to look at me.

"Well, boss, I gave you my end of it, comin' in," Hoddy said. "Want me to go over it again? All right. In Bonneyville, we found half a dozen people who can swear that Kettle-Belly Sam Bonney was making preparations to protect those three brothers an hour before Ambassador Cumshaw was shot. The whole town's sorer than hell at Kettle-Belly for antagonizing the Hickock outfit and getting the place shot up the way it was. And we have witnesses that Kettle-Belly was in some kind of deal with the z'Srauff, too. The Rangers gathered up eight of them, who can swear to the preparations and to the fact that Kettle-Belly had z'Srauff visitors on different occasions before the shooting."

"That's what we want," Stonehenge said. "Something that'll connect this murder with the z'Srauff."

"Well, wait till you hear what I've got," Parros told him. "In the first place, we traced the gun and the air-car. The Bonney brothers bought them both from z'Srauff merchants, for ridiculously nominal prices. The merchant who sold the air-car is normally in the dry-goods business, and the one who sold the auto-rifle runs a toy shop. In their whole lives, those three boys never had enough money among them to pay the list price of the gun, let alone the car. That is, not until a week before the murder."

"They got prosperous, all of a sudden?" I asked.

"Yes. Two weeks before the shooting, Kettle-Belly Sam's bank account got a sudden transfusion: some anonymous benefactor deposited 250,000 pesos—about a hundred thousand dollars—to his credit. He drew out 75,000 of it and some of the money turned up again in the hands of Switchblade and Jack-High and Turkey-Buzzard. Then, a week before you landed here, he got another hundred thousand from the same anonymous source and he drew out twenty thousand of that. We think that was the money that went to pay for the attempted knife-job on Hutchinson. Two days before the barbecue, the waiter deposited a thousand at the New Austin Packers' and Shippers' Trust."

"Can you get that introduced as evidence at the trial?" I asked.

"Sure. Kettle-Belly banks at a town called Crooked Creek, about forty miles from Bonneyville. We have witnesses from the bank.

"I also got the dope on the line the Bonney brothers are going to take at the trial. They have a lawyer, Clement A. Sidney, a member of what passes for the Socialist Party on this planet. The defense will take the line of full denial of everything. The Bonneys are just three poor but honest boys who are being framed by the corrupt tools of the Big Ranching Interests."

Hoddy made an impolite noise. "Whatta we got to worry about, then?" he demanded. "They're a cinch for conviction."

"I agree with that," Stonehenge said. "If they tried to base their defense on political conviction and opposition by the Solar League, they might have a chance. This way, they haven't."

"All right, gentlemen," I said, "I take it that we're agreed that we must all follow a single line of policy and not work at cross-purposes to each other?"

They all agreed to that instantly, but with a questioning note in their voices.

"Well, then, I trust you all realize that we cannot, under any circumstances, allow those three brothers to be convicted in this court," I added.

There was a moment of startled silence, while Hoddy and Stonehenge and Parros and Thrombley were understanding what they had just heard. Then Stonehenge cleared his throat and said:

"Mr. Ambassador! I'm sure that you have some excellent reasons for that remarkable statement, but I must say—"

"It was a really colossal error on somebody's part," I said, "that this case was allowed to get into the Court of Political Justice. It never should have. And if we take a part in the prosecution, or allow those men to be convicted, we will establish a precedent to support the principle that a foreign Ambassador is, on this planet, defined as a practicing local politician.

"I will invite you to digest that for a moment."

A moment was all they needed. Thrombley was horrified and dithered incoherently. Stonehenge frowned and fidgeted with some papers in front of him. I could see several thoughts gathering behind his eyes, including, I was sure, a new view of his instructions from Klüng.

Even Hoddy got at least part of it. "Why, that means that anybody can bump off any diplomat he doesn't like. . . ." he began.

"That is only part of it, Mr. Ringo," Thrombley told him. "It also means that a diplomat, instead of being regarded as the representative of his own government, becomes, in effect, a functionary of the government of New Texas.Why, all sorts of complications could arise. . . ."

"It certainly would impair, shall we say, the principle of extraterritoriality of Embassies," Stonehenge picked it up. "And it would practically destroy the principle of diplomatic immunity."

"Migawd!" Hoddy looked around nervously, as though he could already hear an army of New Texas Rangers, each with a warrant for Hoddy Ringo, battering at the gates.

"We'll have to do something!" Gomez, the Secretary of the Embassy, said.

"I don't know what," Stonehenge said. "The obvious solution would be, of course, to bring charges against those Bonney Boys on simple first-degree murder, which would be tried in an ordinary criminal court. But it's too late for that now. We wouldn't have time to prevent their being arraigned in this Political Justice court, and once a defendant is brought into court, on this planet, he cannot be brought into court again for the same act. Not the same *crime*, the same *act*."

I had been thinking about this and I was ready. "Look, we *must* bring those Bonney brothers to trial. It's the only effective way of demonstrating to the public the simple fact that Ambassador Cumshaw was murdered at the instigation of the z'Srauff. We dare not allow them to be convicted in the Court of Political Justice, for the reasons already stated. And to maintain the prestige of the Solar League, we dare not allow them to go unpunished."

"We can have it one way," Parros said, "and maybe we can have it two ways. But I'm damned if I can see how we can have it all three ways."

I wasn't surprised that he didn't see it; he hadn't had the same urgency goading him which had forced me to find the answer. It wasn't an answer that I liked, but I was in the position where I had no choice.

"Well, here's what we have to do, gentlemen," I began, and from the respectful way they regarded me, from the attention they were giving my words, I got a sudden thrill of pride. For the first time since my scrambled arrival, I was really *Ambassador* Stephen Silk.

CHAPTER VIII

A COUPLE of New Texas Ranger tanks met the Embassy car four blocks from the Statehouse and convoyed us into the central plaza, where the barbecue had been held on the Friday afternoon that I had arrived on New Texas. There was almost as dense a crowd as the last time I had seen the place; but they were quieter, to the extent that there were no bands, and no shooting, no cowbells or whistles. The barbecue pits were going again, however, and hawkers were pushing or propelling their little wagons about, vending sandwiches. I saw a half a dozen big twenty-foot teleview screens, apparently wired from the courtroom.

As soon as the Embassy car and its escorting tanks reached the plaza, an ovation broke out. I was cheered, with the high-pitched *yipeee!* of New Texans and adjured and implored not to let them so-and-sos get away with it.

There was a veritable army of Rangers on guard at the doors of the courtroom. The only spectators being admitted to the courtroom seemed to be prominent citizens with enough pull to secure passes.

Inside, some of the spectators' benches had been removed to clear the front of the room. In the cleared space, there was one bulky shape under a cloth cover that seemed to be the air-car and another cloth-covered shape that looked like a fifty-mm dual-purpose gun. Smaller exhibits, including a twenty-mm auto-rifle, were piled on the friends-of-the-court table. The prosecution table was already occupied—Colonel Hickock, who waved a greeting to me, three or four men who looked like well-to-do ranchers, and a delegation of lawyers.

"Samuel Goodham," Parros, beside me, whispered, indicating a big, heavy-set man with white hair, dressed in a dark suit of the cut that had been fashionable on Terra seventy-five years ago. "Best criminal lawyer on the planet. Hickock must have hired him."

There was quite a swarm at the center table, too. Some of them were ranchers, a couple in aggressively shabby workclothes, and there were several members of the Diplomatic Corps. I shook hands with them and gathered that they, like myself, were worried about the precedent that might be established by this trial. While I was introducing Hoddy Ringo as my attaché extraordinary, which was no less than the truth, the defense party came in.

There were only three lawyers—a little, rodent-faced fellow, whom Parros pointed out as Clement Sidney, and two assistants. And, guarded by a Ranger and a couple of court-bailiffs, the three defendants, Switchblade Joe, Jack-High Abe and Turkey-Buzzard Tom Bonney. There was probably a year or so age different from one to another, but they certainly had a common parentage. They all had pale eyes and narrow, loose-

lipped faces. Subnormal and probably psy-
chopathic, I thought. Jack-High Abe had his
left arm in a sling and his left shoulder in a plaster
cast. The buzz of conversation among the spectators altered its tone subtly and took on a note of
hostility as they entered and seated themselves.

The balcony seemed to be crowded with press
representatives. Several telecast cameras and
sound pickups had been rigged to cover the front
of the room from various angles, a feature that had
been missing from the trial I had seen with Gail on
Friday.

Then the judges entered from a door behind the
bench, which must have opened from a passage-
way under the plaza, and the court was called to
order.

The President Judge was the same Nelson who
had presided at the Whately trial and the first
thing on the agenda seemed to be the selection of a
new board of associate judges. Parros explained
in a whisper that the board which had served on
the previous trial would sit until that could be
done.

A slip of paper was drawn from a box and a
name was called. A man sitting on one of the front
rows of spectators' seats got up and came forward.
One of Sidney's assistants rummaged through a
card file he had in front of him and handed a card
to the chief of the defense. At once, Sidney was on
his feet.

"Challenged, for cause!" he called out. "This
man is known to have declared, in conversation at
the bar of the Silver Peso Saloon, here in New
Austin, that these three boys, my clients, ought all
to be hanged higher than Haman."

"Yes, I said that!" the venireman declared. "I'll repeat it right here: all three of these murdering skunks ought to be hanged higher than—"

"Your Honor!" Sidney almost screamed. "If, after hearing this man's brazen declaration of bigoted class hatred against my clients, he is allowed to sit on that bench—"

Judge Nelson pounded with his gavel. "You don't have to instruct me in my judicial duties, Counselor," he said. "The venireman has obviously disqualified himself by giving evidence of prejudice. Next name."

The next man was challenged: he was a retired packing-house operator in New Austin, and had once expressed the opinion that Bonneyville and everybody in it ought to be H-bombed off the face of New Texas.

This Sidney seemed to have gotten the name of everybody likely to be called for court duty and had something on each one of them, because he went on like that all morning.

"You know what I think," Stonehenge whispered to me, leaning over behind Parros. "I think he's just stalling to keep the court in session until the z'Srauff fleet gets here. I wish we could get hold of one of those wrist watches."

"I can get you one, before evening," Hoddy offered, "if you don't care what happens to the mutt that's wearin' it."

"Better not," I decided. "Might tip them off to what we suspect. And we don't really need one: Sir Rodney will have patrols out far enough to get warning in time."

We took an hour, at noon, for lunch, and then it

began again. By 1647, fifteen minutes before court should be adjourned, Judge Nelson ordered the bailiff to turn the clock back to 1300. The clock was turned back again when it reached 1645. By this time, Clement Sidney was probably the most unpopular man on New Texas.

Finally, Colonel Andrew J. Hickock rose to his feet.

"Your Honor: the present court is not obliged to retire from the bench until another court has been chosen as they are now sitting as a court in being. I propose that the trial begin, with the present court on the bench."

Sidney began yelling protests. Hoddy Ringo pulled his neckerchief around under his left ear and held the ends above his head. Nanadabadian, the Ambassador from Beta Cephus IV, drew his biggest knife and began trying the edge on a sheet of paper.

"Well, Your Honor, I certainly do not wish to act in an obstructionist manner. The defense agrees to accept the present court," Sidney decided.

"Prosecution agrees to accept the present court," Goodham parroted.

"The present court will continue on the bench, to try the case of the Friends of Silas Cumshaw, deceased, versus Switchblade Joe Bonney, Jack-High Abe Bonney, Turkey-Buzzard Tom Bonney, et als." Judge Nelson rapped with his gavel. "Court is herewith adjourned until 0900 tomorrow."

CHAPTER IX

THE trial got started the next morning with a minimum amount of objections from Sidney. The charges and specifications were duly read, the three defendants pleaded not guilty, and then Goodham advanced with a paper in his hand to address the court. Sidney scampered up to take his position beside him.

"Your Honor, the prosecution wishes, subject to agreement of the defense, to enter the following stipulations, to wit: First, that the late Silas Cumshaw was a practicing politician within the meaning of the law. Second, that he is now dead, and came to his death in the manner attested to by the coroner of Sam Houston Continent. Third, that he came to his death at the hands of the defendants here present."

In all my planning, I'd forgotten that. I couldn't let those stipulations stand without protest, and at the same time, if I protested the characterization of Cumshaw as a practicing politician, the trial could easily end right there. So I prayed for a miracle, and Clement Sidney promptly obliged me.

"Defense won't stipulate anything!" he barked. "My clients, here, are victims of a monstrous con-

spiracy, a conspiracy to conceal the true facts of
the death of Silas Cumshaw. They ought never to
have been arrested or brought here, and if the
prosecution wants to establish anything, they can
do it by testimony, in the regular and lawful way.
This practice of free-wheeling stipulation is only
one of the many devices by which the courts of
this planet are being perverted to serve the corrupt
and unjust ends of a gang of reactionary landowners!"

Judge Nelson's gavel hit the bench with a crack
like a rifle shot.

"Mr. Sidney! In justice to your clients, I would
hate to force them to change lawyers in the middle
of their trial, but if I hear another remark like that
about the courts of New Texas, that's exactly what
will happen, because you'll be in jail for contempt! Is that clear, Mr. Sidney?"

I settled back with a deep sigh of relief which
got me, I noticed, curious stares from my fellow
Ambassadors. I disregarded the questions in their
glances; I had what I wanted.

They began calling up the witnesses.

First, the doctor who had certified Ambassador
Cumshaw's death. He gave a concise description
of the wounds which had killed my predecessor.
Sidney was trying to make something out of the
fact that he was Hickock's family physician, and
consuming more time, when I got up.

"Your Honor, I am present here as *amicus
curiae*, because of the obvious interest which
the Government of the Solar League has in this
case . . ."

"Objection!" Sidney yelled.

"Please state it," Nelson invited.

"This is a court of the people of the planet of New Texas. This foreign emmisary of the Solar League, sent here to conspire with New Texan traitors to the end that New Texans shall be reduced to a supine and ravished satrapy of the all-devouring empire of the Galaxy—"

Judge Nelson rapped sharply.

"Friends of the court are defined as persons having a proper interest in the case. As this case arises from the death of the former Ambassador of the Solar League, I cannot see how the present Ambassador and his staff can be excluded. Overruled." He nodded to me. "Continue, Mr. Ambassador."

"As I understand, I have the same rights of cross-examination of witnesses as counsel for the prosecution and defense; is that correct, Your Honor?" It was, so I turned to the witness. "I suppose, Doctor, that you have had quite a bit of experience, in your practice, with gunshot wounds?"

He chuckled. "Mr. Ambassador, it is gunshot-wound cases which keep the practice of medicine and surgery alive on this planet. Yes, I definitely have."

"Now, you say that the deceased was hit by six different projectiles: right shoulder almost completely severed, right lung and right ribs blown out of the chest, spleen and kidneys so intermingled as to be practically one, and left leg severed by complete shattering of the left pelvis and hip-joint?"

"That's right."

I picked up the 20-mm auto-rifle—it weighed a good sixty pounds—from the table, and asked him if this weapon could have inflicted such wounds. He agreed that it both could and had.

"This the usual type of weapon used in your New Texas political liquidations?" I asked.

"Certainly not. The usual weapons are pistols; sometimes a hunting-rifle or a shotgun."

I asked the same question when I cross-examined the ballistics witness.

"Is this the usual type of weapon used in your New Texas political liquidations?"

"No, not at all. That's a very expensive weapon, Mr. Ambassador. Wasn't even manufactured on this planet; made by the z'Srauff star-cluster. A weapon like that sells for five, six hundred pesos. It's used for shooting really big game—super-mastodon, and things like that. And, of course, for combat."

"It seems," I remarked, "that the defense is overlooking an obvious point there. I doubt if these three defendants ever, in all their lives, had among them the price of such a weapon."

That, of course, brought Sidney to his feet, sputtering objections to this attempt to disparage the honest poverty of his clients, which only helped to call attention to the point.

Then the prosecution called in a witness named David Crockett Longfellow. I'd met him at the Hickock ranch; he was Hickock's butler. He limped from an old injury which had retired him from work on the range. He was sworn in and testified to his name and occupation.

"Do you know these three defendants?" Goodham asked him.

"Yeah. I even marked one of them for future identification," Longfellow replied.

Sidney was up at once, shouting objections. After he was quieted down, Goodham remarked that he'd come to that point later, and began a line of questioning to establish that Longfellow had been on the Hickock ranch on the day when Silas Cumshaw was killed.

"Now," Goodham said, "will you relate to the court the matters of interest which came to your personal observation on that day."

Longfellow began his story. "At about 0900, I was dustin' up and straightenin' things in the library while the Colonel was at his desk. All of a sudden, he said to me, 'Davy, suppose you call the Solar Embassy and see if Mr. Cumshaw is doin' anything today; if he isn't, ask him if he wants to come out.' I was workin' right beside the telescreen. So I called the Solar League Embassy. Mr. Thrombley took the call, and I asked him was Mr. Cumshaw around. By this time, the Colonel got through with what he was doin' at the desk and came over to the screen. I went back to my work, but I heard the Colonel askin' Mr. Cumshaw could he come out for the day, an' Mr. Cumshaw sayin', yes, he could; he'd be out by about 1030.

"Well, 'long about 1030, his air-car came in and landed on the drive. Little single-seat job that he drove himself. He landed it about a hundred feet from the outside veranda, like he usually did, and got out.

"Then, this other car came droppin' in from outa nowhere. I didn't pay it much attention; thought it might be one of the other Ambassadors that Mr. Cumshaw'd brung along. But Mr. Cumshaw turned around and looked at it, and then he started to run for the veranda. I was standin' in the doorway when I seen him startin' to run. I jumped out on the porch, quick-like, and pulled my gun, and then this auto-rifle begun firin' outa the other car. There was only eight or ten shots fired from this car, but most of them hit Mr. Cumshaw."

Goodham waited a few moments. Longfellow's voice had choked and there was a twitching about his face, as though he were trying to suppress tears.

"Now, Mr. Longfellow," Goodham said, "did you recognize the people who were in the car from which the shots came?"

"Yeah. Like I said, I cut a mark on one of them. That one there: Jack-High Abe Bonney. He was handlin' the gun, and from where I was, he had his left side to me. I was tryin' for his head, but I always overshoot, so I have the habit of holdin' low. This time I held too low." He looked at Jack-High in coldly poisonous hatred. "I'll be sorry about that as long as I live."

"And who else was in the car?"

"The other two curs outa the same litter: Switchblade an' Turkey-Buzzard, over there."

Further questioning revealed that Longfellow had had no direct knowledge of the pursuit, or the siege of the jail in Bonneyville. Colonel Hickock had taken personal command of that, and had left Longfellow behind to call the Solar League Embassy and the Rangers. He had made no attempt to move the body, but had left it lying in the driveway until the doctor and the Rangers arrived.

Goodham went to the middle table and picked up a heavy automatic pistol.

"I call the court's attention to this pistol. It is an

eleven-mm automatic, manufactured by the Colt
Firearms Company of New Texas, a licensed sub-
sidiary of the Colt Firearms Company of Terra."
He handed it to Longfellow. "Do you know this
pistol?" he asked.

Longfellow was almost insulted by the question. Of course he knew his own pistol. He recited
the serial number, and pointed to different scars
and scratches on the weapon, telling how they
had been acquired.

"The court accepts that Mr. Longfellow knows
his own weapon," Nelson said. "I assume that this
is the weapon with which you claim to have shot
Jack-High Abe Bonney?"

It was, although Longfellow resented the qualification.

"That's all. Your witness, Mr. Sidney,"
Goodham said.

Sidney began an immediate attack.

Questioning Longfellow's eyesight, intelligence, honesty and integrity, he tried to show
personal enmity toward the Bonneys. He implied
that Longfellow had been conspiring with Cumshaw to bring about the conquest of New Texas by
the Solar League. The verbal exchange became so
heated that both witness and attorney had to be
admonished repeatedly from the bench. But at no
point did Sidney shake Longfellow from his one
fundamental statement, that the Bonney brothers
had shot Silas Cumshaw and that he had shot
Jack-High Abe Bonney in the shoulder.

When he was finished, I got up and took over.

"Mr. Longfellow, you say that Mr. Thrombley
answered the screen at the Solar League Embassy," I began. "You know Mr. Thrombley?"

"Sure, Mr. Silk. He's been out at the ranch with Mr. Cumshaw a lotta times."

"Well, beside yourself and Colonel Hickock and Mr. Cumshaw and, possibly, Mr. Thrombley, who else knew that Mr. Cumshaw would be at the ranch at 1030 on that morning?"

Nobody. But the aircar had obviously been waiting for Mr. Cumshaw; the Bonneys must have had advance knowledge. My questions made that point clear despite the obvious—and reluctantly court-sustained—objections from Mr. Sidney.

"That will be all, Mr. Longfellow; thank you. Any questions from anybody else?"

There being none, Longfellow stepped down. It was then a few minutes before noon, so Judge Nelson recessed court for an hour and a half.

In the afternoon, the surgeon who had treated Jack-High Abe Bonney's wounded shoulder testified, identifying the bullet which had been extracted from Bonney's shoulder. A ballistics man from Ranger crime-lab followed him to the stand and testified that it had been fired from Longfellow's Colt. Then Ranger Captain Nelson took the stand. His testimony was about what he had given me at the Embassy, with the exception that the Bonneys' admission that they had shot Ambassador Cumshaw was ruled out as having been made under duress.

However, Captain Nelson's testimony didn't need the confessions.

The cover was stripped off the aircar, and a couple of men with a power-dolly dragged it out in front of the bench. The Ranger Captain identified it as the car which he had found at the

Bonneyville jail. He went over it with an ultra-violet flashlight and showed where he had written his name and the date on it with fluorescent ink. The effects of AA-fire were plainly evident on it.

Then the other shrouded object was unveiled and identified as the gun which had disabled the air-car. Colonel Hickock identified the gun as the one with which he had fired on the air-car. Finally, the ballistics expert was brought back to the stand again, to link the two by means of fragments found in the car.

Then Goodham brought Kettle-Belly Sam Bonney to the stand.

The Mayor of Bonneyville was a man of fifty or so, short, partially bald, dressed in faded blue Levis, a frayed white shirt, and a grease-spotted vest. There was absolutely no mystery about how he had acquired his nickname. He disgorged a cud of tobacco into a spittoon, took the oath with unctuous solemnity, then reloaded himself with another chew and told his version of the attack on the jail.

At about 1045 on the day in question, he testified, he had been in his office, hard at work in the public service, when an air-car, partially disabled by gunfire, had landed in the street outside and the three defendants had rushed in, claiming sanctuary. From then on, the story flowed along smoothly, following the lines predicted by Captain Nelson and Parros. Of course he had given the fugitives shelter; they had claimed to have been near to a political assassination and were in fear of their lives.

Under Sidney's cross-examination, and coaching, he poured out the story of Bonneyville's wrongs at the hands of the reactionary landowners, and the atrocious behavior of the Hickock goon-gang. Finally, after extracting the last drop of class-hatred venom out of him, Sidney turned him over to me.

"How many men were inside the jail when the three defendants came claiming sanctuary?" I asked.

He couldn't rightly say, maybe four or five.

"Closer twenty-five, according to the Rangers. How many of them were prisoners in the jail?"

"Well, none. The prisoners was all turned out that mornin'. They was just common drunks, disorderly conduct cases, that kinda thing. We turned them out so's we could make some repairs."

"You turned them out because you expected to have to defend the jail; because you knew in advance that these three would be along claiming sanctuary, and that Colonel Hickock's ranch hands would be right on their heels, didn't you?" I demanded.

It took a good five minutes before Sidney stopped shouting long enough for Judge Nelson to sustain the objection.

"You knew these young men all their lives, I take it. What did you know about their financial circumstances, for instance?"

"Well, they've been ground down an' kept poor by the big ranchers an' the money-guys. . . ."

"Then weren't you surprised to see them driving such an expensive aircar?"

"I don't know as it's such an expensive—" he shut his mouth suddenly.

"You know where they got the money to buy that car?" I pressed.

Kettle-Belly Sam didn't answer.

"From the man who paid them to murder Ambassador Silas Cumshaw?" I kept pressing. "Do you know how much they were paid for that job? Do you know where the money came from? Do you know who the go-between was, and how much he got, and how much he kept for himself? Was it the same source that paid for the recent attempt on President Hutchinson's life?"

"I refuse to answer!" the witness declared, trying to shove his chest out about half as far as his midriff. "On the grounds that it might incriminate or degrade me!"

"You can't degrade a Bonney!" a voice from the balcony put in.

"So then," I replied to the voice, "what he means is, incriminate." I turned to the witness. "That will be all. Excused."

As Bonney left the stand and was led out the side door, Goodham addressed the bench.

"Now, Your Honor," he said, "I believe that the prosecution has succeeded in definitely establishing that these three defendants actually did fire the shot which, on April 22, 2193, deprived Silas Cumshaw of his life. We will now undertake to prove . . ."

Followed a long succession of witnesses, each testifying to some public or private act of philanthropy, some noble trait of character. It was the sort of thing which the defense lawyer in the Whately case had been so willing to stipulate. Sidney, of course, tried to make it all out to be part of a sinister conspiracy to establish a Solar

League fifth column on New Texas. Finally, the prosecution rested its case.

I entertained Gail and her father at the Embassy, that evening. The street outside was crowded with New Texans, all of them on our side, shouting slogans like, "Death to the Bonneys!" and "Vengeance for Cumshaw!" and "Annexation Now!" Some of it was entirely spontaneous, too. The Hickocks, father and daughter, were given a tremendous ovation, when they finally left, and followed to their hotel by cheering crowds. I saw one big banner, lettered: 'DON'T LET NEW TEXAS GO TO THE DOGS.' and bearing a crude picture of a z'Srauff. I seemed to recall having seen a couple of our Marines making that banner the evening before in the Embassy patio, but . . .

CHAPTER X

THE next morning, the third of the trial, opened with the defense witnesses, character-witnesses for the three killers and witnesses to the political iniquities of Silas Cumshaw.

Neither Goodham nor I bothered to cross-examine the former. I couldn't see how any lawyer as shrewd as Sidney had shown himself to be would even dream of getting such an array of thugs, cutthroats, sluts and slatterns into court as character witnesses for anybody.

The latter, on the other hand, we went after unmercifully, revealing, under their enmity for Cumshaw, a small, hard core of bigoted xenophobia and selfish fear. Goodham did a beautiful job on that; he seemed able, at a glance, to divine exactly what each witness's motivation was, and able to make him or her betray that motivation in its least admirable terms. Finally the defense rested, about a quarter-hour before noon.

I rose and addressed the court:

"Your Honor, while both the prosecution and the defense have done an admirable job in bringing out the essential facts of how my predecessor met his death, there are many features about this case which are far from clear to me. They will be

320

even less clear to my government, which is composed of men who have never set foot on this planet. For this reason, I wish to call, or recall, certain witnesses to clairfy these points."

Sidney, who had begun shouting objections as soon as I had gotten to my feet, finally managed to get himself recognized by the court.

"This Solar League Ambassador, Your Honor, is simply trying to use the courts of the Planet of New Texas as a sounding-board for his imperialistic government's propaganda . . ."

"You may reassure yourself, Mr. Sidney," Judge Nelson said. "This court will not allow itself to be improperly used, or improperly swayed, by the Ambassador of the Solar League. This court is interested only in determining the facts regarding the case before it. You may call your witnesses, Mr. Ambassador." He glanced at his watch. "Court will now recess for an hour and a half; can you have them here by 1330?"

I assured him I could after glancing across the room at Ranger Captain Nelson and catching his nod.

My first witness, that afternoon was Thrombley. After the formalities of getting his name and connection with the Solar League Embassy on the record, I asked him, "Mr. Thrombley, did you, on the morning of April 22, receive a call from the Hickock ranch for Mr. Cumshaw?"

"Yes, indeed, Mr. Ambassador. The call was from Mr. Longfellow, Colonel Hickock's butler. He asked if Mr. Cumshaw were available. It happened that Mr. Cumshaw was in the same room with me, and he came directly to the screen. Then

Colonel Hickock appeared in the screen, and inquired if Mr. Cumshaw could come out to the ranch for the day; he said something about superdove shooting."

"You heard Mr. Cumshaw tell Colonel Hickock that he would be out at the ranch at about 1030?" Thrombley said he had. "And, to your knowledge, did anybody else at the Embassy hear that?"

"Oh, no, sir; we were in the Ambassador's private office, and the screen there is tap-proof."

"And what other calls did you receive, prior to Mr. Cumshaw's death?"

"About fifteen minutes after Mr. Cumshaw had left, the z'Srauff Ambassador called, about a personal matter. As he was most anxious to contact Mr. Cumshaw, I told him where he had gone."

"Then, to your knowledge, outside of yourself, Colonel Hickock, and his butler, the z'Srauff Ambassador was the only person who could have known that Mr. Cumshaw's car would be landing on Colonel Hickock's drive at or about 1030. Is that correct?"

"Yes, plus anybody whom the z'Srauff Ambassador might have told."

"Exactly!" I pounced. Then I turned and gave the three Bonney brothers a sweeping glance. "Plus anybody the z'Srauff Ambassador might have told. . . . That's all. Your witness, Mr. Sidney."

Sidney got up, started toward the witness stand, and then thought better of it.

"No questions," he said.

The next witness was a Mr. James Finnegan; he was identified as cashier of the Crooked Creek

National Bank. I asked him if Kettle-Belly Sam Bonney did business at his bank; he said yes.

"Anything unusual about Mayor Bonney's account?" I asked.

"Well, it's been unusually active lately. Ordinarily, he carries around two-three thousand pesos, but about the first of April, that took a big jump. Quite a big jump; two hundred and fifty thousand pesos, all in a lump."

"When did Kettle-Belly Sam deposit this large sum?" I asked.

"He didn't. The money came to us in a cashier's check on the Ranchers' Trust Company of New Austin with an anonymous letter asking that it be deposited to Mayor Bonney's account. The letter was typed on a sheet of yellow paper in Basic English."

"Do you have that letter now?" I asked.

"No, I don't. After we'd recorded the new balance, Kettle-Belly came storming in, raising hell because we'd recorded it. He told me that if we ever got another deposit like that, we were to turn it over to him in cash. Then he wanted to see the letter, and when I gave it to him, he took it over to a telescreen booth, and drew the curtains. I got a little busy with some other matters, and the next time I looked, Kettle-Belly was gone and some girl was using the booth."

"That's very interesting, Mr. Finnegan. Was that the last of your unusual business with Mayor Bonney?"

"Oh, no. Then, about two weeks before Mr. Cumshaw was killed, Kettle-Belly came in and wanted 50,000 pesos, in a big hurry, in small bills.

I gave it to him, and he grabbed at the money like a starved dog at a bone, and upset a bottle of red perma-ink, the sort we use to refill our bank seals. Three of the bills got splashed. I offered to exchange them, but he said, 'Hell with it; I'm in a hurry,' and went out. The next day, Switchblade Joe Bonney came in to make payment on a note we were holding on him. He used those three bills in the payment.

"Then, about a week ago, there was another cashier's check came in for Kettle-Belly. This time, there was no letter; just one of our regular deposit-slips. No name of depositor. I held the check, and gave it to Kettle-Belly. I remember, when it came in, I said to one of the clerks, 'Well, I wonder who's going to get bumped off this time.' And sure enough . . .'"

Sidney's yell of, "Objection!" was all his previous objections gathered into one.

"You say the letter accompanying the first deposit, the one in Basic English, was apparently taken away by Kettle-Belly Sam Bonney. If you saw another letter of the same sort, would you be able to say whether or not it might be like the one you mentioned?"

Sidney vociferating more objections; I was trying to get expert testimony without previous qualification . . .

"Not at all, Mr. Sidney," Judge Nelson ruled. "Mr. Silk has merely asked if Mr. Finnegan could say whether one document bore any resemblance to another."

I asked permission to have another witness sworn in while Finnegan was still on the stand, and called in a Mr. Boone, the cashier of the Pack-

ers' and Brokers' Trust Company of New Austin.
He had with him a letter, typed on yellow paper,
which he said had accompanied an anonymous
deposit of two hundred thousand pesos. Mr. Finnegan said that it was exactly like the one he had
received, in typing, grammar and wording, all but
the name of the person to whose account the
money was to be deposited.

"And whose account received this anonymous
benefaction, Mr. Boone?" I asked.

"The account," Boone replied, "of Mr. Clement
Sidney."

I was surprised that Judge Nelson didn't break
the handle of his gavel, after that. Finally, after a
couple of threats to clear the court, order was
restored. Mr. Sidney had no questions to ask this
time, either.

The bailiff looked at the next slip of paper I gave
him, frowned over it, and finally asked the court
for assistance.

"I can't pronounce this-here thing, at all," he
complained.

One of the judges finally got out a mouthful of
growls and yaps, and gave it to the clerk of the
court to copy into the record. The next witness
was a z'Srauff, and in the New Texan garb he was
wearing, he was something to open my eyes, even
after years on the Hooligan Diplomats.

After he took the stand, the clerk of the court
looked at him blankly for a moment. Then he
turned to Judge Nelson.

"Your Honor, how am I gonna go about swearing him in?" he asked. "What does a z'Srauff
swear by, that's binding?"

The President Judge frowned for a moment.

"Does anybody here know Basic well enough to translate the oath?" he asked.

"I think I can," I offered. "I spent a great many years in our Consular Service, before I was sent here. We use Basic with a great many alien peoples."

"Administer the oath, then," Nelson told me.

"Put up right hand," I told the z'Srauff. "Do you truly say, in front of Great One who made all worlds, who has knowledge of what is in the hearts of all persons, that what you will say here will be true, all true, and not anything that is not true, and will you so say again at time when all worlds end? Do you so truly say?"

"Yes. I so truly say."

"Say your name."

"Ppmegll Kkuvtmmecc Cicici."

"What is your business?"

"I put things made of cloth into this world, and I take meat out of this world."

"Where do you have your house?"

"Here in New Austin, over my house of business, on Coronado Street."

"What people do you see in this place that you have made business with?"

Ppmegll Kkuvtmmecc Cicici pointed a three-fingered hand at the Bonney brothers.

"What business did you make with them?"

"I gave them for money a machine which goes on the ground and goes in the air very fast, to take persons and things about."

"Is that the thing you gave them for money?" I asked, pointing at the exhibit air-car.

"Yes, but it was new then. It has been made broken by things from guns now."

"What money did they give you for the machine?"

"One hundred pesos."

That started another uproar. There wasn't a soul in that courtroom who didn't know that five thousand pesos would have been a give-away bargain price for that car.

"Mr. Ambassador," one of the associate judges interrupted. "I used to be in the used-car business. Am I expected to believe that this . . . this being . . . sold that air-car for a hundred pesos?"

"Here's a notarized copy of the bill of sale, from the office of the Vehicles Registration Bureau," I said. "I introduce it as evidence."

There was a disturbance at the back of the room, and then the z'Srauff Ambassador, Gglafrr Ddespttann Vuvuvu, came stalking down the aisle, followed by a couple of Rangers and two of his attachés. He came forward and addressed the court.

"May you be happy, sir, but I am in here so quickly not because I have desire to make noise, but because it is only short time since it got in my knowledge that one of my persons is in this place. I am here to be of help to him that he not get in trouble, and to be of help to you. The name for what I am to do in this place is not part of my knowledge. Please say it for me."

"You are a friend of the court," Judge Nelson told him. "An *amicus curiae*."

"You make me happy. Please go on; I have no desire to put stop to what you do in this place."

"From what person did you get this machine that you gave to these persons for one hundred pesos?" I asked.

Gglafrr immediately began barking and snarling and yelping at my witness. The drygoods importer looked startled, and Judge Nelson banged with his gavel.

"That's enough of that! There'll be nothing spoken in this court but English, except through an interpreter!"

"Yow! I am sad that what I did was not right," the z'Srauff Ambassador replied contritely. "But my person here has not as part of his knowledge that you will make him say what may put him in trouble."

Nelson nodded in agreement.

"You are right: this person who is here has no need to make answer to any question if it may put him in trouble or make him seem less than he is."

"I will not make answer," the witness said.

"No further questions."

I turned to Goodham, and then to Sidney; they had no questions, either. I handed another slip of paper to the bailiff, and another z'Srauff, named Bbrarkk Jjoknyyegg Kekeke took the stand.

He put into this world things for small persons to make amusement with; he took out of this world meat and leather. He had his house of business in New Austin, and he pointed out the three Bonneys as persons in this place that he saw that he had seen before.

"And what business did you make with them?" I asked.

"I gave them for money a gun which sends out things of twenty-millimeters very fast, to make death or hurt come to men and animals and does destruction to machines and things."

"Is this the gun?" I showed it to him.

"It could be. The gun was made in my world; many guns like it are made there. I am certain that this is the very gun."

I had a notarized copy of a customs house bill in which the gun was described and specified by serial number. I introduced it as evidence.

"How much money did these three persons give you for this gun?" I asked.

"Five pesos."

"The customs appraisal on this gun is six hundred pesos," I mentioned.

Immediately, Ambassador Vuvuvu was on his feet. "My person here has not as part of his knowledge that he may put himself in trouble by what he says to answer these questions."

That put a stop to that. Bbrarkk Jjoknyyegg Kekeke immediately took refuge in refusal to answer on grounds of self-incrimination.

"That is all, Your Honor," I said, "And now," I continued, when the witness had left the stand, "I have something further to present to the court, speaking both as *amicus curiae* and as Ambassador of the Solar League. This court cannot convict the three men who are here on trial. These men should have never been brought to trial in this court: it has no jurisdiction over this case. This was a simple case of first-degree murder, by hired assassins, committed against the Ambassador of one government at the instigation of another, not an act of political protest within the meaning of New Texan law."

There was a brief silence; both the court and the spectators were stunned, and most stunned of all were the three Bonney brothers, who had been watching, fear-sick, while I had been putting a rope around their necks. The uproar from the rear of the courtroom gave Judge Nelson a needed minute or so to collect his thoughts. After he had gotten order restored, he turned to me, grim-faced.

"Ambassador Silk, will you please elaborate on the extraordinary statement you have just made," he invited, as though every word had sharp corners that were sticking in his throat.

"Gladly, Your Honor." My words, too, were gouging and scraping my throat as they came out; I could feel my knees getting absurdly weak, and my mouth tasted as though I had an old copper penny in it.

"As I understand it, the laws of New Texas do not extend their ordinary protection to persons engaged in the practice of politics. An act of personal injury against a politician is considered criminal only to the extent that the politician injured has not, by his public acts, deserved the degree of severity with which he has been injured, and the Court of Political Justice is established for the purpose of determining whether or not there has been such an excess of severity in the treatment meted out by the accused to the injured or deceased politician. This gives rise, of course, to some interesting practices; for instance, what is at law a trial of the accused is, in substance, a trial of his victim. But in any case tried in this court, the accused must be a person who has injured or killed a man who is definable as a practicing politician under the government of New Texas.

"Speaking for my government, I must deny that these men should have been tried in this court for the murder of Silas Cumshaw. To do otherwise would establish the principle and precedent that our Ambassador, or any other Ambassador here, is a practicing politician under—mark that well, Your Honor—under the laws and government of New Texas. This would not only make of any Ambassador a permissable target for any marksman who happened to disapprove of the policies of another government, but more serious, it would place the Ambassador and his government in a subordinate position relative to the government of New Texas. This the government of the Solar League simply cannot tolerate, for reasons which it would be insulting to the intelligence of this court to enumerate."

"Mr. Silk," Judge Nelson said gravely. "This court takes full cognizance of the force of your arguments. However, I'd like to know why you permitted this trial to run to this length before entering this objection. Surely you could have made clear the position of your government at the beginning of this trial."

"Your Honor," I said, "had I done so, these defendants would have been released, and the facts behind their crime would have never come to light. I grant that the important function of this court is to determine questions of relative guilt and innocence. We must not lose sight, however, of the fact that the primary function of any court is to determine the truth, and only by the process of the trial of these depraved murderers-for-hire could the real author of the crime be uncovered.

"This was important, both for the government of the Solar League and the government of New Texas. My government now knows who procured the death of Silas Cumshaw, and we will take appropriate action. The government of New Texas has now had spelled out, in letters anyone can read, the fact that this beautiful planet is in truth a *battleground*. Awareness of this may save New Texas from being the scene of a larger and more destructive battle. New Texas also knows who are its enemies, and who can be counted upon to stand as its friends."

"Yes, Mr. Silk. Mr. Vuvuvu, I haven't heard any comment from you . . . No comment? Well, we'll have to close the court, to consider this phase of the question."

The black screen slid up, for the second time during the trial. There was silence for a moment, and then the room became a bubbling pot of sound. At least six fights broke out among the spectators within three minutes; the Rangers and court bailiffs were busy restoring order.

Gail Hickock, who had been sitting on the front row of the spectators' seats, came running up while I was still receiving the congratulations of my fellow diplomats.

"Stephen! How *could* you?" she demanded. "You know what you've done? You've gotten those murdering snakes turned loose!"

Andrew Jackson Hickock left the prosecution table and approached.

"Mr. Silk! You've just secured the freedom of three men who murdered one of my best friends!"

"Colonel Hickock, I believe I knew Silas Cumshaw before you did. He was one of my instructors at Dumbarton Oaks, and I have always had the deepest respect and admiration for him. But he taught me one thing, which you seem to have forgotten since you expatriated yourself—that in the Diplomatic Service, personal feelings don't count. The only thing of importance is the advancement of the policies of the Solar League."

"Silas and I were attachés together, at the old Embassy at Drammool, on Altair II," Colonel Hickock said. What else he might have said was lost in the sudden exclamation as the black screen slid down. In front of Judge Nelson, I saw, there were three pistol-belts, and three pairs of automatics.

"Switchblade Joe Bonney, Jack-High Abe Bonney, Turkey-Buzzard Tom Bonney, together with your counsel, approach the court and hear the verdict," Judge Nelson said.

The three defendants and their lawyer rose. The Bonneys were swaggering and laughing, but for a lawyer whose clients had just emerged from the shadow of the gallows, Sidney was looking remarkably unhappy. He probably had imagination enough to see what would be waiting for him outside.

"It pains me inexpressibly," Judge Nelson said, "to inform you three that this court cannot convict you of the cowardly murder of that learned and honorable old man, Silas Cumshaw, nor can you be brought to trial in any other court on New Texas again for that dastardly crime. Here are your weapons, which must be returned to you. Sort them out yourselves, because I won't dirty my fingers on them. And may you regret and feel shame for your despicable act as long as you live, which I hope won't be more than a few hours."

With that, he used the end of his gavel to push the three belts off the bench and onto the floor at the Bonneys' feet. They stood laughing at him for a few moments, then stopped, picked the belts up, drew the pistols to check magazines and chambers, and then began slapping each other's backs and shouting jubilant congratulations at one another. Sidney's two assistants and some of his friends came up and began pumping Sidney's hands.

"There!" Gail flung at me. "Now look at your masterpiece! Why don't you go up and congratulate him, too?"

And with that, she slapped me across the face. It hurt like the devil; she was a lot stronger than I'd expected.

"In about two minutes," I told her, "you can apologize to me for that, or weep over my corpse. Right now, though, you'd better be getting behind something solid."

CHAPTER XI

I TURNED and stepped forward to confront the Bonneys, mentally thanking Gail. Up until she'd slapped me, I'd been weak-kneed and dry-mouthed with what I had to do. Now I was just plain angry, and I found that I was thinking a lot more clearly. Jack-High Bonney's wounded left shoulder, I knew, wouldn't keep him from using his gun hand, but his shoulder muscles would be stiff enough to slow his draw. I'd intended saving him until I'd dealt with his brothers. Now, I remembered how he'd gotten that wound in the first place: he'd been the one who'd used the auto-rifle, out at the Hickock ranch. So I changed my plans and moved him up to top priority.

"Hold it!" I yelled at them. "You've been cleared of killing a politician, but you still have killing a Solar League Ambassador to answer for. Now get your hands full of guns, if you don't want to die with them empty!"

The crowd of sympathizers and felicitators simply exploded away from the Bonney brothers. Out of the corner of my eye, I saw Sidney and a fat, blowsy woman with brass-colored hair as they both tried to dive under the friends-of-the-court table at the same place. The Bonney brothers sim-

ply stood and stared at me, for an instant, unbe-
lievingly, as I got my thumbs on the release-studs
of my belt. Judge Nelson's gavel was hammering,
and he was shouting:

"Court-of - Political-Justice-Confederate-Conti-
nent-of-New-Texas-is-herewith-adjourned-recon-
vene-0900-tomorrow. *Hit the floor!*"

"Damn! He means it!" Switchblade Joe Bonney
exclaimed.

Then they all reached for their guns. They were
still reaching when I pressed the studs and the
Krupp-Tattas popped up into my hands, and I
swung up my right-hand gun and shot Jack-High
through the head. After that, I just let my subcon-
scious take over. I saw gun flames jump out at me
from the Bonneys' weapons, and I felt my own
pistols leap and writhe in my hands, but I don't
believe I was aware of hearing the shots, not even
from my own weapons. The whole thing probably
lasted five seconds, but it seemed like twenty
minutes to me. Then there was nobody shooting
at me, and nobody for me to shoot at; the big room
was silent, and I was aware that Judge Nelson and
his eight associates were rising cautiously from
behind the bench.

I holstered my left-hand gun, removed and replaced the magazine of the right-hand gun, then
holstered it and reloaded the other one. Hoddy
Ringo and Francisco Parros and Commander
Stonehenge were on their feet, their pistols
drawn, covering the spectators' seats. Colonel
Hickock had also drawn a pistol and he was covering Sidney with it, occasionally moving the muz-
zle to the left to include the z'Srauff Ambassador
and his two attachés.

By this time, Nelson and the other eight judges

were in their seats, trying to look calm and judicial.

"Your Honor," I said, "I fully realize that no judge likes to have his court turned into a shooting gallery. I can assure you, however, that my action here was not the result of any lack of respect for this court. It was pure necessity. Your Honor can see that: my government could not permit this crime against its Ambassador to pass unpunished."

Judge Nelson nodded solemnly. "Court was adjourned when this little incident happened, Mr. Silk," he said.

He leaned forward and looked to where the three Bonney brothers were making a mess of blood on the floor. "I trust that nobody will construe my unofficial and personal comments here as establishing any legal precedent, and I wouldn't like to see this sort of thing become customary . . . but . . . you did that all by yourself, with those little beanshooters? . . . Not bad, not bad at all, Mr. Silk."

I thanked him, then turned to the z'Srauff Ambassador. I didn't bother putting my remarks into Basic. He understood, as well as I did, what I was saying.

"Look, Fido," I told him, "my government is quite well aware of the source from which the orders for the murder of my predecessor came. These men I just killed were only the tools.

"We're going to get the brains behind them, if we have to send every warship we own into the z'Srauff star-cluster and devastate every planet in it. We don't let dogs snap at us. And when they do, we don't kick them, we shoot them!"

That, of course, was not exactly striped-pants

diplomatic language. I wondered, for a moment, what Norman Gazarian, the protocol man, would think if he heard an Ambassador calling another Ambassador Fido.

But it seemed to be the kind of language that Mr. Vuvuvu understood. He skinned back his upper lip at me and began snarling and growling. Then he turned on his hind paws and padded angrily down the aisle away from the front of the courtroom.

The spectators around him and above him began barking, baying, yelping at him: "Tie a can to his tail!" "Git for home, Bruno!"

Then somebody yelled, "Hey, look! Even his wrist watch is blushing!"

That was perfectly true. Mr. Gglafrr Ddespttann Vuvuvu's watch-face, normally white, was now glowing a bright ruby-red.

I looked at Stonehenge and found him looking at me. It would be full dark in four or five hours; there ought to be something spectacular to see in the cloudless skies of Capella IV tonight.

Fleet Admiral Sir Rodney Tregnaskis would see to that.

FROM REPORT
OF SPACE-COMMANDER STONEHENGE
TO SECRETARY OF AGGRESSION, KLÜNG:

. . . so the measures considered by yourself and Secretary of State Ghopal Singh and Security Coördinator Natalenko, as transmitted to me by Mr. Hoddy Ringo, were not, I am glad to say, needed. Ambassador Silk, alive, handled the thing much better than Ambassador Silk, dead, could possibly have.

. . . to confirm Sir Rodney Tregaskis' report from the tales of the few survivors, the z'Srauff attack came as the Ambassador had expected. They dropped out of hyperspace about seventy light-minutes outside the Capella system, apparently in complete ignorance of the presence of our fleet.

. . . have learned the entire fleet consisted of about three hundred spaceships and reports reaching here indicate that no more than twenty got back to z'Srauff Cluster.

. . . naturally, the whole affair has had a profound influence, an influence to the benefit of the Solar League, on all shades of public opinion.

. . . as you properly assumed, Mr. Hoddy Ringo is no longer with us. When it became apparent that the Palme-Silk Annexation Treaty would be ratified here, Mr. Ringo immediately saw that his status of diplomatic immunity would automatically terminate. Accordingly, he left this system, embarking from New Austin for Alderbaran IX, mentioning, as he shook hands with me, something about a widow. By a curious coincidence, the richest branch bank in the city was held up by a lone bandit about half an hour before he boarded the space-ship. . . .

FINAL MESSAGE
OF THE LAST SOLAR AMBASSADOR TO NEW TEXAS
STEPHEN SILK

Copies of the Treaty of Annexation, duly ratified by the New Texas Legislature, herewith.

Please note that the guarantees of non-intervention in local political institutions are the very

minimum which are acceptable to the people of
New Texas. They are especially adamant that
there will be no change in their peculiar methods
of insuring that their elected and appointed public officials shall be responsible to the electorate.

DEPARTMENT ADDENDUM

After the ratification of the Palme-Silk treaty, Mr. Silk remained on New Texas, married
the daughter of a local rancher there (see file
on First Ambassador, Colonel Andrew
Jackson Hickock) and is still active in politics on that planet, often in opposition to
Solar League policies, which he seems to an-
ticipate with an almost uncanny prescience.

Natalenko re-read the addendum, pursed his
thick lips and sighed. There were so many ways
he could be using Mr. Stephen Silk . . .

For example—he looked at the tri-di star-map,
both usefully and beautifully decorating his
walls—over there, where Hoddy Ringo had gone,
near Alderbaran IX.

Those were twin planets, one apparently settled by the equivalent descendants of the Edwards
and the other inhabited by the children of a
Jukes-Kallikak union. Even the Solar League Ambassadors there had taken the viewpoints of the
planets to whom they were accredited, instead of
the all-embracing view which their training
should have given them. . . .

Curious problem . . . and, how would Stephen
Silk have handled it?

The Security Coördinator scrawled a note comprehensible only to himself. . . .

THE WORLDS OF H. BEAM PIPER